Life As a Loser

Will Leitch

Life As a Loser

ARRIVISTE PRESS
Boston

Arriviste Press, Inc.
2193 Commonwealth Ave.
Boston, MA 02135

ISBN 0-9746270-0-3

Portions of this book were previously published on the Web sites Blacktable.com, Ironminds.com, TheSimon.com and Haypenny.com.

To Bryan, Sally and Jill

Table of Contents

FOREWARD

By Tom Perrotta

Yeah, Will Leitch is a loser. A small-town Midwesterner adrift in the big city—a guy who used to sport a "feathered mullet," no less—temping and drinking and smoking too much, and generally trying to keep his head above water in the doldrums of the high-tech bust economy. It's a sorry, all-too-familiar tale of early promise squandered and hard lessons learned. The talented college journalist who ditches his safe job at *The Sporting News* for a shot at the big time (*The New York Times*, no less), then jumps on the Internet bandwagon of the late nineties, only to find himself unemployed, crashing on soon-to-be-ex-friends' couches ("It's getting crowded in here. You understand, Will, right?"), borrowing money he can't pay back, carrying all his worldly possessions in a single suitcase. His parents are starting to worry about him. He's not doing so great with the ladies, either.

It would be a sad story, except that Leitch isn't that kind of writer. It's not that he doesn't feel sorry for himself—Leitch can be a bit whiny at times, though I'd have to say he's earned the right—it's just that he's able to cut through the haze of self-pity to see himself with remarkable clarity and self-deprecating humor. If you don't believe me, just read "Consolation Prize," the hilarious and quietly heartbreaking chronicle of Leitch's public humiliation on a second-rate game show. And for all of his bad luck and bad timing, Leitch never loses his perspective about the truly important stuff, as he shows in the affecting "Pretend Sandwiches," in which he returns to his hometown of Mattoon, Illinois, and visits an old acquaintance who's living in a trailer and struggling just to get enough to eat. When his host starts talking about a ham and cheese sandwich as if it were some unearthly luxury, Leitch has an epiphany about the difference between a career setback and real poverty: "I'm broke. A recent financial disaster of mine may end up costing me one of my closest friends. I haven't had any income in three months. But I am not starving. I have people who care for me, who will watch over me, who will bail me out when I've screwed up. I have a margin for error, a margin I've certainly used."

This collection isn't a memoir in the technical sense. It's a collection of Internet columns, and as such, a kind of grab bag. You'll get Leitch's take not only on what it feels like to wash out with the rest of Internet whiz kids, but on baseball, sex, music, cats, drinking, old girlfriends, growing up in Mattoon, and anything else that happened to be on his mind when he wrote these columns. And yet, taken together, these pieces make for a vivid, funny, and occasionally moving portrait of a particular moment in our cultural history, and of Leitch himself. The guy may be a loser, but he's also a survivor, and a writer well worth reading.

INTRODUCTION

This is a book. I don't know if it's any good or not, or whether it will appeal to you, or if it has long-term growth potential. It is just a bunch of incoherent ramblings and self-indulgent excuses to settle scores with girls who didn't like me in high school. To be honest with you, it kind of jumps all over the place. There's no particular reason for me to write a book. I have no tragic story to tell. I am not going blind, no one in my family has died, I have not dragged myself out of the projects, elevating to new heights in a stirring story of human resilience. I'm just a stupid Midwestern kid who had his own Web site and wrote about his life often enough that it only seemed logical to shoehorn some run-on sentences into a book.

I will warn you right now: This is the whitest book you will ever read. Anybody with any soul will find plenty to mock here. I am not dope, fresh, funky, rad or wack. I am not an original gangsta. I have no bitchas on my jock. I do not ride in my 5.0 with the hatchtop down so my hair can blow. There are no girlies on standby, waiting just to say hi.

I have a bad back. I need laser eye surgery. I have mother issues. I wonder where all the cowboys have gone. I have a sticky film on me that just won't rinse away. I let the game come to me, I take it one game at a time. I will not give you cysts. I am not the punky QB known as McMahon. I pick you up in the morning and make you feel good the whole day long. I could use a third nostril. I did not give you lockjaw.

Notes: I have edited a few people out of this story, and I've occasionally changed names, and I've moved shit around, but you figured that already. I do not talk about our family dog, Daisy, even though she's quite a fine dog. I have a friend I used to date named Heather, but she doesn't really fit in the story, so she's not in here. Sorry, Heather. My friend Mike gets shorted as well, even though he is related to former Chicago lead singer Peter Cetera.

This is not a Christian book, either. The only references to the Almighty are in blasphemous exclamations, like, "Oh my God!" "Sweet Jesus!" and "Holy fucking Christ on a stick!" I plan on asking forgiveness for these transgressions at some point, but not until this book sells a lot of copies and I become rich. Even then, though, I do not plan on tithing.

This book is a collection of weekly columns, also called "Life as a Loser," which began in April 1999 and ran, pretty much weekly, for nearly five years. It is depressing to me, as I read through this book, that these are the "best" of that series. Surely, I wrote something better than this. The columns have been heavily edited, but it's important to note that they were written over a length of time and, thus, follow your fearless narrator through considerable periods of change. Hopefully you'll be able to follow along; they're in chronological order, or something close to it anyway. If you get confused, just put the book away and start flipping through something by David Foster Wallace. He's much easier to understand.

Nevertheless, the column has run in several incarnations in several different publications, including an alternative weekly in Fort Myers, Florida, a city that surely has been begging for an alt-weekly for years. (I believe it ran next to "Edna's Steam Room Gossip and "Great Recipes for Rice Krispy Treats.") But mostly, this column has run on the Internet.

There is a stigma involved in writing on the Internet that I do not understand. Dan Savage can write about the proper way to remove a guinea pig from a vagina, and it's taken as gospel. But a piece of journalism that would be at home in Esquire or The New Republic is somehow, just because it's posted on the Web, lessened. This is a problem of perception that will be corrected in upcoming years. The future of literature and journalism is right there in your Web browser, if you know where to find it. The fact that this book is in print doesn't, in my mind, legitimize what I've done any more than it would if I printed my columns out on an 8 ½ by 11 piece of cardboard paper and lined my cat's litter box with them. (Though I will confess that a book does make it more likely that girls will talk to me. Which, of course, is the only reason any of us do this anyway.) The notion that Web writers are undisciplined hacks sitting alone in a basement firing angry screeds at the world is idiotic, and serves only to deprive the world of some of the best writing out there.

OK, I'm off the soapbox.

Writing the column has served as catharsis, as any creative endeavor is, but mainly it has been to make people laugh, and let them know that there's somebody else out there as lost and confused and hopeful as they are. (And at least they're better looking.) I would love to go into more up-with-people blather here, about how the workers have the means of production and how the world is a kind and gentle place, but, frankly, I hope the book will speak for itself. Besides, the Cardinals are on, the cat needs to be fed and I have bills to pay. The story doesn't end with the book, you know.

Thank you for buying this book. I swear it's all true.

Enjoy.

CONSOLATION PRIZE

When I was a young boy growing up in Mattoon, Illinois, a small town about an hour south of the University of Illinois and two hours east of St. Louis, my world was limited. I knew baseball, cartoons, my bike (one of those nasty-ass banana-seat ones; one my dad made me put a huge, awful, orange flag on the back so the cars could see me) and television. My heroes were small ones. Ozzie Smith. Willie McGee. Voltron. Link, from The Legend of Zelda. That kid down the street who could dunk on an eight-foot hoop. My cousin Denny, who could swallow 10 bugs and not gag once.

And Michael Larsen, an unemployed ice cream truck driver from some city no one had ever heard of, with a life nobody wanted.

You might have read about Mr. Larsen. He showed up one day on CBS's *Press Your Luck* (in case you've forgotten, *Press Your Luck* was that show where you tried to avoid the whammies—odd little animated trolls who took all your money away—on some electronic board; it was a very dumb, very addictive game) and wowed the audience and the host by consistently missing the whammies and racking up free turns and more money. He did this over and over until he had compiled winnings upwards of $110,000. Everyone was convinced he'd somehow hacked into the master switchboard or done something equally illegal.

But Larsen was far too pathological to sink to such depths. Larsen—perhaps in between shifts on the ice cream truck—recorded episode after episode of *Press Your Luck* and studied them, freeze-framed them, scoured them for clues. He figured out how the system worked. He learned which box lit up after which box, how quickly it went, when it was smart to hit the plunger so it would land on big money and free turns. He did the paperwork and calculated how much he could win. He came to the show armed and ready.

And sure enough, he just kept winning. My favorite part of the show was when, deciding he had won enough, he had to finish out his final few "plunges." In all the rigmarole, he'd lost his concentration and was off rhythm. He had to finish out his turn, with a hundred some-odd-thousand dollars in the bank, and he actually had to press his luck. And he pulled it off.

I don't know what he did once he went home with his winnings, but you can bet he didn't hop back on that ice cream truck. I'm sure he bolted, left where he was, onto something better, something bigger. Something real.

I loved Michael Larsen. He stuck it to the man and improved his life... on national television. That's the big time, baby, and game shows were their bright, beeping centerpiece. I bought all the home games, borrowed my friends' computer games and practiced, practiced, practiced. Hard work would buy my golden ticket. TV! I didn't even know anyone who had been on TV before; I think a teacher from Mattoon once got arrested for sleeping with a student, and they had him on the news with a jacket over his head. I wasn't sure exactly how I would reach the outside world, but game shows seemed a much better bet than that.

I'm told a lot of people went outside and frolicked when they were children, enjoyed the freedom of youth bathed in sunshine and innocence. I even think I saw a few of them from my window while I was immersing myself in *Family Feud, Sale of the Century, Joker's Wild, Tic-Tac-Dough, Card Sharks*. This, my friends, was showbiz: flashing lights, obscenely jovial hosts, lovely parting gifts, the ecstasy of a ringing bell, the agony of an unforgiving buzz. A seed was planted, a dream was born, a dream that an unassuming young boy from Southern Illinois could one day grow up and make it big on the national platform. I spent years waiting for that break, that chance to prove my mettle in front of the entire world. Or at least a basic cable audience.

I sacrificed much, including my dignity and physical well-being, by joining the high school quiz-bowl team. It was my training, the penance I had to pay for the fame, fortune, and *Price Is Right* home game that awaited me.

Quite a few years later, in May 1997, at the tender age of 21, I was scheduled to graduate from the University of Illinois at Urbana-Champaign. Like every red-blooded college senior in the age before Web startups, I was freaked out about finding a job. And I had more to think about than just myself.

Her name was... well, let's just call her Jennifer. She was some piece of work. I'd met her in an advertising class. At the time, I'd just broken up with a psychotic, depraved, desperate woman who had worked with me at the student newspaper, and I was looking for no one, nothing in particular, just a place where I could shut the door and not be screamed at for being attracted to that guest star on *Friends*, a place where I could just be left the fuck alone for a while.

Jennifer was different than the neurotic, unwashed masses of college journalists I'd typically hung out with. First off, she was blond and beautiful, sleek and refined, one of those girls from a rich family who would do anything in her power to make sure you didn't know it. The first thing you noticed about her was not her hair, or her face, or her breasts, though they were all awfully tempting. It was her eyebrow ring.

Right there, above her left eye, was a little silver ring, jabbed through her skin and twisted, so set in there that you figured if she ever took it out, her face would just plum fall off. It was so odd for it to be there; she didn't have any tattoos, she appeared to wash her hair on a regular basis, and she was open and funny rather than off-putting and confrontational. I'd never actually spoken to a woman with an eyebrow ring before. It was jarring how sexy the eyebrow ring looked on her. It was like Julia Roberts with a bone through her cheek... beauty with a splash of surreal brutality. My first impression was that she would probably be a hellion in bed, then bite my head off afterwards.

She didn't notice me at first, not in that class, mainly because I was fat then and, like all of my college classes, I skipped too often to have much permanence whatsoever. But one afternoon, for no clear reason, she decided to sit smack in the middle of Mike and me. Mike was a co-worker at the student newspaper, my roommate, and my best friend. It was strange to see someone outside our messy, dysfunctional little *Daily Illini* family circle actually make an attempt to communicate with us, so we were enthralled. Plus she was fucking hot. Did I mention the eyebrow ring?

"Hey, guys, I understand you all work at the newspaper?"
Uh-huh, uh-huh, yes, yes.
("She was talking to me, dude." "Fuck you, man, she was talking to me!").

"Well, listen, I was thinking I might like to do some writing for the paper. I actually need a summer job; do you guys publish over the summer?"

Mike, after winning a knockdown, drag-out battle with me for the position a couple months earlier, was the editor-in-chief of the paper; I was the managing editor. But Mike, because he actually gave a shit about his career, had an internship set up in nearby Peoria, leaving me, who just wanted to get piss drunk all summer in Champaign, to run the paper for three months. So, yes, we did publish, and yes, I was in college, yes, I could care less about the semantics of professionalism, and yes, I was going to make sure this hot fucking girl with the eyebrow ring had a summer job.

Jennifer came on board as a summer staff writer, and, thanks in no small part to alcohol, we hit it off big time. You wouldn't have thought so upon a first meeting, but we had quite a bit in common. For example, we both were heavy drinkers and smokers. We both were into Weezer. We both thought she was really fucking hot. We both... well, I'm sure there was other stuff. It's been a few years.

We were quickly in "love." We lasted through the summer and were even stronger as school started. We were so in love she filmed me vomiting after 18 1/2 shots of Three Wise Men (a Johnny Walker, Jack Daniels, Jim Beam combo shot, an evil concoction designed to break men's souls) and didn't even pan away. I now was 21 years old and was about to graduate. It all started to make sense. I was starting to grow up, and it was time to do what I was supposed to do.

My father married my mother when he was 21 and she was 20. In Mattoon, if you're 24 and not married, you're probably gay. (An ominous label in Mattoon.) Time was a-wasting. I was nuts about Jennifer. And graduation was rapidly approaching.

We had only been dating for about four months, but it felt right. I mean, she could play guitar at parties! She could roll the perfect joint! She gave incredible back rubs! We had all any relationship needed to survive. Heck, I liked her so much, she lost the eyebrow ring, and I still found her dead sexy. (It was tough, I admit, to remain aroused by the loss of her navel ring, however. She took it out and a long string of pus oozed out for days afterwards. I think it helped her lose 10 pounds. I think it had the same effect on me.)

Heavy D: *Now that we'd found love, what were we gonna do... with it?*

It was time to act. One night, when we went to Mattoon over Thanksgiving, we sat shitty drunk at a local watering hole, avoiding various obnoxious former classmates. (Any trip to a bar in Mattoon ultimately functions as a pseudo high school reunion.) She looked at me for a moment, raised an eyebrow and smiled.

I returned the look.

I speak: "Are you thinking what I'm thinking?"
She speaks: "Well, I do have to pee."

That's not what I meant.
"I know."
Do you want to do it? I've had it on the mind for a while now.
"So have I."
All right then. Do you want to say it first? Or should I?
"I don't know. It's scary."
Not as scary as that guy's mullet.
"That's pretty scary."
Mattoon's pretty scary.
"I've noticed."
Jennifer... I think we should get married.

(Pause. Smile. Quiet glance downward. Doves flutter in the distance. Somewhere, a bell is chiming.)

"That's not what I was thinking."
Oh. Really?
"No. Just kidding. Sorry."
Jerk.
"Yeah, I think maybe we should."
Good. I almost threw up there for a second.

And we were off. I told my parents the next night that I was going to ask her. My father belabored me for not having a job yet. (He called it a "*J.O.B., Jaaaaaaaaaaaaaaaaab,*" implying an accent he doesn't have and continuously called Jennifer "that Jessica girl.") My mother was shockingly supportive. She began to cry, then took me to her jewelry chest. She opened it up, dug around for a while and pulled out a small ring.

"This was my engagement ring. It was also your grandmother's. I want you to have it, and I want you to give it to Jen. If it's not too (more crying) small." We hugged. She cried some more.

Then I think she vacuumed for a while.

It was too small—hands like Shaq, Jennifer had—even though it had fit both my mother and my grandmother perfectly. I zipped out to a jewelry store and had it resized, then I drove 140 miles up I-57 to Kankakee, where Jennifer lived. The importance of tradition weighed heavily, and I felt the next honorable step in the process would be do ask Jennifer's parents for her hand in marriage. I arrived, and Jennifer and her brother bolted; they knew why I was there.

For whatever berserko reason, Paul and Jami loved me, and they gave me their blessing. Paul waddled over to me and told me if I were to enter the family, I would have to have a glass of whiskey with him. I'd never drank whiskey before—in college, it was box of wine or bust—but I struggled through a couple of carafes of Crown Royal. Been drinking whiskey heavily since then… way too much, in fact; thanks a lot, Paul.

At the end of the night, the entire family gathered in a circle. Paul made an announcement: "If you are to enter this family, you will have to go through the gauntlet, our hazing. It is time for the Bundy Family Zerbet." I had no idea what a zerbet was; I thought I was about to eat ice cream. No such luck. Paul went over to Jennifer, lifted her shirt to her navel (no pus, thank God) and blew on her stomach, making sounds suspiciously like a fart. She giggled madly. She then did it to her brother, who did it to me, who did it to her mom. We then switched places in the circle. I shit you not, people.

Everyone went to bed, and Jennifer and I went out for a cigarette. I told her I had some papers in the car I needed to wrangle up—*smooth*—and opened the glove compartment, where the engagement ring conveniently... wasn't located. Fuck. Where is that sumbitch? I fumbled around for a few minutes until Jennifer started getting annoyed, then finally found it. I did the whole spiel; on bended knee, glazed over eyes (the Crown Royal helped), it-would-be-an-honor-if-you-would-be-my-wife, that whole business. She said yes and started to weep; we then went inside and passed out before we had a chance to properly consummate the engagement.

We were engaged. I had a fiancée. January 5, 1998 was to be the date.

Graduation. About two months before school ended, I received wonderful news: *U. The National College Magazine*, an obtuse monthly publication that was distributed in college newspapers across the country, called me and asked me to apply for their fellowship position. Every year, *U.* took four recent college graduates (journalism majors preferably), brought them out to Los Angeles, set them up with an apartment, and let them run a magazine. It sounded like a pretty sweet deal to me: cheap apartment, right on the beach in Santa Monica, nice salary, tons of writing opportunities.

Most important... it was in Los Angeles. The big time. The goal since birth had been to escape my small town and prove that I was bigger than factory work and marrying a cousin. I didn't want to be an electrician like Dad. (Frankly, I couldn't change a light bulb.) I wanted to see the world, find out if I could make it somewhere on this big planet. Sure, Mattoon was nice enough, quaint, Mayberry-esque... but I was an adventurer, an explorer, a man with much to do and say and show the world.

Los Angeles? Los freaking Angeles? Me? Shit, dude... I could make a name for myself out there. Once I arrived there, nothing could go wrong. The world would be my proverbial chicken coop... I would take the place over. There would be no stopping me.

Jennifer loved the idea of Los Angeles, so with her blessing, I applied. They called me for a phone interview. I tried to be alternately:

Wacky:
("Yeah, I live with a woman now, so that wouldn't be a problem. The only thing I have issue with now is that she keeps leaving the damn seat up.")

Serious:
("Journalism is in my bones," or some shit...)

Responsible:
("I've run a staff of 10 people!")

Complimentary:
("What *U. Magazine* does, you just don't get that anywhere else. It's killer!")

Worldly:
("Yeah, um, I've been to Chicago once or twice.")

The call came a week later; they wanted me, don't care that I'm engaged, stay at the apartment until the fiancée arrives (she was coming out a month after I was to plan the wedding and save some money), cool, excited to work with you.

Poof, whammo... I was in Los Angeles. I started the job, covering film and television, waiting for Jennifer to arrive. She gave me daily updates on how the wedding progress was coming, in which I did a lot of "yes, dear," and "I'm sure that's tough," and "I agree, having rotating swans across the front lawn to welcome wedding goers is entirely necessary." And we counted the days until she'd arrive.

Meanwhile, I had a job to do. Basically, I just assigned stories and went to film screenings, taking calls from pathetic publicity people about why I should see this movie, review this show, listen to this band. One day, a press release from Buena Vista Entertainment came across my desk.

COMEDY CENTRAL TO DEBUT GAME SHOW "WIN BEN STEIN'S MONEY" IN JULY blared the headline. I remembered Ben Stein, the former Nixon speechwriter, as the morose, charisma-challenged schoolteacher in *Ferris Bueller's Day Off* and *The Wonder Years*. I knew he was a professor at nearby Pepperdine University, but only because I read the press release. Supposedly there was this new television program where Ben Stein would not only host a game show, but also actually play against the contestants. The gimmick: Anyone who could beat Ben Stein would win $5,000, Stein's payment for the episode. If he beat you, he kept his cash.

Then I caught the end:

Those wanting to become a contestant on "Win Ben Stein's Money" can call 818-234-4022 and leave their name, address, age and phone number.

Ding! We have liftoff! Of course! A game show! My chance! Imagine what the boys in Mattoon would think if they flipped on their TV and saw good old Will buzzing in and answering questions with that shit-eating grin on his face! They'd know I made it then! I'd be a hero!

I wasted no time. Dial, dial, dial: Busy. Fuck. Dial, dial. An answering machine. I left my information. I waited by the phone. The next day—they were far more desperate for contestants at this infant period of the show—Shoshana, the "talent coordinator" for *Win Ben Stein's Money*, called. I needed to come to so-and-so building at so-and-so time, where I would take a trivia test and then have my "charisma quotient" evaluated. It was on.

I showed up and took some test, and they weeded out anyone who didn't score high enough. I made the cut, proceeding to sit in a group of people and slap playing cards on a table when it was time to buzz in. I tried to be funny and charming when I buzzed in and picked my categories, but I ended up only answering one question correctly: In what city was Northwestern University located? (Evanston, you moron.) We were shuffled out, and it seemed my chance had been blown. I quickly forgot about the whole thing. Jennifer had arrived.

Her first night, in an attempt to be romantic, I booked us at a hotel overlooking the ocean. Jennifer ended up sick; she spent half the evening vomiting, the other half crying, presumably over the strain of leaving her home, family and all she'd ever known. We were off and running. I asked her if she had the flu. She said it was something like that.

She moved into my apartment, already stacked with four people, and we searched the greater Los Angeles area for a place for the two of us to lay some roots. She also searched for an advertising job, just like Amanda on *Melrose Place*, our favorite Wednesday night TV show.

Then the call came. It was Shoshana. "Will, you've been selected to be on *Win Ben Stein's Money*. Congratulations! You film in two weeks, so start studying up. Ben's a tough competitor!"

I put down the phone and hugged Jennifer, exhilarated that I'd finally made it. It was my time! Welcome to The Show, kid. I couldn't contain myself. I was hopping around the apartment, laughing, loony, exultant. I was going to be on television! Will Leitch! From Mattoon! I leapt into the bathroom and began practicing my intro in the mirror. "Yes, my name is Will Leitch, I'm a writer, originally from Southern Illinois, living in L.A. now, and boy, lemme tell you, this city's crazy. Smoggy, I tell ya. It's so smoky here, the other day, I went outside and thought I was on fire. Started stopping, dropping, and rolling. Oh!" Talent agents would see the show, realize they had a blazing new talent on their hands, and climb all over themselves to sign me. Money, fame and the other trappings of comedy stardom would roll right in.

Jennifer seemed indifferent, which I found curious, but she had been sick again the night before. I started studying up, poring through encyclopedias and playing countless games of Trivial Pursuit. But no amount of last minute cramming would ultimately make much difference; I'd been training my whole life for this.

The fortnight passed, and we still hadn't found an apartment. I was a bit more into the process than Jennifer was; every place we saw, she hated. That was fine; I was a family man now, and finding an apartment was the type of real-life business that husbands are supposed to attend to. I also searched around for jobs for Jennifer; she tended not to like any of them either. Too stuffy, too corporate, too boring, too "L.A." Money was also beginning to become a problem; my job was nice, but it wasn't set up to support two people. And Jennifer was presumably still planning a wedding, deciding which invitations to use, what color the bridesmaids should wear, whether we should have a three- or four-course meal. The stress was starting to mount.

But it didn't matter because we had each other, and we had this incredible, exhilarating new life ahead of us. And we had Ben Stein.

The night before my 8 a.m. taping, Jennifer and I caught a movie and came back to my apartment for some wine and relaxation. Bed by 10 p.m. Must be well-rested. She was unusually quiet all evening. Nerves, surely. After all, her future husband was about to take the entertainment world by storm. That kind of impending jolt of fame can make one skittish. Would she be able to handle the spotlight? Would her private life be interrupted? And what would we do about those blasted paparazzi?

We had this wonderful porch at our apartment. It overlooked Schatzi's, a fancy-pants wine restaurant owned by future statesman Arnold Schwarzenegger. I would sit out there and overlook the city, remind myself that I really did live here, reading and smoking and dreaming. Later on, I would include much, much alcohol in that equation, but for this night, at this point, it was just some Boone's Farm.

Around 11 p.m., Jennifer came out to the porch, where I'd been plotting my impending global domination. She had the oddest look on her face, and she appeared to have been crying. I asked her what was wrong. She told me to sit down. I *was* sitting. I told *her* to sit down. I tried to hug her, comfort her. This had been happening a lot. What was wrong this time?

The speech was quick. It had clearly been rehearsed. This was not the first time she had said it. It was just the first time I'd been around to hear it.

She exhaled deeply. "Will, I've been doing a lot of thinking. And I've decided... well, I don't think I'm ready to get married. I don't think I want to be, I don't think I can be, with anyone right now. I just think I need to be alone for a while. I was thinking of maybe getting away, maybe leaving all of this big world, getting more in touch with nature, maybe hiking through the mountains, finding myself. I just... I just can't marry you."

Remember that scene in *Goodfellas,* when Joe Pesci realizes that he's about to be killed? He looks almost content, glad to finally, once and for all, *know.* Glad to finally stop running, glad to stop worrying, glad it's finally *over.*

My reaction was nothing like that. Mine only included the bullet to the head.

It is tempting to lie here. It is tempting for me to tell you that I took this news like a man, with a stiff upper lip, stoic demeanor, chiseled features, rugged humor. It is tempting to say that I told Jennifer that I supported her, that I understood, that much has happened in the past few months and it's been very stressful. I would like to say I kept my dignity.

No. I whined. I bawled. I begged. I crawled. I whimpered. I screamed. I dragged through the muck, pleading for a chance, weeping, wailing. It was pathetic. Imagine Meryl Streep in *Sophie's Choice,* minus the Nazis and the kids. My face caved in on itself. It was messy and endless.

This went on for about seven hours. "I feel terrible," she said. "I never meant to hurt you," she said. "It's not you, it's me," she said. I won't delve into the details of all that happened, mainly because I've either forgotten them or blocked them out, but eventually, I blearily looked at my watch—the one she bought me for Christmas, a nice one, Dakota Quartz—and realized it was 6:45 a.m.

She mentioned we should get going. She then paused and handed me her engagement ring.

Showtime. I changed clothes—we were halfway to the studio when I realized my pants were on backwards—and headed to Studio City. We mulled around with other contestants and their wives and husbands for a while—"I hear Ben's a fucking genius, man. I'll be happy to get out of here with a parting gift." "Screw that. I'm here to win." "Anybody have an aspirin?"—and eventually a producer came out to direct me backstage and Jennifer, hereafter referred to as the "ex-fiancée," to the front row seating area. They placed me in the makeup chair, which, as you can probably guess, was dearly needed.

"Hey, Will, are you ready to WIN SOME OF BEN STEIN'S MONEY?!" Some producer guy with a nasty comb-over was bellowing to my nostril. He looked like he'd been up all night too, albeit with more stimulants. He mentioned that we needed to go over some biographical information before we started. Okey-doke.

"OK, you're a film critic, you love Woody Allen, and you're single but engaged, right?"

Ha. Funny you should mention that. I informed him, through a random smattering of grunts and clicking sounds that, in fact, *craziest* thing happened to me on the way to the show. He frowned the frown of the terminally cheery and said "Don't worry, Will, we won't even mention it." Mention what?

It was time. I stumbled onto the set and shook hands with Ben Stein, and his trusty sidekick Jimmy Kimmel made some small talk and tossed a tired—so tired—smile toward the ex-fiancée in the crowd. My opponents were a flighty woman who was trying to pass the bar exam and a compact, angry-looking young man who told me in the waiting room that he'd been rejected for *Jeopardy* and figured this was the next best thing. (Ben was scared of him during the intro. So was I.)

Stein came out to huge applause from the bused-in crowd, who were paid 20 bucks and given lunch for their day of canned excitement. I found out later that a couple of the homeless and hungry asked Jennifer before the show who she was rooting for, and why. She mentioned I was her... well, she wasn't sure what I was. They were confused. Who wasn't?

The other two contestants shared some witty on-air banter with Kimmel. Then it was my turn.

Quoth the Kimmel: "And our final contestant is Will Leitch. He's a film critic who loves Woody Allen and, I hear, just got unengaged last night. Wow. That's amazing. How are you feeling today, Will?"

Man.
Man.
Man.
Man, man, man, look at those bright bright bright bright bright lights they've got on the set. They are mighty pretty! How do they make them that bright? Do they need special amps? Wonder if Letterman does that? Probably not, as cold as he keeps his set. When police interrogate suspects, do they keep them that bright? Wonder if the sun started out that way, as a really bright light on a set, and then worked and struggled and kissed ass enough to become the center of our solar system that we now know and love. It's a long road to the top.

I stared ahead, transfixed. Hey, I wonder, could I name all the Phoenix brothers? The Baldwins? What's the name of that guy Willie McGee was traded for? Did Mom and Dad ever smoke pot together? Is it true Bob Hope lives with a commune of dwarfs in Palm Springs? Remember Mr. Smithson in high school English? He was my favorite teacher. Hope he's doing well. I bet he was gay. We always thought he was. It must have been tough being a gay schoolteacher in Mattoon, if he was indeed gay. And did I sign my name on that third-grade spelling test for Mrs. McRoberts? You get no credit if you don't sign your name, you know. I'm sure I did. But you never remember those things. You know, I'm really beginning to believe that Bill Clinton probably wasn't that popular in grade school. It's tough; I bet he was always the last guy picked in dodge ball. He sure showed them though. And what a strange sport dodge ball was. It seems odd to think that our recreational activity when we were eight was taking large plastic balls and whipping them at the heads of our classmates. Hard to imagine our parents and teachers let us do that. Do the kids today play dodge ball? Or do they just trade Pokemon cards? Is that fad over yet? Does it even count as a fad? I think raves might be a fad. I don't know much about them. I'm never invited to them; I think I just read about them in *Time*. Now, I'm new to this whole "rave" thing, with all the "kids" "raving," "having fun" and "enjoying their time at a 'rave.'" I'm not "hip" with the "rave" mainly because I'm a "dork" with a sticky film that just won't "rinse away." You know, I think I might be out of soap. I've been borrowing my roommate's, but eventually she's going to notice. I'm a bit of a slob, and she might yell at me. I hate to be yelled at. Remember that one time, on ESPN, when Jim Everett, quarterback for the Los Angeles Rams, started yelling at host Jim Rome to stop calling him "Chris Evert" because he was injured all the time. Everett, obviously incensed at being compared to a women's tennis star, albeit one who accomplished more in one month than Everett did in his entire career, pushed him over and they had to stop the show. I wonder if that was staged. I hate it when people think the NBA is fixed. It's impossible. I remember when I had my cat fixed. I felt so bad for him; I bet sometimes he pisses on my head when I'm asleep as revenge. I probably deserve it. Seems like a relatively insensitive thing to do to a fellow guy, even if he is a cat. Hey, what is it exactly that Cat Stevens changed his name to? Isn't he a Muslim now? Or a Hindu? Heck, I don't know. I hate the word "niggling." It seems wrong, wrong, wrong. You know, I've always felt Denzel Washington was screwed out of his Oscar for *Malcolm X*. He lost to Al Pacino in *Scent of a Woman*, which was just a terrible movie. I think Al lost his mind in the mid-'80s. Now he just screams all the time. HOO-HA! HOO-HA! HOO-HA! IF I WAS HALF THE MAN I WAS 10 YEARS AGO I'D TAKE A FLAME THROWER TO THIS PLACE! HOO-HA! HOO-HA! HOO-HA! MOTHERFUCKING HOO-HA! HOO-HA!

"Will? Will? You with us there, buddy? Hey, Will!"

The sight of the show's producer, snapping a finger in my face and chanting my name, awakened me from happy happy land, hoo-ha, hoo-ha. I acknowledged his presence with a wave and a confused cold fish limp handshake. He looked at me like I'd accidentally set the Mona Lisa on fire and didn't realize it yet.

"So, you really got unengaged last night, huh? Jesus."
"Am I on TV?"
"No, we stopped tape. Are you going to be OK?"
"Um... oh, yeah, let's go. I want to WIN BEN STEIN'S MONEY!"

I didn't dare look in the audience. After a brief break, in which my corner men applied substance to my cuts and told me to stick the body, hit the one in the middle, set him up with the jab, hang in there, you're up on points, they started up again, and Kimmel—or, as he's known around my family these days, That Bastard—coerced me into doing a wretched Woody Allen impression that became a running joke throughout the show. I do not do a Woody Allen impression.

They even mocked me in the bonus round, to which I did not advance. The game was on, and I knew that Kareem Abdul-Jabbar was the all-time leading NBA scorer and that Mary McDonnell had been nominated for an Oscar for *Dances With Wolves*. But my scalloped reflexes failed me when asked where Lee Harvey Oswald was shot (*in the back* was not the right answer, I'm afraid), and the law lady edged past me into the next round. Ben Stein gave me his heartfelt good-byes, made fun of my Allen impression and then, off camera, patted me on the back and told me to hang in there. Bless him. Bless that Fascist, racist son of a bitch. Fucking Nixon man. I should have known.

The ex-fiancée left for the Appalachian Mountains a week later. She hiked around for a few months, then returned to her parents' home. Upon arriving, she learned she had inherited three million dollars from her grandfather. She packed up and moved to Vermont, to be with the birds and trees and things.

And I never saw her again.

About a month and a half later, *Win Ben Stein's Money*, featuring Ben Stein, Jimmy Kimmel and one shriveled corpse of a man aired on Comedy Central, and I received congratulatory calls from all my friends in Mattoon for finally striking the big time. But they all wondered one thing: If I was out in Los Angeles all this time, near the beach and sand and sun, why was it that looked so pale?

IMBECILE IN THE OUTFIELD

W hen I was 6 years old, my father, a somewhat talented athlete as a teen before joining the Air Force, decided his bookish son—the one who had been chided by teachers for reading *Mom, the Wolfman and Me* during recess—needed to start playing baseball, if only to get him off the damn couch.

In my hometown, 5- to 7-year-olds were herded into something called tee-ball, where you attempted to hit the stationary ball off a piece of black plastic, and since you couldn't strike out, you were going to sit there, with scoffing parents and mean-ass kids staring intently, until you just hit the friggin' thing, for Christ's sake. For kids like me, for whom a baseball was that thing the other kids threw at you while you were studying Judy Blume, this was a long and laborious process. In the field, a coach once had to run out and remind me to face the batter and, for the love of God, please quit chewing on my glove.

In retrospect, I realize how difficult it must have been for my proud father, an electrician and a man's man who certainly received countless ribbings from other men's men whose sons didn't run to third base when they finally hit the ball. By the time his son at last earned a base hit, then walked to the dugout because he was so used to being thrown out, the stoic Bryan Leitch had reached his boiling point.

(*Note: Mr. Leitch explains, "I just figured you were going to turn out gay, which would be fine, as long as you could hit the cutoff man."*)

As a last-ditch effort, my father dragged me away from my Bugs Bunny cartoon one Saturday morning and drove me to Busch Stadium, where his beloved Cardinals were facing the then-potent Montreal Expos. Keith Hernandez hit a home run, Willie McGee stole three bases, and Ozzie Smith made one of his gravity-defying double plays. It was breathtaking. To my dad's amazement, I was hooked.

Next thing he knew, I was memorizing Johnny Mize's 1943 statistics, sneaking a radio into my room at night to listen to Jack Buck, and showing a newfound vigor in my tee-ball league. Years passed, and I discovered movies, alcohol and pubic hair, but my passion for baseball never waned. It got to the point where I tried out for the freshman football team to get in shape for baseball tryouts, although I eventually had to quit because I was failing biology. (I was too afraid of wasps to do the bug collection.)

By my junior year, I had made the varsity baseball team at my adopted position: catcher. Well, a more accurate description would be to say my adopted position was scorekeeper and the guy put in right field in 14-3 blowouts. I excelled at both, particularly scorekeeping, where I inspired the wonder of my more adrenaline-enhanced teammates—who were constantly amazed by my ability to figure out that if you were batting 3-for-8, your average was .375. ("Dude, man, if they ever have a draft for scorekeepers, you'll go in the first round!")

I dealt with such indignities with aplomb, mainly because April was rapidly approaching. For the first time in the history of Mattoon High School, the varsity baseball team was traveling to Busch Stadium to play an exhibition with county rival Charleston before a Cardinals-Phillies game. I was returning to the genesis of my love affair with America's pastime, and best of all, his hand forced by public sentiment, Coach Simpson was going to let everyone play, even the schleps with the pencils. (I'd slugged a whopping 2-for-6 in 18 games coming in.)

A little bit about Mark Simpson. He was a young man, just older than 30, a gym teacher who wore sweat pants everywhere, presumably even at his own wedding, to a plastic blonde whose presence never failed to stir the loins of Mattoon's finest power hitters. He'd happened to take over the team as Mattoon's greatest class of baseball players was passing through. Simpson, however, had decided this team's success (16-2 going into Busch) was a measure of his own genius as coach, something of which he never failed to remind us. He was the type of guy who, when going out to comfort a struggling pitcher, would say, "Jeez, they're really killing you out here. What's wrong with you?" He was a vain, pathetic little twerp, and he was openly mocked and generally reviled by his players. But his team won, so our small, baseball-mad town saw him as a bit of a savior.

And Coach Simpson had no use for me. He'd once flat-out told me that I was on his team because a friend of his was close with the coach of my scholastic bowl team and thought it would be "good for me" to hang around. If there was anyone on the team causing him to quiver about the "Everybody Plays" philosophy, it was his pet scorekeeper, the guy who once sheepishly informed him that this was a poor time to intentionally walk the opposition's best hitter, considering the bases were loaded.

Oh boy, was I going to show Coach Simpson. Like all bench-dwellers, when I finally got my chance to shine, I was going to prove everyone wrong. My teammates, constantly startled by my encyclopedic knowledge of former Cardinal Dane Iorg's on-base percentage with two outs against left-handed pitchers in the fourth inning, surprised me by rallying around me in my quest for Busch Stadium glory. One even remarked to the local paper, "He's the biggest Cardinal fan we know. We really want him to get a hit."

We entered the stadium through the players' gate—*Hey, check it out, Pedro Guerrero's car!*—and walked onto the Astroturf field. Glancing at the lineup card, I noticed I was batting 14th—desperate times called for desperate measures—and playing right field in the third and sixth innings. After waving to my family and my girlfriend in the stands, I trotted out to right field in the bottom of the third, filled with awe and with Mattoon ahead 3-0.

It had rained the night before, so much so that many panicked players feared the game might be canceled. We played on, but the field was still wet. Damp. Slippery.

With two outs, a runner on second, and a sandy-haired corn-fed kid at the plate, our pitcher threw an outside fastball that was lifted into, of all places, right field. A lifelong catcher, I'd never felt quite at home in the outfield, but I nonetheless camped comfortably under this lazy fly.

A flashback. The night before the game: 11 p.m., Central Standard Time. Thanks to a defective air conditioner in our hotel, the embattled warriors were sweating profusely and unable to sleep. Coach Simpson stormed angrily into our room and grumbled that we were switching hotels because this goddamned place couldn't get its collective shit together. We hurriedly gathered our things, and, as I realized while dressing for the game the next morning, my cleats had been lost in the transition. That left me with my sneakers for the game.

Tennis shoes and a wet field. Not good. I glided—OK, glided is what pros do; I shambled—to the left about half a step. That step was not there. My right shoe gave way, and next thing I knew, I was lying on wet turf with my sneaker sitting next to me and the ball far, far, beyond me. A teammate later told me Coach Simpson, upon witnessing this spectacle, spat something that rhymed with "Boo clucking sidiot."

My one shoe and I sprinted to the wall, where I grabbed the ball and fired it back toward the infield, but the sandy-haired kid had long since crossed the plate. In the next day's paper, our late, beloved local sports editor listed his hit as a home run and didn't even mention my spill, bless his heart. At least the sandy-haired kid can tell his grandkids he hit a home run in Busch Stadium and have the proof to back it up.

In the stands, my father tried to save me—and himself—more shame. When another parent witnessed this spectacle, he asked, "Yikes, who is that out there?"

"Um, I think it's that Alexander kid," my dad answered, mercifully.

I ended up getting two hits and an RBI, and we won the game handily. But the die had been cast with Coach Simpson. I batted just once more the rest of the season, and once he even bitterly kept score himself, as if I treasured the duty.

The next season, we played again at Busch Stadium, but I was too disillusioned at that point to expect much of a shot at redemption. In the fifth inning, when we were down by two runs, I came up with runners on first and third and two out. Simpson gave me the take sign on the first pitch, a beauty right down the middle that allowed our runner to steal second. I fouled the second pitch straight back, and the Charleston pitcher reared back to fire what had to be the best curveball of his life, and I struck out. We ended up losing, and I batted only twice the rest of the season.

After that second game, my dad and my best friend came down to the field to offer their condolences. When my father left, carefully avoiding the other fathers, my friend's dad came down to offer me a bit of baseball expertise.

"Bad time to strike out, Will."

Yeah, thanks. Jerk.

MUSICAL DESPAIR

My cousin Denny is about the coolest guy I know. He's studying to be a grade school teacher, he lives alone in a spacious house with velvet Elvis paintings, and on the side, he races motorcycles professionally. Considering this is a guy with whom I bathed when we were younger—well, is 22 considered "younger"?—I feel like something must have gone wrong at some point. He's got this really kick-ass life, and I type my woes into a word processor while cleaning up cat shit and picking my nose.

I've tried to improve my social standing in respect to my cousin, but there is one way I am certain I will never match him. Denny, in addition to all that other stuff, plays guitar in a rock band, writes his own songs, and jams with friends in a back room of his house, which is decorated generously with various amplifiers, drum sets and static pedals. (I don't know what a static pedal is, but he mentioned it one time, and it sounded cool. *Static. Pedal.* I like it.)

Whenever we're at a party together, someone will inevitably ask him to break out his guitar. He'll be sheepish about it, but he'll end up busting it out and rocking, and every woman in the place eventually will be at rapt attention. When I break out my word processor at parties, I never garner quite the same reaction. Denny's obviously a hip guy in more than one way, but his musical prowess certainly impresses people the most. He didn't play any instruments as a kid, but one day he picked up a guitar and just started pouring his soul into it.

No matter her place in society or her proclivities toward spontaneous gestures, I've yet to find a woman who can resist a guy who teaches little kids, races motocross, and writes ballads. So, as I tend to do when I notice someone who seems to have a better idea of how to live life than I do, I decided to try to shamelessly copy Denny. It was time to become a musician.

I'd tried this before. In high school, a friend was starting a band and wanted a lead singer. I'd never sang much before, but I was always looking to try new things, especially if they helped me meet girls. We had a little jam session at his parents' house, and he broke into Led Zeppelin's "Rock 'n' Roll." I just tried to keep up, but yeah, I felt I was belting out the tunes with the requisite amount of soul.

I was mistaken. My friend told me I had a "good punk voice," but, um, that wasn't quite what this band was all about. "Maybe if you knew how to play guitar, you'd know how notes work." Yes. That.

I gave up any pretense of singing when the music teacher at my high school, upon witnessing my audition for the school play, told me, "Will, you're perfect for the part (Nathan Detroit in *Guys and Dolls*), but seriously, we've got to do something about that voice." I played Big Jule instead.

OK, fine. Can't sing. Got it. But I had plenty of friends who played guitar. Maybe I could do that. When I moved to Los Angeles, I had a roommate who had a working guitar and an amp. Well, until I got a hold of it. After I got home from work, I would plug in and start rocking out, randomly scratching out unrecognizable sounds that sounded beautiful to me. This agonizing noise—strangely, every time I left for work in the morning, four dogs would be lying dead at our front door—ended when, while trying to compose a particularly difficult death metal selection, I snapped two strings on the guitar. I offered to replace them, but my roommate insisted that wasn't necessary. *Seriously, Will, don't fix it. It doesn't need to be played again. I mean it.*

I'd had enough of this fly-by-night informal training. If I was going to learn to play an instrument, I would have to do it the right way and take lessons. I couldn't afford a nice electric guitar and amp, so I figured I'd go in another direction. It was time for some ivory tickling.

I would learn to play the piano. It didn't seem that difficult; I mean, I type all day every day, and I use my fingers to do that. You use your fingers to play the piano. Pretty much the same principle, right?

I had visions of a New Year's Eve in an unnamed big city, overlooking the downtown skyline, my girlfriend in an evening gown and I in a tuxedo, surrounded by our closest friends. I raise my glass of bourbon for a toast. "This one is for my friends, who have given me a wonderful year and will give me many wonderful years to come." I sit down at a grand piano and play a beautiful ode to fellowship, the passage of time and happiness. When I finish the composition, the room is absorbed, my friends pat me on the back, my girlfriend kisses me, strangers tip their top hats in respect. Preferably a music executive then shows up, offers me a record contract and tells me he will make me a star, but that part is optional.

I bought a little Casio keyboard for practice and signed up for lessons with a friendly elderly woman in town. Every Wednesday night, for the reasonable price of $12 a half hour, I headed to her home. The plan was for her to turn me into Mozart or, at the very least, Little Richard. Adding up the details, I guessed it would take me about, oh, a couple months before I was ready to take my show on the road. There would then be groupies.

My first warning sign that things weren't heading in quite the direction I'd hoped occurred in my first lesson. My instructor, Resa, informed me I would have to unlearn everything I knew about music, which wasn't all that much. "None of that rock 'n' roll stuff, that noise," she preached. "You must appreciate the discipline of counting and measures. The piano is an instrument of science and mathematics, and you must treat it as such." Well, Mrs. Miyagi, I suspect Axl Rose would disagree with you, but I'll play along.

The first selection in the book, *The Older Beginner Piano Course* (a.k.a., *Why Didn't You Learn This Shit When You Were Seven Like Everybody Else?*) was "Au Clair de la Lune," the French folk song that monkeys can play. I had no sooner made a lame joke about how maybe I needed to save this song from the German folk song on the adjoining page when Resa tersely tapped me on the knuckles—I'm lucky she didn't slam the damn piano door on my fingers—and reiterated, "Concentrate! There is no time for jokes. You must immerse yourself in the notes." But I just wanted to rock, rock hard, rock steady rock, steady rockin' all night long.

I sucked it up though, and eventually I did learn how to play "Au Claire" as well as "When the Saints Go Marching In," "Down in the Valley," and of course, "Mary Had a Little Lamb." I thought I was progressing at a pretty solid pace. Until one night, when I arrived about 15 minutes early for my lesson.

Resa was working with some snot-nosed, six-year-old Stepford child, a demonically angelic little girl with bows in her hair who was tapping out a magnificent version of Brahms' "Hungarian Dance No. 5." (How do Hungarians dance, by the way? I imagine it being manly, and hairy.) I watched as Resa gently turned the page and the little shit seamlessly transitioned into the Swan Lake theme. The lesson was then over, and she hugged Resa and told her she couldn't wait until next Thursday's recital. She asked if she could stay and listen to my lesson while she was waiting for her mom. Resa tried to hide her reluctance, but I noticed it. The kid stayed.

Well, old man Will sat down and clunked his way through "Michael, Row the Boat Ashore," feeling fortunate he hit any key, let alone the right one. Resa tried to remain patient. She told me, "You know, Will, it's OK to use both hands," but her exasperation was quietly evident. Kids, however, have no such restraint, and I heard a sickly sweet voice rise up behind me with, "Boy, you stink."

The piano gods later smiled on Resa. Our lessons ended about a month later when she and her family moved away. At our last one, she gave me the number of another teacher, but I got the impression she'd rather another colleague not be subjected to me. I staggered through a final version of "Lightly Row." Her look during the performance implied she felt it wasn't written to sound like silverware being dropped on the floor. I bade her, and my musical career, adieu.

Denny is fully aware and sympathetic of my thwarted desire to be a rock star, so he threw me a bone a couple weeks ago. His band was playing at a local watering hole, and in between songs he called for me to come onstage. To imaginary cheers, I sauntered on up and prepared for my moment of glory.

"OK, this is a new number we're doing. Will, you'll know what to do."

He then broke into a rousing version of the Peanuts theme song, and I realized I was not there to sing or drum or strum but instead to jump around and bob my head up and down just like Linus and the gang did on the cartoons. I was, of course, the dancing monkey for the crowd to mock, but I played along. It was fun, actually.

And, if I do say so myself, I *rocked*.

PHISH SCHOOLING

I like to think that, when it comes to music, I'm pretty open-minded. My favorite artists range from Bob Dylan to the Wu-Tang Clan to Nirvana to Lauryn Hill to Radiohead to the Beatles to R.E.M. to Liz Phair to Miles Davis to the Flaming Lips to Meat Loaf. Pretty much the only genre of music I can't tolerate is country music, and that's probably a subconscious rebellion against my Mattoon roots. Or maybe I just heard "If the South Would Have Won, We'd Have It Made" one too many times.

It takes quite a bit for me to openly reject a new artist. My friend Tim introduced me to Son Volt, and next thing you knew, I not only had all their CDs, but Uncle Tupelo's and Wilco's as well. My friend Mark mentioned how cool that new Outkast song was, and whammo, I had the entire Outkast oeuvre on my shelf. I even accompanied my friend Matt to an Elton John concert, though I did blanch at holding hands.

But there is one band, and one band only, that all my friends appear to love, and I just don't get it. I've fought lovers, family members, colleagues, even pets about it, but I've yet to find one positive aspect of the music of Phish.

Two of the most prominent women in my life have been Phish-heads. My sister Jill has a boyfriend named J. (just J, not Jay or Jaye, but J. Period.) who is as passionate about the band as she is. Jill and J. are students at the University of Illinois, but that's just their part-time job. Mainly they go to Phish shows and say things like, "You don't see Phish. You *experience* Phish." When I asked Jill how she liked the last show she'd been to, she said it was, "the bomb shit," which I guess means it was adequately pleasant.

The much more problematic Phish fan in my life was my ex-fiancée, who was a much more loose and fun person than me. She simply could not understand why I didn't realize that Phish was the closest thing to orgasm one could experience without being alone—you know, let's not get into that—and she considered me quite the fuddy-duddy for not enjoying their "music." We even once had a fight that ended with her telling me that I could take Kurt Cobain and shove him up my ass.

I actually once attempted to attend a show with her, but her Phish friends couldn't help but notice the glowing NERD sign imprinted on my forehead. After three songs, I sighed and accepted that I couldn't have looked more out of place if I was wearing a bow tie and praying toward Mecca, and I was banished to the parking lot to wait for her.

I guess I didn't understand how important Phish was to her—I mean, she did move to Burlington, Vermont, after inheriting her millions—but once she left me, I figured my days of pretending to be able to stand Phish were over.

Then I moved to St. Louis and made new friends, many of whom were Phish fanatics. (I'm sorry: Phish Phanatics.) They attempted to turn me on to the band, but I explained that my history with the band was probably too much to overcome. My friends trudged on, undaunted. A couple months ago, my friend Maggie invited me to a Phish concert at some place called Alpine Valley in Wisconsin, with the hope I might be converted. Now, I like Maggie quite a bit, but I couldn't imagine any situation where I could possibly enjoy hanging out with 65,000 people just like my ex-fiancée, except younger, poorer, and more stoned.

That said, I decided it was time to move on with my life, quit sitting around the apartment and lamenting what had once been, and, goddammit, go to the friggin' concert. Many people I respected were Phish fans, and because I had yet to *experience* Phish, perhaps this could be just the thing to pull me out of my three-year-plus doldrums. OK, Maggie, I'll go.

Five of us (Maggie, her husband, a soon-to-be-married couple, and I) packed into a rented minivan to head off on our savage journey to the heart of the American Dream. There's something very un-hippie, I think, about taking a soccer-mom-mobile, complete with automatic doors, temperature gauges and child seats, to a Phish show; to be fair, though, it *was* quite a comfortable ride.

Not only was my accompanying quartet big Phish fans, they were also married, or close to it, so it was fun to play the crazy single guy throughout the trip. Sample conversation:

Husband: Should we have gotten off at that exit?
Wife: Listen, do you want to drive?
Husband: Hey, I was just trying to help. Don't jump all over me. Maybe if you wouldn't leave your crap lying all over the house...
Wife: You want to help? Sit back there and shut the hell up.
Will: Does anybody have the Doritos?

I sat in the very back for the six-hour trip, trying not to be noticed and wondering what the odds were that I would run into the ex-fiancée at the concert. (Conclusion: About 1-in-112,500,000, accounting for the 65,000+ crowd and for the fact she lived 1,500 miles away.) But this concert was not about meeting long-lost loves. It was about exorcising old demons, about showing that Ghost of Ex-Fiancées Past that, doggone it, Will could relax and have a fun time at a Phish show. I could hop around and look at the dancing bears— there were dancing bears, right? Or was that something else?—and be loose and one with nature too. All I needed was the means.

I needed to get inside the Phish mindset, understand what it was that was holding me back, what made my various associates so cool for liking them and me so lame for not. I had to find that ideal Phish fan, in its own environment, and study its habits.

Alpine Valley was an obscenely over packed venue which featured enough lawn seating to hold the populations of Rhode Island, Delaware and Guam. To our immediate left in the parking lot, I witnessed a gaggle of kids who appeared to have swiped Dad's Pathfinder for the weekend, reaching the heaven of having a place to light up without worrying if Mom was coming down the stairs. If they were a day over 16, I'd be shocked. I quickly remembered how I looked at people my age when I was 16, and I realized that I didn't like the way those punks were looking at me.

"Hey, nice van, dudes!" an Acne Nation member spat at me to a random smattering of giggles and grunts from his cohorts. I was only 23, but I'm constantly aware of my own mortality, so it was important for me to bond with them.

"So guys, you pumped for the concert? Motherfuckin' PHISH, yeah!" I was reaching, but I wasn't sure they'd be able to tell the difference. They couldn't.
"Fuck no, dude, we're just here to smoke some dope and grill some brats, yeah!" We were in Wisconsin.
"Oh, you guys aren't Phish fans?"
"Oh, some of their shit's OK, but their solos go too long, like forever. We don't even have tickets. We'll just be out here, gettin' fucked up!" The Pathfinder inhabitants cheered.

I was unfazed. Surely, not everyone there was around only to have a safe place to smoke pot away from Mom and Dad. I was aware of a crazed Phish contingent, people willing to follow them around the world, and I was determined to find it.

Once we got settled on the lawn, I found a most peculiar man who not only dressed like Hunter S. Thompson, but also seemed to be trying to channel Dr. Gonzo. He had the whole package: doofy fisherman's cap, crazy Hawaiian shirt, cigarette holder jutting out of his mouth from a dangerous angle. He even talked in the sporadic, between-clenched-teeth manner of Thompson, so much so that I wondered whether this wasn't something he brought out just for the concert. I was preparing to ask him why exactly he decided that his muse would be an ether-swilling madman who hadn't written anything worthwhile in 20 years, but I couldn't get my own damned cigarette lit and was interrupted by a pleasant-looking goateed gentleman who mercifully offered me a light.

"You don't quite look like you belong," he said. He was right. Unlike the sarong-clad, dirty-haired, bead-adorned average Phish-goer, I was wearing a black Old Navy t-shirt and a pair of almost ridiculously yuppie slacks, and my hair had a Pat Riley-esque amount of gel in it.

My new friend was from New Hampshire. "This is my first time in Wisconsin." Pause. "Of course, why the hell do I go anywhere? I've been to Vermont, New York, Hawaii, they all look the same. The only reason I've been anywhere is to see Phish. So, yep, here I am, in Wisconsin. I'll be in Illinois tomorrow, I think."

Now we were getting somewhere.

I pushed. "So, if you don't mind me asking, what is it about Phish that makes you willing to sacrifice everything in your life just to follow them around? Is it their music? Is it the atmosphere? Is it the pot?"
"Listen, society wants you to get a job, have a family, get a credit card. I don't want any part of that. I just want to be free, ride the music, man."
"OK, but can't you 'ride the music' at home? Can't you 'ride the music' to, say, Nirvana? What is it specifically about Phish that has changed your life?"
"Man, if you don't know, I can't tell you."

I was obviously butting my head against a wall, but still willing to dig deeper. But the conversation ceased as the band took the stage. They launched into some song I didn't know, and I prepared myself for the apparent mind-altering sound that I was about to experience for the first time.

What can I tell you? I'll try to be nice about it. I still don't get it. That kid in the Pathfinder was right; their solos *did* go on too long. It was just a bunch of idiotic, bouncy-happy music, a bunch of forget-life-and-just-hop-around-like-an-idiot gibberish that I tuned out about halfway through. The music was nice enough, I guess, but I kept waiting for Pete Townshend to show up, smashing guitars and *rocking*, for chrissakes.

'Twas not to be. The band took an intermission, during which I tried in vain to find my sister, the ex-fiancée or, at the very least, God, and then they played a few more interminable songs. I understand that they played a song they hadn't played in years, because the guy with the lighter all of a sudden started jumping up and down, screaming, knocking over his companion and making us all giggle. All in all, underwhelming.

Eventually, the show ended, and I had found neither a reason to pursue Phish further nor an understanding of why anyone would slavishly follow them anywhere. We got back to the van, where our underage friends were still hanging out, smoking, grilling, and philosophizing.

"You know what's so awesome about Phish concerts?"
What's that, Paco?

"It's all about gettin' fucked up, hangin' out with my boys and scopin' out the hippie bitches.

"Actually, it's mainly about the bitches."

Trust me, kid, it's not worth the effort.

KISS THE GIRLS AND WATCH THEM FLY

I've kissed 19 women in my life. Typically, I'm told that number is somewhat low, but it doesn't seem like it to me. Nineteen people who would share something as intensely personal and uniquely human as a kiss? With me? I'd settle for that many people who will *talk* to me.

I've been doing a lot of thinking about this lately, and I've decided that No. 20 is going to have to be special. I'll be officially out of the teens, and I plan on celebrating the occasion more appropriately than I did No. 10. (I never told Niki Ziegler she pushed me into double digits; I thought I was too mature for such a thing. Balderdash!)

Confession: You might find me to be a borderline psychopath for doing such a thing, but I have a list of every woman I've ever kissed, in chronological order. I also have an alphabetical list, but I don't bring that one out too often. I've always kept up an unofficial list—you know, like horse racing results; pretty much accurate, but you've got to check every last detail first—but only recently have I etched it into stone. This list is very important to me, but I'd have to talk to my mother before I tried to determine any particular reason why.

Having such a list might seem trivial or even offensive to you, but, I swear, this isn't some kind of notches-on-the-bedpost exercise in self-congratulation; it's sincere. I look at the names of these 19 women in wonder. Am I one of their more embarrassing partners? If asked if they had ever kissed me, would they admit it? Do they think of me fondly? Do they think of me at all? Considering that I've haven't spoken with any of the 19 in the last month, I guess I know the answers to those questions.

Looking at such a list is a most disconcerting activity. It's like reading the story of my life in outline form: Met this girl in the church youth group; met this one at the movie theater; met this one at the college newspaper; met this one in Los Angeles; met this one while recovering from the breakup of my engagement. The list exposes my flaws and excesses. The first time I kissed the first nine had nothing to do with alcohol; nine of the last 10 were during or after drinking.

I'm a big baseball fan, so it's fun to do statistical breakdowns of the list. Of the 19, six are married, two are engaged, three have children, 16 have college degrees, six have graduate degrees. Ten were from my hometown, four from college, five from the scary grownup world. Weirdly, 12 on the list are older than I am, including a shocking nine in a row. I don't know what that means, exactly; my only guess is that I reminded them of a little brother they picked on all the time, and they were trying to make amends.

The women fall into different categories. Some were one-time aberrations, random occurrences that likely would be forgotten if it weren't for the self-doubting kid with the word processor dredging them up from their rightful home in the subconscious (Traci, Amy, Jennifer, Kim, Angela, and Danielle: 31 percent).

Then you have the false alarms, the ones I thought were a big deal at the time but turned out to be, in retrospect, fond footnotes in the sand (Barbara, Andrea, Kyla and Michelle: 21 percent). Like any human, I've had my share of the people who would have every right to hate me. (Well, I was kind of a jerk, and they probably do.) I either stopped calling them, or I met someone else, or I simply left town without a proper goodbye. Before you lash out at me, dear reader, make your own list, and see how many of these there are on yours (Amanda, Rachel, Niki, Laura, Carrie… an alarming 26 percent). Strangely, I've only really had one relationship that started with no expectations, ended with no expectations and had nothing all that crazy happen in between. Kind of a perpetual dating holding-pattern. (Sorry, Joan, wherever you are: 5 percent).

Then there are the ones who stick in your craw, the ones you never quite get over, the ones who pop up in your dreams every once in a while just to haunt you. They're the ones most likely to spur one to write a column to try to come to mental terms with the 19 women one has kissed. These might have ended badly, but what's most important is that they ended, and I haven't quite come to terms with it. These women are the ones that if I ran into one of them on the street, I'd probably hide under a table, and whimper. They were too beautiful, too smart, too hip, too beloved by all to be wasting their time with me. Most common phrase overheard when we were together: "Well, I'm sure he's got qualities we don't know about." It was of course inevitable they would eventually move on to bigger, better, and less neurotic things (Betty, Diane and the ex-fiancée: 15 percent).

I've always thought it might be cool to track down all 19 and find out what they're up to, try to find some common theme among all of them to help me understand why I do some of the things I do, why I've turned out the way I have. After researching all their lives, I'd probably have enough material for a book. I'm sure it would never work though. Seems like such a project is destined to be titled *19 Restraining Orders*.

Which leads us to today. Now, understand, I'm hardly actively searching for No. 20. Good thing: Anyone reading this has probably already eagerly dismissed themselves from competition. And I'm in no hurry. In fact, 19 sounds like a good number to end on. It's about in tune with what I'm used to; right on the precipice of a milestone, a new horizon, but stopping agonizingly short.

Nineteen is probably too many anyway. I have a good friend who has kissed only one person, his wife. They have a beautiful child, a happy home, and matching 401K plans. They even have one of those cross-stitched wall hangings on their wall that says, "God Bless this Mess." I have posters of Woody Allen movies about longing, loss, and the absence of God on my wall. I'm sure my friend isn't haunted by old girlfriends in his dreams. I'm sure he doesn't have various women across the country who, if they think of him at all, snicker about how he sweated too much, stroked their hair too much or often smelled terrible. I think I like his life a little more; less complicated.

But one thing is certain. If there is a No. 20, I'll have to tell her. Though I have a feeling if I do tell No. 20, I'll be on the search for No. 21 pretty soon thereafter. Very good chance of that, actually.

(Note: This column was written almost four years ago. Your author wishes to point out that he has since kissed more than 19 people. He doesn't remember the name of No. 20.)

ADULT WORLD

It is clear I am not cut out for the corporate world. I don't mean the corporate world of insider trading, guys screaming "buy" and "sell" into their cell phones and foreclosing on family farms. That world is as foreign to me as Mars. I mean the grownup world, the place where you earn a salary, pay bills, put money into 401k plans, and try to stay upwardly mobile. I'm perfectly content to sit here all day and tell you about Woody Allen's new film and whether my cat and I are getting along, but the world doesn't seem too crazy about that idea. Since the world, like the playground bully, is bigger than me, it tends to win.

I've told you a bit about my current job, but let me tell you a little more. According to the stack of unused business cards sitting next to my ashtray, I'm an Associate Editor/Online at *The Sporting News* in St. Louis, Missouri. What this means is that four days a week, I update *The Sporting News* Web site with fresh stories, snazzy headlines, compelling photos and various subterfuge I can throw up there without anyone noticing. On a fifth day, I come in and write a column about college football, called "The Blitz," in which I try desperately to make games like Idaho vs. Eastern Washington sound remotely interesting. I also take a lot of smoke breaks and watch a bunch of NBA games.

My job is nice enough, I guess; I make a decent living, have many friends at work, and am at least somewhat respected by my colleagues and my helpful and pleasant superiors. But, well, I dunno. I'm a snot-nosed kid, and I'm just inexperienced enough in this business to think there has to be more out there.

When I was an idealistic college student who planned on ruling the world, I never imagined I'd be straining to come up with a headline for the Padres-Expos game at 1:30 in the morning, hoping to hurry home because my cat hasn't been fed yet. I guess I just didn't think I would ever use "helpful superiors" as a justification for why I like my job. We all go through this painful realization that the real world isn't near what we thought it would be, I suppose, but understand, I was only in college two years ago and haven't quite come to terms with it yet.

As you may know, my true loves are movies and books, and working in sports has never really felt all that comfortable. I covered Illinois basketball in college, and I was close to my ultimate opinion on sports reporting as a long-term career when Michigan basketball player Robert Traylor simply refused to wrap a damned towel around himself during an interview in the Wolverines locker room. (I now know why they call him "Tractor.") When I came back to press row and found four bloated beat reporters whining about the chicken at the buffet table, I pretty much decided sports was to be watched with a beer in hand, not a pencil.

Still, after circumstances including the breakup with my ex-fiancée, a film critic position that fell through, and a general drunken malaise, I ended up at *The Sporting News*, and I was happy to be there. Everyone was extremely friendly, and my old friends were impressed I had an e-mail address that ended with *.com* rather than *.edu*. But by the time my daily column on baseball was killed, in part because it was "too writery," I realized that if I was going to get to where I wanted to go—wherever that was—it would have to be elsewhere. Eventually, anyway.

That said, I liked where I was and didn't see any immediate need to get some boring city-council beat job just because I wanted to write. Then my *deus ex machina* came soaring in. A friend informed me of a job opening at *The New York Times* on the Web, an arts/living producer position that involved, well, producing the arts/living section, I guess. It likely wouldn't increase my writing opportunities, but jeez, it was *The New York Times*, and given a choice of barely writing at *The Sporting News* or barely writing at *The New York Times*, I'd go with the *Times*.

Plus, I figured what better place for a young, neurotic wannabe writer guy than New York City? At the very least, I'd be hanging out with other artsy-fartsy writer people, and I'd either have constant creative inspiration or realize that everyone was better than me and resign myself to middle management.

I sent my résumé and all the particulars to my editor's contact at the *Times*, an engaging woman named Meredith who spoke with me for a while, then suggested I head out to New York for an interview. I was dumbfounded; as excited as I was about the possibility of moving to New York and working for *The New York Times*, I'd never really thought they would actually consider a kid two years out of college who could barely write his name in the ground with a stick. But they set up the flight reservations and everything, and after my mother made an emergency trip to St. Louis to prepare me—"Will, you are not going to wear that fish tie into the offices of *The New York Times*"—next thing I knew, still stunned, I was on a plane to New York City.

I had never been there before.

I'm not a big fan of airplanes, not because I'm afraid of crashing, but just because you inevitably have to sit next to people who, if you're lucky, only have a crying baby with which to annoy you. Fortunately, it was an under-booked flight, so I had my own pair of seats to stretch across, but I still found a way to be irritated.

In the seat in front of me, some guy about my age, maybe a little older, was reading a book called *Seven Ways to Peace and Happiness*. Now, I've always been of the belief that if you need a self-help book to help you survive, the world would be better off without you anyway, so to torture myself and take my mind off the interview, I found myself looking over his shoulder. The book was by Tony Robbins or Zig Ziglar or Zed Zappa or some other idiot, and the guy in front of me was currently on a chapter called "Eight words that can transform your life." I don't know what those eight words were—it's not easy to read over someone's shoulder in a plane, you know—but I have a few ideas:

Quit reading books and do something with yourself.
There is no peace and happiness; grow up.
Self-help books fill the voids in your brain.
Don't sit ahead of cynical assholes on planes.

By the time the guy in front of me was dutifully studying the wisdom of "At least once a day, tell yourself, 'Self, I will be happy today.' And you will be," I retreated to my own world. I got to thinking about how much I hate the interview process. I spend most of my life thinking I'm constantly failing everyone's internal test on how to live anyway, and job interviews simply amplify this process times 50. This time, the test is external, and it's someone you don't know doing the judging.

Every single flaw I merely dwell on in everyday life, I obsess about to the point of mania before a job interview. On the ride to the airport for my departing flight, I interrogated my friend Matt about my: a) hair, b) tie, c) socks, d) complexion, e) suit jacket, f) hair, g) waistline, h) tie, i) armpit smell, j) breath, k) hair. After the third hair mention, Matt began smacking me.

How much did I want this job? I caught myself, while making notes for the interview, doodling "leitch@nytimes.com" in the margins, like some junior high girl writing "Mrs. Tammy DiCaprio" on her three-ring binder. This job would mean everything. At least my small-town relatives would have an answer when they asked my parents, "Seriously, why isn't Will married yet?" ("Oh, he lives in New York. You know how those people are.") There would have been a definite direction in my life, if not a vague one. It is not wise to hang your happiness on whether a group of strangers deem you worthy, but, well, it was all I had.

Anyway, my plane finally landed and I picked up my luggage. (The guy with the self-help book was greeted by a beautiful woman. Of course.) I hailed the first cab of my life and headed to Manhattan, which for the first time I would recognize as something other than a great Woody Allen movie.

I checked into the hotel and went upstairs for my twenty-minute break until I was supposed to arrive at the interview. I cleaned up a little, went over my notes for some last-minute cramming and smoked a dearly needed cigarette. Then it was interview time.

I knew I was in trouble when I walked in wearing my best suit and was greeted by some casually dressed friendly people who nevertheless looked at me like the new kid in class who just moved here from some snooty prep school. My nerves got the best of me for a while, but I pulled it together. I said all the right things, made silly jokes, and mentioned how much fun it appeared everyone was having. During the next two days, they were going to show me how their system worked and I was actually going to participate in a night shift, so I jotted down copious notes, hoping to impress them with my Web expertise.

Everything went as well as could be reasonably expected, and, save for a few stray questions about why I wasn't eating when everyone else was—I eventually admitted a strange addiction to Dexatrim—I think I had them thinking I was adequately normal and qualified for the job. When I left, I had a cigarette with Meredith, who seemed, not that I possess much knowledge about these things, as if she were optimistic about hiring me. She told me they would let me know in "one to three weeks," which, given past experiences, I assumed would be about 10 days, tops. I bid her adieu and headed back to the hotel. Ten hours later, I was on a plane, heading back to St. Louis.

Of course, when I arrived, all my friends wanted to know how the interview went, and, when pressed, I had to admit, I felt it had gone pretty well. You never know about such matters, I said, but if I had a chance in the first place, I didn't blow it, which for me is 95 percent of the battle. All I could do now was wait.

About a week and a half after I got back, around the time I was staying home all day desperately waiting for a phone call, I received an e-mail from a woman I'd met at the *Times* named Inger. She was a fellow arts producer with whom I would work if I got the job. Her e-mail said that she was happy to meet me while I was out there, and that I had mentioned I had some ideas for the site. Could I please send those to her? Well, I thought I'd spent the three days out there telling them all about my ideas for the site, but I was nevertheless happy to oblige, putting together a term-paper-like manifesto in about two hours, finishing close to midnight. I hoped it was adequate. The *Times* called two of my four references later in the week and I prepared myself for the evidently impending call.

I spent about as much time preparing as a high-school girl going to her senior prom. Every morning, I'd wake up at 10, shower and jot notes on my word processor until I had to be at work at 5, expecting the phone to ring any second. Oh, it did ring. Salesperson, friend from college, another salesperson, mother, cousin, another salesperson, friend from work. But still, as we rapidly approached the three-week deadline, I didn't hear a thing.

As you can probably guess, I handled this stressful period of purgatory with my typical panic. I get stressed out when I order drinks; when I'm waiting to find out where I'll be spending the next few years of my life, I'm borderline catatonic. Still, I realized there was simply nothing I could do, so I waited. And I waited. When I got bored, I'd take a break, and then I would wait some more. Lather, rinse, repeat.

Now, I know you're expecting some big dramatic end to this. I have tried to build suspense. I am not sure I did well.

Well, guess what, folks? It has been three months—count 'em!—since I left the interview, and, in the one scenario I didn't anticipate in the slightest… I still don't know if I got the job. I've had a bit of correspondence with people at the *Times*, and they keep telling me to hang on. That's fine, but nevertheless, this needed to be written about. I'm losing my mind here.

It's likely there's some kind of statute of limitations on writing about job interviews, and it's got to be less than three months. This column might not be wise, but it's honest.

One thing's certain. Whether it's at *The Sporting News* or at *The New York Times*, I'm not getting a 401k plan. I don't have to grow up if I don't want to.

(Note: The author ended up getting the job and moving to New York. He was there for three months before leaving for an upstart dot-com. It was one of the poorer decisions of his adult life. But we're getting to that.)

CAN'T FIGHT THIS FEELING

One of my least favorite things when I was living in Los Angeles was being known as Midwestern Guy. For some reason, when you live on either coast but didn't grow up there, you are subject to ridicule and mockery. I've heard 'em all: *Hey, Will, do you miss the corn? Hey, Will, you Midwesterners sure can drink! Hey, Will, ever bed your cousin?* Perhaps the best example of the mindset: A friend who lives in New York told me about how she was talking to a guy at a party, and when she told him she was from Illinois, he responded icily, "Well, someone has to be from Illinois, I guess."

Still, having friends who grew up outside the Midwest has forced me to re-evaluate some of the things I do. I guess you can take the boy out of Mattoon, Illinois, but it takes the Jaws of Life, a salad fork, one of those Bobcat diggers, and a powerful leaf blower to even try to extricate Mattoon from the boy.

I'll admit to drinking Anheuser-Busch products, saying "doggone it to heck" on occasion, and thoroughly enjoying a night of bowling from time to time. I have been cow-tipping; I used to have a mullet and, given the opportunity, I'll put John Cougar Mellencamp on every jukebox in the Tri-County area. I'm not afraid to say it, folks: I was born in a small town... used to daydream in that small town... that's probably where they'll bury me. HEY!

However, I don't want the Midwestern thing to be my rep when I move to New York next week. As I found out when I made friends with people from Los Angeles—and even Chicago—it's difficult to be taken seriously once you tell someone you wore a jean jacket with Poison and Warrant buttons during your sophomore year in high school. Can't imagine seriously discussing Dylan Thomas poems with artsy New Yorkers if they know my favorite movies as a kid could be found in the Ernest oeuvre.

Changing misconceptions will be one of my top priorities once I get to New York, and I'm willing to wear black turtlenecks and smoke cloves to do it. (That's what they do there. Seriously. I read about it once.) There's one very Midwestern vice, however, that I will not apologize for, and I can only hope the artsy folk can deal with it. When you're talking fun, drunken social activities, I won't lie, I find few more fun than... are you ready?... *karaoke*.

You don't think I'm a dork, do you?

There's a place called TomE's near my apartment, a ragtag saloon with plenty of big-haired women and guys wearing Confederate-flag hats. It's a rough-and-tumble place, full of guys who bring their pool cues with them to their factory jobs so they don't have to stop at home before the bar. They sell pitchers of Natural Light and Busch for four bucks, and you drink out of plastic cups with ads for local garages on the sides. Every Friday and Saturday are karaoke nights. No matter where I am each weekend, if you listen closely, you can hear TomE's beckoning me, singing its siren song of "I Will Survive," vexing me.

I will say—in an attempt to sound all postmodern and in favor of performance art—there is an obviously strong kitsch factor involved in a Midwestern karaoke night. I've been to them too many times to count, and I've learned what you can bank on each time:

✓ A group of three to six drunk women, friends from work or old college cheerleaders, will sing "Love Shack."

✓ Some guy with sideburns will do an Elvis song.

✓ The most meek, quiet, shy woman in a gaggle of friends will eventually be persuaded to live a little and go up and sing something like "I Will Always Love You," "My Heart Will Go On," or "Wind Beneath My Wings," then smile sheepishly, go back to her table and be congratulated by her friends for her courage. My favorite example of this was an obscenely overweight woman who gave a rousing rendition of "What A Feeling (Flashdance)," complete with a chair turned backwards and violent Jazzercize gyrations. All she was missing were the headbands, leotard and someone to pour water over her.

✓ Some guy in a cowboy hat will do either a Hank Williams song, or if he's particularly hip, Bon Jovi's "Wanted Dead or Alive." He will sing with a proud snarl, particularly the line, "I'm a cowboy! On a steel horse I ride!"

✓ A dumb, drunk frat guy will think he's being really funny by doing a song with the word "sex" in the title (although I've never had the heart to tell him that George Michael is gay, so he's probably singing to a man.

This is wonderful entertainment over a few pitchers of beer, and I don't mean to mock these people too much. There's something achingly sincere about each of these performances. That's the beauty of karaoke. It's a time to cut loose and forget you have an efficiency expert coming in next week and that your cable bill is a week overdue. I do enjoy laughing at these people, but it's not cynical. Karaoke is no place for cynics. If you're not willing to play along with a 40-year-old welder trying to channel Tom Jones, then you can go to your tofu bars, hippie, and leave the soul to us.

When you're at karaoke, you see people at their naked, truest selves, using a song to remember or mark one of the happier times in their life. Sure, when Bernice tries to belt out "R-E-S-P-E-C-T," she sounds more like Pat Boone, but that's not the point. In her mind, she *is* Aretha Franklin—for five minutes anyway—and if you're too heartless to let her have that moment and witness the freedom she's obviously reveling in by being someone else, well, we don't want you around anyway.

And if she's so out of tune it makes your back hair stand at attention? That's just all the more fun.

Anyway, the last time I went, I was with a group of five who were not regular karaoke participants. None of my friends planned on actually singing, heavens no, but I figured if I went up first, and they consumed a few pitchers of Busch, they'd give it a shot. My name was called. I'd kept my song choice a secret, and I followed a woman who had the audacity to sing KISS's "Beth" with a straight face. (KISS is the exception to the karaoke rules; if someone sings a KISS song, you have every right to openly mock them, and even, perhaps, pour beer on their head.)

My moment had come. As the song began, I thought back to junior high school, at the roller skating rink, when all my friends had girlfriends and I had to sit and eat Fritos in the common area. There was one particularly popular song for the slow, hand-in-hand skate at the time, and it used to always depress me. But now it was my turn:

"I can't fight this feeling any longer. And yet I'm still afraid to let it flow. What started out as friendship has grown stronger..."

As I wailed out REO Speedwagon's "Can't Fight This Feeling," my friends were at first horrified, then a little worried; then they started to laugh. And then they started to smile. I was up there singing REO Speedwagon—REO Speedwagon!—wildly out of tune but with every bit of feeling and, yeah, dammit, all the sexiness I could muster. I serenaded a woman in the front row, and I think I even might have made her friend blush.

I was ghastly, embarrassing, and more than a little drunk, but when you're up on stage singing REO Speedwagon to a group of strangers, you have little time to think about that. A waitress even walked by the table where my friends were laughing and chided them for making fun of me. I found that adorable.

I don't know what my future friends in New York would do, but my Midwestern friends eventually got up and sang with me. They had a damned good time.

Now, let's see if we can get those folks in the Village to do some cow-tipping...

LIVING IN SQUALOR... AND FEAR

My junior year of college, I had a roommate named Ryan. He was a nice enough guy, who worked with me at the *Daily Illini*. We got along adequately, but we were both closer to our third roommate, Mike, than we were to each other. I actually lived with both of them the summer before my junior year, in one of those glorious sublets for losers left behind in Campustown in July, and we figured it would be a good test run for the upcoming year.

Since it wasn't really our apartment, and since we were going to be bolting in August anyway, I never felt particularly compelled to make certain our living arrangements were pristine. That is to say, I never cleaned the place, or even my own small segment of it, in the three months we lived there. When I moved out, I left before Ryan did and headed home to Mattoon for a couple of weeks of R&R before school started up again. We had no security deposit to answer to, so I didn't find it all that necessary to clean up any of the random shit lying around our apartment, namely three-week old pizzas, empty beer cans, and some sort of substance around the ring of the toilet that resembled human hair, although I couldn't be sure.

Ryan was a neat freak, and he just couldn't stand leaving the apartment in such disarray. So he figured he'd tidy the place up a bit, assuming I'd done somewhat of the same before I bolted. Wrong. I'd left about 15 dirty, nasty-ass washcloths lying in the shower and various paraphernalia strewn across the kitchen floor. I'd even failed to pick up some socks that were in the corner of my room.

Needless to say, Ryan was plenty pissed. I came home to a smirking father who spat, "You've got a message on the machine." It was Ryan, spewing forth a stream of profanities and basically saying that I was a disgusting waste of flesh, and that next time, I was peeling my own damn underwear off the wall. My memory has faded, but I think Ryan's signoff was "Asshole." It was that or "Prick." I don't remember exactly.

I was reminded of this episode recently because, for the first time in about a year and a half, now that I live in New York, I have a roommate. When I lived in Los Angeles, four of us shared a big-ass apartment meant for two people. I was lucky enough to have two close friends as fellow dwellers, and the third roommate was enough of an idiot that I didn't have to deal with him, so my inherent slob quality was taken as a personality eccentricity rather than as grounds for execution.

When I moved to St. Louis, I was determined to live by myself. This wasn't because I didn't like my previous roommates; I just wanted to have the experience of being able to sit in my boxer shorts at 3 a.m., spill nachos on myself, read an Andy Rooney book and answer to no one. And I enjoyed it; it's always nice when you have the freedom to just dump your ashtray on the carpet, rather than get up and walk all the way over to the trash. I'd picked up about 75 percent of my current bad habits in St. Louis, and I loved them all. I didn't think it would be a big problem; I had no plans to have a roommate other than a cat in the near future, so why try to be clean? For that matter, why try any self-improvement at all if you don't have to?

Then came my unexpected move to New York. Initially, I had planned on living in the *Times*-supplied hotel right by the office for a month, during which time I would go through the hell of finding an apartment in this city. I knew it would be daunting, but I figured the month would be more than enough time to deal with sleazy brokers and the stench of paying $1,200 for glorified closet space.

Then my friend Brian contacted me. Brian worked with me at *The Sporting News*. A sports nut like me, he became one of my best friends at *TSN*, mainly because we shared a healthy appreciation of the NBA Live PlayStation game and we saw the world in similar ways. When I arrived at *TSN*, I knew nobody, and my friend Chris took me under her wing and introduced me to the social circle. Feeling I should do the same for new faces, I warmed to Brian immediately, even though, as he informed me in our first conversation, he didn't drink and was a devout Methodist.

I do, and I'm not.

(One of my favorite moments of my first week in New York was when Brian's parents were here helping him get set up and cooking us breakfast; I was halfway through mine before I realized that, oh yeah, we're supposed to pray first... But I'm getting ahead of myself.)

Brian quickly became one of my favorite people in the world, and when he told me he'd taken a job at Fox Sports in New York, I was deeply saddened to see him leave. But then after the *Times* finally called me, and after Brian had his first nasty broker experience in New York, he rang me up and introduced the possibility of us being roommates. The deal: He would find a place, I'd send him a check, and bam, I'd have a place to live. No fuss. Having heard all the horror stories about finding an apartment here, I figured, yeah, Brian, go ahead and do all the dirty work. The check will be in the mail if and when you find a place. For that, I figured I could deal with having a roommate and not being able to smoke in the apartment.

Well, Brian found a place in Greenwich Village: I checked it out with New York friends; they said it was cool, and just like that, I was here. Neither of us had much time to worry too much about the particulars; we had a place, and we didn't have to pay a broker fee—non-New Yorkers: do you realize a broker fee is two month's rent and non-refundable? Mission accomplished.

Now came the hard part—preventing Brian from killing me for as long as possible.

Don't get me wrong; Brian and I have been getting along fabulously so far, and we've spent each Sunday since I got here watching the NFL playoffs, playing PlayStation, and just hanging out. I've had a bit of a personal crisis of late, and Brian, as always, has been a valued confidant—even if his advice is usually, "You're an idiot." I think we'll have a lasting friendship. But when the honeymoon is over, when we settle into our lives here, those cute, weird little things that I became accustomed to when I was living by myself will start to become real annoying, real fast.

Brian appears to have done this roommate thing more recently than I have, or he's just far more organized than me, because there's all this stuff I didn't know I was supposed to do. Like, what's the deal with this whole bill-paying thing? I mean, I know you have to do it, but on time? Really? What if you'd rather go out to the bar? How important are lights, anyway?

It's already obvious that the practical things that need to be done in an apartment are all being taken care of by Brian. He set up our voicemail, got all our utilities turned on and has written down all the bills that are due, letting me know when and how much to pay. He left me a note the other day saying we should get a dry-erase board for the refrigerator so we wouldn't need to use notebooks all the time. Good idea; I wouldn't have come up with it. He also left me a note telling me he had done the dishes; I didn't even know we *had* dishes.

We're fortunate because nothing is too dirty yet, but I'll be honest with you: I didn't clean my toilet once when I lived in St. Louis. That seems like the type of thing that Brian might expect to be done once in a while. It's not that I don't want to do it (although I don't); the problem is that I just never notice things like a dirty commode. I think a lot of it has to do with my lack of a sense of smell, which is also why Brian will probably get real annoyed by the litter box real quick.

Oh, and there's my room. We have one of those railroad apartments where Brian has to walk through my room to get to his. That seems like something that would bother him more than it would bother me, but the problem is, nothing bothers me. Not dirt, not smell, not dust.

Most of my stuff has yet to arrive from St. Louis, so my room is basically random suitcases and unopened boxes all over the floor. Brian is the type of guy who would probably start putting stuff away, somewhere. Not me. I'm perfectly content to just let everything sit there, unorganized. But when you have to walk through an eyesore—and underwear lying everywhere—just to get to your room, a normally mild-mannered Methodist might veer toward a life of murderous fury.

Then there are the supplies normal people need to survive. When I was in St. Louis, I would never buy anything until a week or two after I ran out of it. I suspect that after a week or two of no toilet paper, Brian might start to protest. It's possible.

Now, nothing has gone wrong so far, not in the slightest. We're getting along great, hanging out, leaving each other roommate notes, getting adjusted to the city. But I know me, and I know I'm a goddamned slob with no idea how to take care of myself. Our saving grace might end up being our radically different schedules; Brian works during the day like a normal human while I have that oh-so-attractive 4 p.m. to 2 a.m. shift.

Ultimately that might be the only way to keep me alive. When I end up unwittingly but inevitably irking the otherwise comely Brian to the point of homicidal rage, I'll just hide until it blows over. Or maybe I'll try to become a better person, make myself cleaner, more considerate, careful and responsible.

OK, let's not get carried away. It's easier to hide. In fact, I think I see a good spot under the bundle of dirty clothes in the kitchen...

WAITING FOR WOODY

Ninety-first and Madison. According to the snazzy Streetwise Manhattan pocket map a friend gave me upon my arrival in New York, I need to hop on the 6 Train at Union Square, ride it to 96th Street and then jaunt five blocks south and two blocks west. I'm $1.50 and a five-minute walk away... from Woody.

When I revealed to close friends that I had accepted a job in New York City, the first question they asked, without exception, was, "So, are you going to stalk Woody Allen when you get there?" I chuckled, let out an amused sigh and then shot them a steely glance and said, "Yes. Of course."

Little bit you should know about me... Growing up in Mattoon, it was difficult to find others like me, other neurotic little simps who would much rather sit and muse and philosophize about love, death and the meaning of it all than swig beers while sitting on the hood of a Corvette in a cornfield. (As I've gotten older, I've learned to combine these things.) The closest I could find was my best friend Tim, and even he was a little too cool for the job. He was smart and read books by Tom Wolfe, too deep for a Shel Silverstein junkie like myself.

Then Tim and I discovered Woody Allen. We were 16 and had only recently discovered that we shared a manic, depraved love of the movies. We were coming to the devotion somewhat late, so we made a practice on Saturday nights—while normal kids were out prematurely ejaculating like 16-year-olds are supposed to—to rent all the famous movies we could find and get caught up. We grabbed *Citizen Kane, Singin' in the Rain, Raging Bull*, the essentials. Then one evening, Tim suggested a film called *Annie Hall*, which I had heard of mainly because I knew Paul Simon was in it.

We brought it back to my home, and it was like nothing I'd ever seen. Here was this nebbishy little man, ethnic in some way I didn't quite know but certainly understood—there are no Jewish people in Mattoon; Catholic is about as eclectic as you get—who was smart, funny, and strangely sad. He was a guy like me, a nerdy bookish type who was trying to figure it all out—relationships, life, death, family, toasters. I was intrigued but not yet hooked. I then, on my own, rented *Play It Again, Sam*, Woody's and Herbert Ross' 1972 valentine to *Casablanca* and the movies.

Now he had me. Woody played Allan Felix, a film writer who was, in turn, klutzy, ridiculous, smart, funny, perverted, weird, and sweet. When his on-screen wife left him, complaining he was a helpless dreamer with no real concrete plans to do anything, I could have cried. I had *found* him; there was another like me. Woody Allen was saying, analyzing, living parts of my life before I'd even realized they had occurred. And yet, somehow, he was a hero, attracting beautiful women and doing the right thing in the end, trying to find a way to make it through the day when he knows it all ends in death anyway, kvetching all the way. Suddenly, seeing Woody Allen, I knew being the way I was was OK, that it wasn't so strange. I was 16, but I knew I'd found my muse.

Oh, was I ever hooked. After Tim and I saw *Husbands and Wives*—my first Woody Allen movie in a theater—and I realized that Woody had ideas about the darker sides of life that made as much sense as anything I'd ever even considered, my friends began to notice a distinct change in me. I began to talk like Woody Allen, stutter like Woody Allen, gesticulate wildly like Woody Allen, walk hunched over like Woody Allen, *think* like Woody Allen. My obsession dominated every aspect of my life, and well, I guess it still does.

Right before Tim—who was a huge Woody fan but intelligent and self-assured enough not to let him take over his entire life—left for film school at the University of Southern California, we got together for a marathon viewing of all Woody's films, 22 at the time. We watched them all, straight through, with occasional visits from sympathetic friends who wondered what exactly had happened to Tim and Will. But we made it, we saw them all, even *September*, and my mom wonders if it might have messed me up even worse than she and my dad could have.

And it's actually gotten more extreme. I've been idolizing Woody and his films for so long, I don't even know where my adopting his persona starts and my own ends. Every fall, when his new film inevitably comes out, it's like a trek to Mecca.

The best birthday I've ever had was my 20th, which I spent in a crowded theater in Champaign, Illinois, watching a sneak preview of *Mighty Aphrodite* with Roger Ebert and other Daily Illini alumni. At the end of the film, Ebert, who through e-mail correspondence knew I was a psychotic Woody fan, waddled over to me and asked what I thought. Ebert, a fellow Southern Illinois boy, had always been an example to me of how hard work and talent can get you out of the twisted cycle of small towns, and he was a secondary hero. When Ebert asked me my opinion, my head exploded and my body burst into flames.

I can tell you who with, where, and when I've seen each Woody Allen movie for the first time. My first published writing was a review of *Manhattan Murder Mystery*. Once, in a fit of extreme boredom and dementia, I even organized an In Defense of Woody Allen club to fight off anybody who dared to smear Woody for that whole Soon-Yi scandal thing. (Tim had moved by that point, so the club had a membership of one.)

Now, for the first time in my life, Woody is not just a figment of my imaginary world anymore. He's right here, here in town, the town where I live. He doesn't play at his Monday night jazz club as often as he used to, so I'm not sure I can find him there. I've frequented a Greenwich Village place called Chumley's—where Woody filmed a scene in *Sweet and Lowdown*—thinking he might show. He hasn't yet.

I've been here a month now, and that's too long to live in the same city as Woody without finding him, telling him how he's changed my life, how lost I would have been without his films and his words and his life. Yeah, true, it's called stalking in some circles, and some people even consider it illegal, but sheesh, Woody should just be happy he has crazed fans, considering, you know, nobody watches Woody Allen movies anymore.

Woody's getting up there in years, and he's recently flirted with the idea of moving to Europe with Soon-Yi. It's clear I'm running out of time. Is it unreasonable for me to think that someone who has meant so much in my life, for better or worse, should cross my path at some point? Doesn't he deserve to know? And if I have to push it along... so be it.

So, the 6 Train at Union Square, to 96th, five blocks south, two blocks west. According to the new issue of *The New Yorker*, Woody and Soon-Yi just moved into a "handsome, double-width Georgian town house" in the Carnegie Hill neighborhood. Easy. Can't miss that.

Maybe if I approach him nicely, with my hands in the air, telling how much of an effect he's had on my life, maybe he won't call the police. Maybe he won't be freaked out. Maybe he won't be scared.

I don't know... would you be?

FALLING OFF THE LEDGE

I don't know if you've ever hung off the balcony of a Santa Monica apartment, teetering dangerously close to crashing to your death onto the deck of a restaurant owned by an enormously popular if somewhat English-language-challenged Austrian movie star, but let me tell you, kids, it ain't fun.

After accepting the job with *U. Magazine*, they set me up with that sweet apartment, where I lived with my two co-workers, Marisa from Florida and Lynda from Michigan. Initially, I had expected to stay there only for a month or two, until the fiancée arrived and we found our own place, full of bliss and domestic tranquility. Obviously, it didn't turn out that way.

One night, about a week after the ex-fiancée announced she was going to leave me and about a week before she did, Lynda, her annoying boyfriend Billy, the ex-fiancée, and I decided to have one of those patented "sit out on the porch and get obnoxiously drunk" nights that I later, after the ex-fiancée left, mastered on my own, thanks very much. Arnold Schwarzenegger's restaurant, Schatzi's, sat directly below our balcony. This was Ah-nuld's personal place, a cigar bar and wine palace that was more intimate, less cheesy, and definitely more expensive than Planet Hollywood.

Also below us was our parking garage, which had one of those brick drawbridge entrances that reached over to the balcony, about 15 feet below. An awning covering Schatzi's saved the filthy-rich Republicans Arnold had over for cigar night from having to look at us undesirables above.

This drunken night, the reality of the ex-fiancée leaving was beginning to seep in, which meant I made a couple more trips to the liquor store than I ordinarily would (say eight, rather than six). The four of us sat and drank and gabbed and gossiped and pretended nothing was wrong, which became increasingly difficult to do as the wine and Rolling Rock continued to flow.

Lynda and the ex-fiancée had become friends in the short month we'd been out in L.A., and even though Lynda's loyalty was to me, she knew what the ex-fiancée was going through. Lynda understood that the ex-fiancée was wracked with guilt because she was destroying a man who loved her but still was unable to be anything but true to herself and her need to figure out what the hell she was doing with her life. Yes. Guilt. She had to have some.

So Lynda and the ex-fiancée decided to make another trip to the liquor store, and I was stuck out on the balcony with Billy, an obnoxious frat guy who, to me anyway, always seemed a little bit unbalanced. Billy glanced out over the awning, pointed to the foot-wide brick overhang 15 feet below and began to boast.

"You know, back in my college days, when I was drunk like this, I would have jumped down on that awning and walked across that thing."

Billy had graduated four months earlier, so obviously his perspective was not to be underestimated.

He continued, "I'm grown-up now, too smart to do it, but it sure would have been fun in college."

Now, readers, today I would just scoff at such a stupid comment. I would. I would. But at the time, after all the alcohol, something he said struck a chord with me.

Consider the situation: There I am, a whimpering shell, watching as the love of my life just leaves me, and I'm putting up little more than a pathetic gasp of protest. I'm spineless, helpless, sad, a schmuck, one of the losers. I've never done anything risky in my life, never chucked everything to move to the wilderness, never done something stupid just because it made me feel *alive*. If I were more of a risk-taker, less of a fuddy-duddy, maybe the ex-fiancée wouldn't be leaving, maybe she'd respect me more, maybe she'd realize she was supposed to be with me, after all.

My state of mind was such that a moron like Billy was starting to make sense to me, and truth be told, it was all I could do not to start crying, fall to my knees, grasp Billy's leg and wailing.

"You know," I choked off, "I bet I could do it. Why not? What do I have to lose. You know, fuck it."

I climbed up on the rail surrounding the balcony, turned myself around and started to move down the 15-foot-wall, hanging on to the rail until I was ready to let go. I then made the mistake that so many movie protagonists had made before me: I looked down.

The realization hit quickly. The fall was much farther than my drunk goggles had anticipated, and there was a very good chance that if I let go, I would plummet to an ignominious death. The awning was... well, it was cloth and it wasn't attached to anything resembling steel that would hold me up. The idea that I could fall on the awning and then walk to the brick overhang was ludicrous; it was much more likely that I'd go through the awning, crashing into the restaurant—which, mercifully, was closed—and smash tables and glass and, if I were fortunate, break only my back.

Hanging there by my fingertips, I looked up at Billy, whose eyes were looking even more vacant than usual. He glanced down at me, aghast, and said, "What the fuck are you doing?" You know you've hit rock bottom when someone like Billy asks you that question and you have nothing even resembling a coherent answer.

At this point, Lynda and the ex-fiancée had gotten back, and Billy quickly filled them in on my predicament. The ex-fiancée began to cry and tried to give me her hand and pull me up. It wasn't happening. My fingers were beginning to slip, and it was only a matter of time before I went down.

A matter of seconds, actually. Looking the ex-fiancée in the eye, I yelped as my last bit of grip loosened, and down I went.

I'd like to say my life flashed before my eyes, but I think I was too busy dealing with the heart attack to have time for much introspection. I hit the awning with what would have been a thud had there been something solid enough for me to thud on, and, somehow, it didn't give. It certainly drooped, and I even heard some pretty haunting ripping sounds, but it held. For a moment.

Now that my life had been spared, I was faced with a different problem. I had no idea how to get up. I couldn't exactly execute a standing 15-foot jump back to the balcony, and the drop to the concrete below was about twice that. So I stood there waiting for the awning to say "enough already" and send me through it, and tried to figure out what to do.

Then the security guy came by. He echoed Billy's previous query about what the fuck I was doing, and I profusely apologized, saying I had too much to drink and was an idiot, which was hardly news to him. He took mercy on me, though, and rather than calling the cops or just shooting me, he stepped back, lit a cigarette, offered up a bemused smile, and watched to see how this imbecile was going to get himself out of this mess. There wasn't anything much more interesting for a security guy to do at 2:30 in the morning, I guess.

I heard another rip. It was time to move, and quickly. I contemplated making the jump to the street, but, having somehow avoided serious injury so far, I thought I'd see if I could continue that streak as long as possible. Lynda, still shocked that her trip to the liquor store had put her stupid roommate close to killing himself, ran to her room and pulled the sheet off her bed. She then rolled it up and tossed it to me.

"Climb."

I was in no position to argue. Lynda and Billy held on to the sheet while the ex-fiancée was drooling in the corner, calculating when she could leave all this insanity. I took the sheet and yanked, putting my feet on the balcony and doing my best Sylvester Stallone in *Cliffhanger* impression. It took about five minutes—and two tries—but, at last, I grabbed a hold of the rail, and Billy and Lynda pulled me up and over. I then sprinted inside and jumped under the covers.

The ex-fiancée left a week later.

It is an awful thing, being hurt, especially when the one causing the hurt is someone you trusted, someone who never meant to hurt you in the first place. It's the type of suffering that'll have you hanging off a balcony, piss-drunk, trying to explain to a security guard what the fuck, exactly, you were doing.

Well, OK. Maybe not you.

LUSH LIFE

It occurs to me, as I enter Month Four of the Great New York Experiment, that I might drink too much.

I don't mean that I'm in that *Leaving Las Vegas*, pints-of-vodka-with-my-Cheerios league, not yet anyway; most of the veins in my face are, as of now, still not visible. I just mean, well, let's just say that after four months here, there are three bartenders who know me by name, four by face, and surely countless others by reputation. I can tell you which places make the best vodka tonics, who has Newcastle on tap, who waters down their Dewar's on the rocks.

I don't drink in the mornings, and unless it's Saturday or Sunday (or Monday... or Tuesday...), I don't drink in the afternoons either. But it's amazing, in this city, how much one's social life revolves around alcohol.

After work—I've left the *Times* for a Web startup; long story—I'll meet a friend or associate for drinks, or I'll grab drinks after a movie, or I'll stop by a party with an open bar, or I'll stop by for drinks to make notes for columns about stopping by for drinks.

I don't think I drink that often, and I never figured those close to me thought I did either. But when college friends visit me, they often mention that they don't remember the last time they were this drunk, and then they remember: It was the last time they were with me.

I think that's because their lives are relatively humdrum, what with their celebrity-handling jobs and random sexual encounters and all. Anyway, it's not like I was ever thought of as the class drunk, the guy who has sudden attacks of 'roid rage when he has a few too many rum and Diet Cokes. I always considered myself the drinking buddy, the person who was always willing to throw back a few with the old pals, always happy to lend an open ear to a buddy in need of counsel or just someone to talk to. And usually they opened up more after a few beers, or a few shots, or maybe just some ether.

Nevertheless, I have a feeling people are starting to talk. More and more, I'm receiving ominous signs.

At my new job, I met with my editor, who informed me that a few new hires would be starting in a couple of weeks. "Eric's excited to meet you, since he's heard you can handle your alcohol. He wants to see if he can out-drink you," he told me. I talked to my old co-worker Clare, who mentioned that she was worried about me leaving because she'd have no one to stay out all night drinking with. People have been classifying me as a "heavy" drinker, though, I must say, I greatly prefer the term "accomplished."

I hit the nadir last week. An old girlfriend had just arrived in town, and we were out, of all things, drinking, when she, with a straight and really not all that concerned face, asked me, "Will, are you an alcoholic?"

When someone whom you think of as somewhat of an occasional admirer—for whatever sick, sadistic reasons—says this to you, you tend to stand up, pay attention, and look deep inside yourself.

Or at least you order another drink and scoff off the comment with a pithy, wiseass comment about the shakes being gone and that's great, not worried anymore, har har, then change the subject to how lovely she looks, yes, yes, quite lovely, and let's move on.

All this said, I don't think I have the intestinal fortitude to become a bona fide we're-all-worried-about-Will alcoholic. I think I started too late. I didn't drink in high school. My fellow nerds and I always felt that we didn't "need" alcohol to have a good time. (God, how silly and naïve we were.) The first time I ever had a sip was at a college-newspaper party the end of my freshman year at which I had vodka forcibly poured down my throat while I was already taking codeine for a head cold. At the end of the night, if I may blatantly steal a Woody Allen line, I tried to take my pants off over my head.

Even then, though, I never really got on the booze bandwagon, and even though I was drinking heavily by the end of college... well Christ, it was college, give a brother a break.

Hey, I've slowed down a bit, even if I have graduated from scraping pennies together for a bottle of Natural Light to scraping dimes together for slugs of Crown Royal. I mean, I've never drunk before work the way I used to drink before exams. That's a step up, right?

Evidently not enough of one, considering the comments. But, jeez, you know, it's hard here, hard not to drink. I don't know how my roommate, who has never sipped alcohol, could possibly do it; the dude goes to a bar and orders a Coke every time. He always has to say it twice, as if that couldn't possibly be what he actually said.

I mean, if I gave up drinking, I'd have to give up all the things that drinking allows me to do, like convince myself my conversation is actually interesting... or dance... or karaoke... or sleep... or, for that matter, sex. I don't know if I'm willing to make those kinds of sacrifices, even if my reputation is starting to become a bit more soiled than I'd like it to be. There are a million different bars in this great city, each with their own stories, their own people and their own price for pitchers.

So bring it on, new guy Eric. I accept your challenge. But let's just keep it between us, OK? People are already starting to talk...

FOULED BALLS

M atters are good. The weather is at last warming up, I'm enjoying my new job, I've finally discovered Napster and, most important, baseball is in full swing.

Nothing could possibly make me feel better than baseball, spring, and the Cardinals in first place.

Like any blue-blooded baseball fan, I'm convinced that this life—the one where I write and edit and whine about my life, the one where I smoke and drink and generally lay waste to the body I was given—is the wrong one, a mistake, a waste of opportunity.

Because I was supposed to be a major-league baseball player.

It's not my fault my youth-league and high-school coaches never figured out my talent, how I was ticketed for the big time, The Show. They're the bastards who didn't play me, who didn't give me the chance to show my stuff on a daily basis. No, they thought their backup catcher would be better off keeping score, warming up the closer, filling the water cooler, keeping the guys loose on the bus.

How wrong they were. I could have done it, you know, played baseball all day. The happiest moments in my life have been on the diamond, chatting it up with the umpires from behind home plate, joking with the hitters, blocking a pitch in the dirt, slapping a hit-and-run single past the out-of-position second baseman, getting clocked in the head by a line drive while I was checking out the redhead in the second row.

There is nothing, nothing in this world I miss more than playing baseball.

I've looked around for recreational leagues, but that's all softball, a bunch of fat guys drinking beer in the outfield, complaining about their jobs and their wives and their kids and their hemorrhoids; goddamn those hemorrhoids. That is not real baseball, the way it's supposed to be played, with fastballs on the inside corner and picking the runner off first, waving a guy home for the play at the plate, it's gonna be close, here comes the throw, shit, they got him, should have held him at third.

No, no, I haven't played actual organized baseball in six years. Six years exactly.

Throughout the Mattoon public youth baseball leagues, I had always been known as a bit of a throwback. Typically, our baseball-mad town would force-feed any kid between the ages of 7 and 15 into one of the locally sponsored teams. Their dads, like mine, would coach them, usually screaming at their sons to compensate for their own misspent youth, steering them quickly from the game. Most of those kids, by the time they were 16 and had a car to get the FUCK away from Mom and Dad, did so and were too busy screwing in the backseat to have time for baseball.

I, however, loved the thinning of the talent ranks. I'd played high school ball, but I mostly sat on the bench and got out of class early to go to cities as exotic as Rantoul and Villa Grove. I ached to play. And in the youth summer leagues, thanks to all those kids who decided baseball was too cerebral and bolted for factory jobs, I got my chance.

We didn't have enough players for an actual league, so we just corralled all the 17- and 18-year-olds left into a traveling all-star team. By the time I was 18 and home for the summer from college, I was ready. It was my last chance at glory, the last time I'd be able to play baseball for a long, long time. And because they had so few players, well, doggone it, the all-stars just wouldn't have any *choice* but to play me.

Plus, all the kids were younger than me, just out of high school at best, and I was the big college boy back in town. I was the grizzled workhorse, the Crash Davis, the vet making one last tour of duty. Everyone knew how much I would miss playing, so I started every game at catcher, in towns as ludicrous as Cerro Gordo, Moweaqua, and Teutopolis.

It was a wonderful summer. I worked on a magazine assembly line, folding double spreads of *Vogue* into a monstrous machine called a collator, made a ton of money, had an older girlfriend, and played baseball. I knew this was my last shot, so I made the most of it and played as well as I ever had, even knocking my only home run of an 18-year career and serving as a calming presence, an extra coach for my younger teammates.

(Either that, or they just saw me as a snooty college kid, pathetically hanging on to the last threads of his youth, taking up a valuable roster spot. Time has dulled my ability to decide which it was.)

Anyway, we came down to the final games, a doubleheader in rival-city Effingham. Now, I don't know how much of a baseball fan you are, but here are a couple things you should know about catchers:

1. Due to the strain on a catcher over the course of a baseball game, it is typical for a catcher to play only one game of a doubleheader, considering that two consecutive games would tire him/her out the way a real sport, such as basketball, does. In baseball, that is not acceptable.
2. Considering that most (male) catchers tend to want to someday reproduce or simply avoid having their groin feel like it's being ripped apart by rabid animals, it is

commonplace for those who play the position (and most positions, actually) to wear something characteristically referred to as a "cup," to protect a region that perpetually needs protection.

OK, so you know that. Now, two things you should know about me:

1. There was no way that I was going to play only one game of that doubleheader, not during my last day on a ball field. My last game ever, on the bench... nada, I'd had that view quite enough, thank you.

2. I had a peculiar way of catching, one I suspect broadcasters wouldn't advise young players to follow. Early on, when I was learning the fundamentals of catching, I found that the best way to make sure no pitch in the dirt ever snuck past you was to throw your mitt in front of your crotch and dive in front of the ball, allowing it to hit only your mitt or your chest protector, nowhere else. That worked for me, and I was known as an excellent defensive catcher, but I was still looking for an edge. So, in order to make certain that I instinctively thrust my mitt where it needed to go, which is the elementary nature of catching after all, I secretly—because no coach in his right mind would allow a player to go without—refused to wear a cup. My glove always was where it was supposed to be. So nothing could go wrong. What could possibly go wrong? Question my tactics, but do not question my results.

My coach, a pleasant and accommodating sort with an almost-cute comb-over hidden under an Anderson Trucking mesh cap, made a compromise with me: "In good conscience as a coach, I can't let you catch both games, Will. Sorry, but how about we put you at, say, third base for the second game? It's the same principle, right? Knock down what's in front of you?"

Even though it had been so long since I'd played the field that I had to borrow a teammate's glove, I agreed with him, and so it was.

In the first game, I threw a runner out, forgot to back up first base on a groundball that cost us a run, went 2-for-4 with 2 RBIs, and walked in my last at-bat. We won 8-5.

I took off my shin guards and chest protector for the last time, sighed, and grabbed some guy named Bill's glove and headed to third base for my final game. I fielded the first couple of ground balls, warm-ups tossed by the first baseman, with relative ease, and when the first batter stepped to the box, I even started up some "hey batter, hey batter" chatter. Our pitcher, an outfielder by position and ultimately a plumber by trade, walked the first guy on four pitches.

A short kid, with no semblance of or potential for body hair, scampered to the plate. I was ready, crouched in anticipation of the double-play ball, ready to scoop, pivot and fire, the way Ken Oberkfell and Terry Pendleton used to do it. Having caught the first game, I even made sure to come in and tell our pitcher that this batter was struggling with the curve.

"I don't have a curveball," the pitcher told me, annoyed.

I'm in position... The pitch.

Short Kid gets an inside "fastball" and slaps it down the line. Hard. So hard, in fact, that it takes one hop, spinning wildly, whistling, and plants itself in my crotch a split second before the glove can make the trip.

As you may know, there is a brief second, before the gnashing and screaming and fuck, fuck, *fuck* happens, where you are able to rationally and disinterestedly understand that you have just been hit in the balls, and it's about to genuinely, all-encompassing, awesome, hurt like a bloody bitch-and-a-half.

I had that second, then collapsed. The spectators gasped, followed by those involuntary snickers that we cruelly cast every time we see someone hit in the groin. The coach came out with an assistant and carried me off the field. That Bill guy with the glove took over.

And I spent the last seven innings of my baseball career with an ice pack under my shorts, keeping score, wondering when school started again.

MAKE SURE YOU CAN GET US SOME MONTEL TICKETS

I have a friend coming into town this weekend. Nice enough guy; we worked at the college newspaper together, then again at *The Sporting News*. Depending on who you talk to, he either a) made me aware of the job, or b) was the reason I got hired. (a: Me, b: everybody else.) He's now a big-shot columnist at *USA Today*, though I've always felt his mug shot looked kinda doofy.

When I lived in L.A., I had, let's see, seven visitors. Some were welcome: My sister trotted out there to get a tattoo on her 18th birthday—a huge-ass butterfly across her stomach, an adornment my parents for some reason blame me for—Cousin Denny visited twice, and my friends Andy and Kyla came out to celebrate their recent engagement. But there was one guy...

His name was John. I'd gone to college with John, and we had a few mutual friends, but I never particularly cared much for the guy. He was spineless and had a tendency to trash you behind your back. Upon graduation, I figured I'd never run into the guy again, and I felt none the worse for it.

About 10 months into my one-year stay in L.A., I received an e-mail from John. He mentioned that he would be out my way in a month or so, and he thought we should hang out. I could swing that, I told him, just let me know, we'll grab a drink or something. He ended up calling about a week later, and his "out my way" had suddenly morphed into: "Hey, would it be okay if I stayed with you while I'm out there?" Another week, and it had degraded further, into: "Hey, let's hang out that week—you can show me around."

In other words, I had to play the cordial host to a guy I didn't even like, doing things I didn't want to do, for an undetermined amount of time. He postponed the trip for one more week, a pivotal move; in that week, I learned I'd notched the job at *The Sporting News* and had just nine more days to stay in Los Angeles, to say goodbye to the old gang. And seven of those days would be with freaking John.

People often ask me, now that I've professed an immediate, deep, and lasting love to New York City, what I thought of Los Angeles. My social group in Los Angeles consisted of my roommates/co-workers Marisa and Lynda, and the Film Nerds, a bunch of people who had gone to USC film school with Tim, my best friend from Mattoon. They were wonderful human beings, just crazy smart, and when I found out I was leaving, I knew I'd miss them all terribly. They were my favorite part of Los Angeles, the people who were my crutches when the ex-fiancée left, lifelong compadres. Leaving them saddened me greatly.

My least favorite part of Los Angeles: The fucking Hollywood Walk of Fame. My God, I bet I saw that stupid thing 30 times. Every single person who came into town: *Let's see the Hollywood Walk of Fame. Oooh, it's George Burns. Oooh, it's Alec Baldwin. Oooh, look how small Lillian Gish's hands were! Hey Will, do you know who Lillian Gish is?*

Every damned person who visited wanted to see the blasted Hollywood Walk of Fame and Mann's Chinese Theatre. Now, if you haven't been to Los Angeles, you might not know that the area surrounding the Walk of Fame is the dirtiest, nastiest, cheesiest, most tourist-infested place on our planet, and I'd be surprised if Neptune has much that could compare, either. It's a bunch of morons with Hawaiian shirts, mullets, and excessive chest hair, futzing around with cameras and snickering about that Rock Hudson exhibit. Best way to describe the Walk of Fame: Right next door, there is a wax museum. If you ever meet anyone who willingly wants to visit a wax museum, neuter them immediately as a civic duty.

Well, guess what John wanted to see. Like every other first-time-to-L.A. visitor, he wanted to see the Walk of Fame, and the place that was in *Swingers*, and the planetarium, and the part of the beach with the most people and syringes. I spent my last week in Los Angeles showing some idiot around town, and thanks to an upcoming "cross your fingers; drink this stuff; you'll be clean" drug test, I couldn't even drink away the pain. I vowed never to be sucked in by tourist friends again.

And now I'm here in NYC, and now everybody I know that's ever wanted to visit New York has an excuse to. This weekend's visitor is the first in a string of people: My uncles and grandmother will be out here at the beginning of July, and then the big one, the one we've all been waiting for: The Leitch family, Bryan and Sally and Jill, will be making its first ever trip to New York City at the end of July. The Clampetts take Manhattan, a very special episode. (Quoth the Mom: "Make sure you can get us some Montel tickets.")

Now, I'm excited to see my old *Sporting News* buddy this weekend, and he's staying for four days, a perfectly reasonable time, enough for us to appropriately hang out but short enough so that we don't become sick of one another. (A friend here at work has someone staying with her "until he finds a job and a place to live." You'd be amazed how often this happens.)

But I'm just trying to think of what people want to do when they visit New York. There are a few givens: Statue of Liberty, Times Square, Central Park, Chinatown. We'll go see a baseball game, and we'll probably scope out the Village a bit.

That's not my life in New York, though; people often forget when they visit that while this is just some fun vacation for them, I live here. If I were to give someone the true New York experience the way that I live it, we'd sit inside writing all day, then we'd go out and drink all night, whine about women, drink some more, then stumble home, either to write some more, play some video games, or pass out. It's a vacation to me, but probably not to him.

I'm just afraid I'll be a terrible host, which is pretty much assured because I've always tried to avoid hosting anyway. I just hope he doesn't mind when I point out everything he wants to see as "Well, that's a tourist trap, only dorks would want to go there, and you're not a dork, so we won't go."

At least I like the guy. Actually, if anybody does happen to know where John is living these days, lemme know... I could use a vacation.

THE BEGINNING

I was all set to wallow this weekend. If ever a weekend were made—no, created—for wallowing, preferably in a huge vat of dripping, gelatinous self-pity, this was the one.

My friend MDS had a wedding reception back in Chicago on Saturday. He had zipped to Vegas a couple of months ago and married his college sweetheart, and this was his first trip back to the Midwest to celebrate with family and friends. I wouldn't have dreamed of missing it.

But, as luck would have it, the weekend had an added little element of hell. I learned the day after I booked my flight that also on June 24 the ex-fiancée would be getting married— just a couple of towns over from MDS's reception.

That's right. By pure happenstance, I was going to be very near to my ex-fiancée, who was marrying some guy who wasn't me.

I was ready to wallow.

I would be with old college friends, ones who knew the ex-fiancée well, my memories of whom will always be linked with her. And they all would know it. This wasn't just MDS's wedding reception, it was a (another) Will support group.

People kept asking me in the days preceding my trip if I would drop by her wedding. Seriously. Listen people... I: a) wasn't invited; b) haven't talked to her since she left; c) was about to marry her, and d) do not want another slip added to the stacks of restraining orders. The idea for the weekend was to suffer quietly, to wonder what time exactly the ceremony would take place, to compare what I imagined this wedding would have been like compared to mine, and to pray for rain. Lots of rain. A deluge. Motherfucking Ark-worthy rain.

So there I was, musing... the ex-fiancée is finally getting married, two years, five months, 16 days later than expected but still right on schedule.

I still have our invitation. You know how, just moments after a team wins the Super Bowl, they have all those hats, the ones that say, "St. Louis Rams, 2000 Super Bowl Champions"? Now, obviously they weren't just put together in the 30 seconds after the horn sounded. Those suckers were pre-printed. Therefore, it stands to reason that the other team had hats made up too. Somewhere, there is a "Tennessee Titans, 2000 Super Bowl Champions" hat.

The ex-fiancée left me in August. We were to be married in January. I am Kevin Dyson, catching Steve McNair's pass at the four-yard line, ducking forward, smacking in to Rams linebacker Mike Jones, who drags me downward. I stretch... desperately reaching for the goal line, arm extended as far as it'll go. But I am four months short of the end zone. From a cherished memento to a morbid collector's item, in the span of one yard... I will always keep my wedding invitation.

I arrived Friday night, and my friend Mike picked me up from Chicago's dreaded Midway Airport. We hit Wrigleyville and drank and drank and drank and drank, pausing for a while to drink. Poor Mike. He had to hear me the whole time. *Maybe we'll run into the ex-fiancée's bachelorette party at some bar here, Mike. Do you think it's a night wedding, Mike? Wonder if they'll have cameras at every table, Mike. She didn't want them at our wedding, but I insisted, Mike. Maybe she has short hair now, Mike. Always thought she might get short hair someday, Mike. Hey, Mike, maybe we should just drop by tomorrow, just for a little bit... maybe?*

Mike's the perfect guy to hang around on weekends like this, because he's smart, stable, caring and, if need be, I can talk him into shit. He put up some resistance. *Will, if you actually drop by that wedding, you're a goddamned psychopath.* But I knew if push came to shove, he'd drive my ass to Kankakee, and we'd see the ex-fiancée's wedding, dammit.

Saturday came. We headed to Lyons, for MDS's reception. I was surprised, immediately, by how few friends of MDS I knew. He was two years behind me in college, and apparently he made about a million friends in those couple of years. To them, I was ancient, a ghost of *Daily Illini* past. Instantly, I was out of place, the weirdo who would fly halfway across the country when they just came from down the street.

But what struck me more was MDS. The wild-haired prophet MDS I knew, the crazed Pied Piper to the complacent, he now was... well, now he was married. He was still brilliant and caustic, instantly puncturing pretensions with nary an eyebrow lifted, but he had changed. He looked sedated, he looked less restless... he looked *happy*. Scared me a little, to be honest.

In addition to me, MDS was also a close friend of the ex-fiancée. I took him aside for a moment and jovially (ha ha, ho ho) reminded him that, hey, MDS, it's not just your day, heh heh, it's also the ex-fiancée's big day, how about that, what a coincidence, har har.

He barely turned his head. "Yeah, Will, that's kinda crazy, you must th- Paula, hi! Oh, it's so good to see you! How are the kids?!" And he was off, and I sat there, alone. Mike invited me to grab a cigarette outside. It was raining.

It was a cheesy reception, like all good-hearted Midwestern wedding receptions are, with the "Hokey-Pokey" and "Macarena" and "YMCA." Some full-full-full-figured woman hopped on the dance floor during "Boot Scootin' Boogie," and her eight-year-old son joined in beside her, jumping up, smiling, laughing, falling down, picking his nose, enjoying the attention. A DJ-for-hire spurred the crowd on. An old man at the end of the open bar sipped a bourbon, smoked a stogie and argued about the Bears with a man who looked to be his son. A new mother breast-fed in the corner.

And somehow... I forgot about it. The entire flight to Chicago, I kept wondering what time the wedding was, when that precise moment was that the ex-fiancée became a wife. Would it be noon? 5 p.m.? 7?

But as the day passed, and I watched 55-year-old women groove to "Mambo No. 5," I lost track of time, and I stopped asking. I met MDS's wife's family, and we played some darts, and we talked about Sammy Sosa, and I answered questions about whom I would vote for in the New York Senate race, and suddenly it was midnight. I turned to Mike.

"I bet the ex-fiancée is married now," I said.
"Yep, I'd certainly think so."
"Well, congratulations to her."

It was kind of dopey-sweet, sad-sack-loser wacky for a while, still lamenting what happened that day on *Win Ben Stein's Money*. It gave me some gravitas, made it clear, *yes, I have suffered; I am still suffering; I know how to feel; I've hurt; look at me*. And, admittedly, it *is* a pretty fucking funny story if it didn't happen to you, one that's provided me plenty of comedic mileage, one I've told a thousand times, one that's guaranteed to provide me with some sympathetic looks, preferably from attractive women.

But it's not cute anymore. Once Jennifer is married, my pining for her and my retelling of my gloomy tale are just, well, *creepy*. Game over. She's married now. She has a husband. She will start a family soon. We are officially in each other's pasts... it's on the books; the law even says so. This chapter is closed.

I saw MDS laughing with his wife's mother, sharing a private joke with a distant cousin, goofing off with his newly acquired nephew. Uncles came over and shook his hand. Her brothers popped him in the shoulder playfully. He was a member of their family. I know some of MDS's ex-girlfriends. They were not there, and they were certainly not on his mind. They were from a different world. He had a new life now.

And, suddenly, I missed New York a whole bunch.

The next day, Mike dropped me back off at the airport, but thanks to bad-weather-in-New-York-related delays, I spent about eight hours sitting in a chair, waiting, thinking. In a moment of extreme boredom, I called home to Mattoon. My mom answered, and I complained to her about how awful this airport was, and how incompetent this airline was, and how I was sick of Chicago and how I just had to get back to Manhattan as soon as goddamned possible.

"Yeah, I always think that when I'm gone for Mattoon for more than a few days," she said. "It means it's home. It's your home now."

We finally took off about 11:30, and I planted my nose on the window and slept. Woke up a little more than an hour later, wiped the grease stain off the glass and glanced out. We were flying over Manhattan on a clear night. The Statue of Liberty was so radiant, so beautiful... the whole damned island lit up and welcoming, wondering why the hell I was gone so long.

Because, contrary to the weather reports—and unlike Chicago—it was not raining in New York. I was fucking home.

GOING... GOING... GONE

So I'm talking to my mother the other day.

It's an odd time for the Leitch family. The new house my father built, about 100 feet from the old house, is finished, and Mom and Dad are moved in. A young husband and wife bought the old place, and they're living there now. I'm not sure they're my parents' type of people. According to Dad, the guy is a full-time firefighter—there are evidently enough fires in Mattoon to facilitate a need for full-time firefighters; who knew?—and he "isn't much of a worker." (The contempt in my father's voice was clear and penetrating.) He basically just sits around a lot, doesn't do much with the yard, isn't down with upkeep. This is about as cardinal a sin as you'll find with my father. My dad works on his new shed and sees his old house, with the grass about two weeks past its optimum mowing date, and he seethes.

I told them this was going to happen, but no one ever listens to me. Dad is starting to feel helpless. He hasn't adjusted to the new house yet, and with his huge project finally finished, he's looking for the next step. Mom's happy with church; Dad goes too, but I've always suspected his support of my Mom's fervor outweighs his own devotion to Catholicism. His kids are running wild, me in New York and Jill in Champaign, and he doesn't really have anybody to guide anymore, no one to yell at. He pretty much just does odds and ends around the house and plays with the dog.

So he's been grumpy lately, which my Mom described in intricate detail. "Honestly, you just can't talk to him sometimes. He's a complete grouch. He's becoming just like his father." Grandpa Leitch was a man who once lobbied the city in which he retired, nearby Toledo, to change a sign that welcomed visitors. It said: "Welcome to Toledo, home of 2,000 happy souls." He, serious as one of his four heart attacks, argued that he was not a happy soul and had little desire to be classified as such to any unsuspecting tourists. His attempts failed, but he did try to talk his grandson into spray-painting, "1,999 happy souls and one nasty grump" on the sign. Would have worked, too, had Mom not caught me.

I tried to cheer up my mom, telling her that Dad is just in a weird place right now, that he's not sure what to do with himself. "Honestly, Mom, he just needs to get away for a while. I think visiting New York will be good for him."

"Oh, let's not get started on that. He's talking about how he has too much to do, how he doesn't have time to head all the way to New York City, about how you're going to be working the whole time anyway. He's just been unbearable lately."

I had suspected something like this might happen. This is Dad's first trip to New York, and it's going to be hard on him. He doesn't like to walk, he doesn't like trash on the streets, and he doesn't like a lot of people around. Like most of America, my dad sees New Yorkers as rude, arrogant pricks who wouldn't know a day of honest work if it slapped them in the face. But even more than that, to him, New York is the unknown, an enormous side of the world he has up to this point chosen to ignore. It's bad enough that his only son lives there; now he has to visit? No thanks.

When planning the itinerary for their visit, I tried to keep this in mind. This was why for the first two days, we're going to a familiar place: a baseball game, Shea Stadium, to see the Cardinals play the Mets.

We all have that revelatory moment with our parents, that instant where we finally look at them and realize that, I'll be darned, they're people too, with the same fears and insecurities and blood and shit and piss that we have. They have just spent years masking these things from you.

Mine with Dad was at a baseball game, of course. It was in 1998, when I had flown in from Los Angeles for a job interview with *The Sporting News*. It was the weekend that Mike Piazza had been traded to the Florida Marlins from the Dodgers, and the Cardinals were to play the Marlins that night. Dad picked me up from the airport, where he gawked at a confused-looking Mr. Piazza himself ("I play for the Marlins?") and headed to the riverboat casino, where we would gamble and drink for a while before heading to Busch Stadium.

I remember the first time I drank with my father. It was when I came home to tell my parents I was going to get married. For some reason, I thought my father would handle the news better than my mom, and I headed with him to a Mattoon pub to chat. We had a few beers, and I broke the news to him. I think he beamed with pride when I ordered a Natural Light. It was wonderful, and, swear to God, I almost teared up when he mentioned that Grandpa would "shit a brick" if Dad ever asked him to have a beer with him. "Never figured I'd have a beer with my son." From then on, he looked almost offended if I had a Diet Coke rather than a shot of the Nat in his presence.

So we hit the casino. I lost a bunch of money on video poker, but we had about seven beers and shambled over to the stadium early to watch batting practice. It was the first time, thanks to the year in Los Angeles, that I'd actually seen Mark McGwire in a Cardinals jersey. It was breathtaking. I'd never seen anyone hit a baseball like that before, just moon shots, blasting into and through the ether. We ordered a couple more beers, bought a scorecard and settled in.

The beer kept flowing. We yakked about mostly baseball at first, whether or not McGwire had a chance at Roger Maris' record (I said no way; he insisted it was possible, the way that guy hits the ball), about the weirdness of Tony LaRussa batting the pitcher eighth, about the possibility of trading for Randy Johnson come July.

I've never seen my father drunk, which is quite an accomplishment, because I've been with him when he's downed about 12 Nat Lights in one setting. One time, when I was 16, he and Mom came back from a Christmas party and yelled at me for dating an older girl my parents didn't approve of with a little more vigor than usual, but I've never classified that as drunkenness, just anger.

But this night, at the game, we just kept downing $5 beers, one after another. The conversation veered in odd directions. We talked about women he'd dated before Mom, about how weird one of my uncles was, about how he always thought that one girl, what was her name, Betty?, was pretty damned attractive, why didn't you stay with her? Considering I never even knew my dad acknowledged any of my dates, this was doubly bizarre.

McGwire stepped to the plate. He was facing Livan Hernandez, one of the lone survivors of the Marlins' binge-and-purge of their World Series champions from the season before. I think Dad and I were talking about how you have to double down when you've got 11 and the dealer's showing 16 when McGwire hit a fly ball to center field.

We leapt up to see if the ball could sneak over the center-field fence. Dad started yelling, "Get! Get! Get!" which he tends to do—he stole it from Cardinals broadcaster Mike Shannon, who drunkenly wails that every pop-up when a ball looks like it might make it over the fence but he isn't sure. The ball landed in the grass area just beyond the wall, and we cheered. "Whew, that one just barely made it!" I exclaimed. "Yeah, that was close," Dad replied.

We had just ordered another beer when a graphic flashed on the JumboTron. "MARK MCGWIRE'S HOME RUN WAS MEASURED AT 545 FEET, THE LONGEST OF HIS CAREER." It was true. The ball hadn't just slipped over the wall; it had bashed against the *St. Louis Post-Dispatch* sign that hung under the upper deck, then it fell into the grass below. You might have heard of this home run; the Cardinals immortalized it by placing an enormous Band-Aid over the sign to make it clear just how far the ball had traveled. McGwire later said, "I don't think I can hit one any better than that."

My father and I had seen one of the longest home runs in the history of baseball; we were just too drunk to notice.

Because we're idiots, after a 10-minute sobering-up period, we drove home. During the two-hour trip to Mattoon, we started getting personal. We talked about my troubles with women, and I openly wondered if it was my fault or if I just had bad luck. Dad then said something to me that haunts me to this day.

"Will, I gotta tell you... I don't know this for sure... but if you've got a small pecker, it's my fault. Sorry about that."

No matter how grumpy my dad might be, no matter how little he might be looking forward to spending a week in New York City, no matter how much he might play everything close to the vest, stoically revealing little about his life or how he feels about anything... I saw the man behind the mask that night. He looked scared and insecure and whacked. He looked a lot like me.

That said, when they get to New York, I think we'll just have Diet Cokes at the game this time.

(Note: It has been brought to the author's attention that it would be wise to mention here that his father is "hung like a goddamn horse," lest he not be invited home for Thanksgiving.)

WU-TANG

W hen I was a child, probably about eight or nine, my family was visiting some neighbor friends for a late-night cookout. As tended to be the case, the adults would sit around the grill and bitch about their marriages, or their jobs, or their children, whatever came to mind after a six-pack or two. We kids were relegated to the yard, free to roam around as long as we were within eyesight and able to stop, drop and roll at a moment's notice. I was running around stupidly, freely, as children are wont to do, when I came across a small kitten, likely a stray. He was gray and dirty and had the cutest little nose. Unlike most cats I'd come across at the time, he didn't seem to mind when I picked him up and did some roughhousing. He was sweet and funny and even jumped up on my lap when I was lying in the grass, daydreaming of Ozzie Smith and E.T. He was the friendliest cat I'd ever come across.

Way back in the Dark Ages, when I was a confused, scared kid retreating from Los Angeles, storing myself in the Midwest comfort of St. Louis, a place that was home to the Cardinals and therefore could contain nothing but joy, I decided that I needed a friend.

After a year of living with as many as seven people in a cramped Santa Monica apartment, I wanted some space. When I took a job at *The Sporting News* and moved halfway across the country, I had only two requirements: First, I had to live alone, no more roommates commandeering the remote; second, I wanted a cat.

A cat seemed like the ideal pet for me. Heck, cats are easy. All you really have to do is feed them and change their litter box. Cats aren't like dogs; they don't need attention. They just go about their own thing, eating, sleeping, shitting, licking themselves. The world of a cat is a blissful one, and it is decidedly solitary. They just go about their merry way, living their content, spoiled little lives, and if you end up playing with them, it's because they have allowed you to.

I loved that concept. As nice as dogs are, you could pretty much smack them upside their head with a two-by-four, and after the cobwebs cleared and the blood was wiped out of their eyes, they'd happily come drooling back for more. Not cats. They don't need you. They're just fine without you, thank you very much. You have to earn the respect of a cat. They figure out whether or not they like you, and then they conclude if you're worth hanging out with. My father has the best way with cats. He has little interest in pets, save for our beloved family golden retriever, Daisy, and he's particularly not a fan of cats. So he just completely ignores them, not even implying any interest in their activities, a difficult task, since there are four of them roaming around his house. What happens? The cats, appreciative of not being picked up and snuggled when they just want to sleep, can't get enough of the guy. He has to peel them off of him anytime he's just trying to watch the ballgame. Dad claims this is also how you're supposed to deal with women, which, well, is a notion that might be of some value.

We were just goofing off. I would grab a leaf, rub it against his nose, then throw it so he could chase it around. He'd grab it in his teeth, bat at it with his paws, knock it across the grass and then scamper after it again. Playing along, I'd swipe it from him, dangle it around his ears and titter as he twirled wildly trying to find it. I even did that trick where you pretend to throw the leaf and keep it in your hand instead, tittering madly as he searched furiously for it. At last, I did wad the leaf up and throw it toward a fence that surrounded the yard and shared a boundary with the neighbor's yard. Out of nowhere, I heard a chain rattling, a growl, a crunch, a shriek and, ultimately, a whimper.

So I decided I wanted a cat. I wouldn't take an apartment that wouldn't let me have one. I didn't care what type of cat; as long as I had a kitten, something whose mind I could shape and warp in my own image. My mother, just pleased her son wasn't 2,000 miles away anymore, went on the hunt and found a woman she worked with at the hospital whose cat had just shot out a litter. The middle one will be perfect for you, she said; he's sprightly and energetic and very affectionate. You'll be living alone. You'll need all the affection you can get.

Thus, on one Sunday afternoon, about two weeks after I arrived in St. Louis, a city in which I knew no one, a furry little tiger runt showed up at 631Geoffrey, announcing his presence by crying and sprinting under the bed. At first, inexperienced in having my own pet, I rushed after him, trying to calm him and instantly make him my friend. I learned quickly enough... just leave him alone. After a few hours, he peeked his head out from under the covers, looked left, looked right, and slowly, slowly, slowly crawled tentatively toward the living room. I tossed him a play toy I'd bought for the occasion. He hopped back, frightened, and bolted out of the room. Within 30 seconds, he was back, gnawing on the toy. I just watched, quietly. A half hour later, he was attacking my feet. An hour after that, he was on my lap, sleeping, and I knew he was mine. Or, more accurately, I was his. I named him Wu-Tang, half after the group I was listening to most heavily at the time and half because I am very white and wanted desperately to seem down.

Many friends of mine had cats, and I thought they treated them too much like, well, too much like cats. They would end up either hiding under the bed anytime company would come over, or they would be the fat blob of hair taking up half the couch, a piece of furniture that needs to be fed. My cat wouldn't be like that, I vowed. He was just my roommate, and he could do whatever he wanted just like any other roommate. Want to sit on the kitchen counter? Dude, go ahead; it's your place too. Want to eat the leftover pizza? Want to scratch up the wooden couch? Want to bite my arm? Hey, it's your prerogative. Who am I to tell you what to do? I have no business telling you how to live your life; like I know what I'm doing.

And he was awesome, the most personable animal this side of a car salesman. He would welcome any visitor with a hop up on the lap and a nibble on the wrist. He was just another guy—having him fixed was an ordeal I lamented for days—and he became more a pal than a household pet. He would fall asleep wherever I ended up at night—whether it be the bed, the couch or, on those particularly rough nights, the bathroom floor—and he ran the place however he saw fit. He even helped me out by charming what few women I could coerce to come over to the apartment. (Sometimes being a guy living alone with a cat has its advantages.)

It has always seemed to me that, in a way, we're closer to our pets than we could ever be to another human being. You can pick your nose, fart, masturbate, whatever, the types of things you could only otherwise do alone, with your pet in the room and not even think twice, not even hesitate. It's a natural closeness. I had that type of relationship with Wu-Tang.

I imagined how insane it would be for Wu-Tang, who as a cat was likely to live for close to 20 years, to go through changes with me, to move to new places, to meet the woman I love, to play with my children. You have a cat for a long time, and, sometimes, they're actually a bit of work. With Wu-Tang, it was a commitment I didn't think twice about making.

Immediately, it was obvious something was wrong. I hurried guiltily over to the fence and saw an enormous dog, blood dripping from its jaws, scurry away. And on the ground, eyes wide wide wide open, was my little kitten. There were two puncture wounds, one just below his neck and one just below his ribcage. The cat was feeling no pain, not yet; it just lay there, in shock, lacking understanding. I was vaguely aware that I might have caused this... if I just hadn't have thrown the leaf near the fence. And then came the gasps. Later that evening, my mother explained that the dog's bite, its horrific CHOMP!, likely broke the kitten's ribs and collapsed its lungs. But all I remember are the gasps. The desperate thrusts for air, a wheeze, a cough, another wheeze. There was simply no air to be found. He wearily lifted his eyes up to me, what happened, oh God I can't breathe, what is going on? I found myself eerily calm. He is going to die. I ran to the bathroom, grabbed a wet rag and ran back out to him. And for the next two hours, until my parents made me leave, I lay there with my gasping kitten, wiping his brow, trying to ease his suffering, making sure he was not alone.

My cat is dying. It started about four months ago, when my roommate Brian complained to me that Wu-Tang, entirely out of character, had urinated on his bed. After buying Brian new sheets and apologizing profusely, I watched as Wu-Tang promptly hopped on my bed and pissed there too. I took him to the vet, who told me he had a urinary infection, common for male cats. He gave me some pills (he gave the cat some too) and told me to make sure he drank plenty of water.

Wu-Tang was better for about a week, but then he was right back at it again, this time not urinating, but instead depositing little droplets of blood across the apartment. It was almost cute; he was conditioned to the litter box, so he would only go on places that weren't the floor, like the bed, or rugs, or pieces of clothing lying around. I rushed him back to the vet, who said his bladder was blocked, or his tract was swelling, or something, I didn't really understand what. He said Wu would need surgery, and that it would cost me about $900. After being laid off by my dream dot-com job the month before, this was clearly money I didn't have just sitting around, but there was no way I was letting my cat suffer. Plus, I think the place was starting to smell. Wu had the surgery and was fine for about a month.

And then last week. I've been in crisis mode lately, and the only solace, the only guy always there for me, has been Wu-Tang. So it didn't escape my attention when I found a dark red spot on a stray newspaper. I called the vet, bitching up a storm about paying 900 bucks for a surgery that would only help for a month.

"Yeah, we were afraid that was going to happen. Listen, we weren't sure at the time, but this is a chronic thing. This isn't going away. We can perform another surgery on him, but this is likely going to happen again in three months, or two, or one. And it's just going to get worse. "

"So what do I do?"
"Well, he's going to be in a lot of pain. I don't think it's right to let him suffer."
"Yeah, but how do I fix him?"
"We're not sure we can."
"Wait, you're not saying... ?"

That's what he was saying.

About a year later, I was riding my bike by the very same house we visited that night. It was the middle of the afternoon. No one was home. I noticed the dog, a big, nasty, mean, ugly dog, sleeping in the neighbor's front yard. Looking around and finding no spies, I hopped off the bike and jumped the fence. Then, with all the strength I could muster, I kicked that dog square in the stomach. I ran off, leaping the fence and pedaling away. I felt little satisfaction. I was just empty.

I'm supposed to take Wu-Tang to the vet tomorrow. I am not certain what the vet will say, but I have a good idea. So now my cat is lying there, on my couch, silent, motionless, in agony. Occasionally he'll move his head, look up, eyes wide wide wide open, and let out an anguished yet muted *rowwrghhhhhhhhhh*, then put his head back down. Christ, is there anything worse than an animal in pain?

The poor fucking thing... just lying there, crying, screaming, wondering what in the world is happening to it... incapable of adequately communicating how much it fucking hurts.

As an "owner," I have little control over my pet's life. I feed him, clean his litter box, make sure he's not living in total filth. That's about all I do. Yet I keep thinking that I've done something wrong, that I fed him the wrong food, or I didn't pay enough attention to him, or I didn't change the litter often enough. I could have done something. This is my fault. It isn't, or so people keep telling me, but it sure feels that way.

Oh, God, he just jumped up here, on my desk, next to my computer. Did he know I was writing this? How did he have the strength to make the leap? He's looking at me. Does he know? Is he aware? Can he understand? Is he angry? Does he know how much he's meant to me? Has he ever known?

Oh, Wu-Tang, I am so sorry. Please forgive me. We have been through so much. I'm sorry.

AN IMAGINARY CONVERSATION BETWEEN WILL LEITCH AND HIS HERETOFORE ODDLY QUIET ID

(Note: After being laid off and learning that New York City had no jobs remaining, the author swallowed his pride and moved back to Mattoon to stay with his cousin, lick his wounds, pay off mounting debts and work on a book that he would never finish. He spent two months there, trying to come up with some answers. He found none.)

Well, boys and girls, I've clocked a week here in my hometown of Nowhere, just off the corner of Oblivion and Nether, and no major disasters so far. Really, I haven't done much of anything. I'm working on my Web site, writing feverishly. That's about it.

I've successfully siphoned myself off from the rest of society. I have no television, no car, no social interaction. Just me, sitting here tap-tap-tapping away, with The Flaming Lips and Nirvana and Radiohead and Bob Dylan providing the soundtrack.

It's so calm here. I haven't heard a single car horn since I arrived. Easy does it. Other than cousin Denny, there aren't many close friends remaining in town, so there is not even the possibility of distraction. Life, for the first time in a while, is feeling good, in place, together, normal. This sojourn has been all I hoped it would be so far, and nothing more. Not a damn thing to do or see exists here, and that's just the way I like it.

Hey Will. It's your id. How's it going?

Quiet, you. Go away. Back off. I'm trying to talk to my readers here. And seriously, can't you come up with a better introduction than, "Hi, I'm your id?" I mean, please. That's such a cheap way to painfully force a contrived concept into this story. You're making me look bad.

Yeah, I'm sure both your readers will be so annoyed by the interruption. Plus, I've been reading some of your last few entries, and I'm getting real sick of your passive-aggressive "woe-is-the-poor-little-loser" bullshit. I've been silent for too long. Besides, I'm just checking in with you. Sure is weird being back in Mattoon, isn't it?

No, not really, actually. Very peaceful. It's pleasant to feel on top of things again.

Kind of a shame your closest friends, other than Denny, have left, isn't it?

Well, it only seems natural. My clique in high school consisted of the people who desperately wanted to leave. Most of them were successful. And it's for the best. If there were anybody else here I wanted to see, it would just serve to get in the way of my work.

So there's nobody here you'd be interested in seeing?

Didn't I just say that? This place is my past. I haven't lived here in seven years.

O... K. Hey, what's that over there? Is that a Mattoon phone book? Yeah, go pick it up.

No.

Fine. In spite of my inherent limitations as a state of being rather than a physically endowed human with free will and arms and legs, I'll do it. Let's see here... hey, what's this on page 78?

That's GAR through GAS.

Yeah, but do you see that name in the second row, about a quarter of the way down? That's Amy Garvey. Do you remember her?

Uh... a little. Maybe?

A little? Maybe? So you don't recognize her as the girl you worshipped all the way through junior high and high school? The one you were about to ask out until Shad, one of your best friends, beat you to it? The one you watched date Shad for a year after that? Come on, Will, you remember Amy Garvey! She's the one you just about asked to the junior homecoming but wimped out. You wrote her long letters that you never delivered. Your friends made fun of you all the time for your thing for her!

Uh... that's all kind of hazy. It's been so long...

So long, huh? Well how about your fifth-year class reunion?

Um, don't know what you're talking about. ANYWAY... back to this column. Hey, readers, have I told you how much I like Woody Allen? I have? I could probably go into it some more. I remember when I first started watching his—

Five years down the line, a supposed grown man, past all those demons. And there you are, there WE are, drinking too much at the reunion, telling tales of Los Angeles, when BAM, there she was. She's had a kid since high school, but she's single now and she looks fantastic. None of this is ringing a bell?

—and then Mia Farrow says to Woody, "How can you have so much hostility about—

And then at the after party, at the grimy bar with peanut shells all over the floor and Queensryche on the jukebox, when you lived out the most boring cliché in the book by actually walking up to her and telling her, "You know, I had a crush on you all throughout high school." Lord! That sure was embarrassing! That wasn't even that long ago. Just three years. Heck, she was pretty drunk that night, probably didn't even understand what you were saying. You never know, Will. If she's still single...

Fine! You got me. That happened. I'm not proud of it. That was your fault anyway. It doesn't matter now; I don't have a thing for her anymore. And you know I have a girlfriend back in New York, and you know I'm crazy about her.

Sure. But I'm not talking about sex here. I'm talking about resolution. Jeez, aren't you curious? Amy's always been an apparition to you, a phantom, this mythic figure with no real basis in reality. She isn't an actual person to you. Yet there she is! Her number is right there! There! You could just call her. You could prove that you didn't just imagine her. She's your little red-headed girl, Will, like from Peanuts! Don't you want to know what she's doing now? What she would sound like? Heck, you could just ask her if she ever liked you, or if she didn't even know you were alive. You can find out what she would have said if you had asked her out before Shad. You would finally know!

You're starting to sound like High Fidelity.

Maybe, but don't pretend it isn't true. You could end all the speculation and wonder right here. Exorcise those demons. All right, you don't buy that? Fine. Turn to page 109. Toward the bottom. Mark Simpson.

Surely you're not suggesting we call my high school baseball coach.

Why not? Don't tell me you don't want to tell him off. Scream at him for humiliating you by making you keep score for a team you were on! We've always thought you'd be in the major leagues right now if he would have just given you a chance to play. But no. It's his fucking fault. And he's right there. Here's your chance.

Listen, I'm just trying to write here. This is a place for contemplation and solitude. You're just trying to make trouble.

Is that right? Okey-dokey, then, last one here, I promise. Turn to page 211.

Sapp? I don't know anyone named Sapp. Unless Warren moved here, and I highly doubt that.

No, no, doofus. This is Mattoon. Taylor is her married name.

Oh. No. You're not really going to bring up—

That's right. We're talking about Betty. Don't even pretend you don't remember.

Uh... um... readers, look over here! I'll talk about my weight issues, or my dad's disappointment in me, or Ben Stein! Yeah, yeah, I was on this game show, see, and—

Haven't told your readers much about her, have you Will? Well, folks, lemme clue you in. Betty was Will's first serious girlfriend, an older girl—Will was 16, she was 21—who was beautiful and smart and saw something in Will other people didn't see, whatever the hell that was. After much trepidation on both ends—not to mention a little fiancé she needed to rid herself of—they finally admitted their mutual attraction and fascination with one another. Will fell hard for her, and she him. Everything was beautiful. Will was suddenly cool, dating some hot older chick—who could drink! And they were great together. But then—

La, la, la, I can't hear my id, la, la, la! I'm sorry, was someone speaking? I didn't hear anyone.

Then Will got cocky, full of himself, and he broke up with her, to date some sophomore who looked up to Mr. Senior Guy. Betty was deeply hurt, but she was temporarily better when Will came crawling back to her the summer before he left for college. To be with him, she broke up another potentially blossoming relationship—a costly move in a town where, at 22, you're an old maid—and all was good, because Will was scared about going to college and needed someone who cared about him. That is, until Will met a college girl, from Chicago and all sophisticated, someone who made him feel smart, and he ended it again, this time for good. Will tried again later, after the Chicago girl turned out to be less than what he expected, but this time Betty had moved on. She was dating a cop, who forbade her from talking to Will anymore, which sounds like an unfair request to make of one's girlfriend but, given Will's history, in retrospect looks quite understandable. And then they ended up getting married. Hey, Will, when's the last time you talked to her?

Uh, I think it's been about six years.

Wow. Six years. The first woman you ever cared about, the one who taught you so much, the one who made you feel important, like there was something special about you, for the first time... her number's right there, on page 211.

I know it is.

But of course you won't call. You won't find out what she's doing. You won't apologize. You're just here for the writing, right? The solitude? The quiet? The peace? No demons lurking around Mattoon, no no. The place is just a joke for your columns, a quaint Mayberry, a place you're through with, right?

Uh... sure.

You're full of shit, Will.

I know.

Now, let's go get a pizza. I'm starving.

Listen, id, I'm trying to lose weight. Give me a break here.

You're such a wuss.

PRETEND SANDWICHES

H is name is Lloyd. He is one of cousin Denny's friends who is eager to meet me, the peculiar guest mysteriously in town from New York. I remember hearing rumors about Lloyd from high school. Big dude. Crazy. Violent. Unstable. Danger. Danger. Don't remember ever meeting him, which is just fine with me.

Before we head out to his place just past the infamous Dead Man's Curve between Mattoon and hated neighbor Charleston, Denny assures me, as I shave pathetic strands of peach fuzz masquerading as facial hair from my face, that Lloyd's a cool guy, that he's different than he was in high school, that he's good people. "He's a fucking funny guy, Will," Denny tells me. "I mean, he's big and can be kind of scary, but he wouldn't hurt a fly. Not anymore."

Not anymore. I once had sex. I don't anymore. That doesn't necessarily mean that if the opportunity afforded itself again, I would not welcome it with obsessive fury. I am not convinced this Lloyd will not kill me. I don't remember the exact details, and it's probably some kind of high school myth, might not even be him, but I recollect hearing a story about Lloyd once. A poor sap had started dating a woman who had just broken up with Lloyd. After school, Lloyd found him. He punched him in the face, flooring him instantly, and then took his head to the curb. There he slammed his foot on his head, twice, knocking out two teeth (or was it three? Four?). He then picked up his limp body and threw it into the mercifully empty road. Lloyd had never met the kid before.

Denny's car is in the shop, with a dead starter likely brought on by a grueling drive to New York City and back, so we drive one of my parents' extra cars, an ancient, early-'70s Caprice Classic, with the same dreary olive green paint job it's had for decades, dubbed somewhat unoriginally "The Green Mile" by my family. Attempts to make it clear to my parents that I do not want to borrow a car while I'm home have fallen on deaf ears, which is fine for tonight. The Mile is enormous and awesome, and I feel powerful behind the wheel. It's a power I worry I might need this evening.

"Lloyd's a little self-conscious about where he lives," Denny tells me as we pull up. At the end of the rocky side road is that unheralded gem of rural living, the trailer. As far as my knowledge of trailers extends, it seems like a nice one, with wood paneling hammered hastily to its side and, as far as I can tell, running water. Too many of my friends grew up living in trailers for me to have any snobbery about these living arrangements, and besides, your average trailer is about three times the size of the typical New York City apartment, including mine. Nevertheless, it's been a while. The unfamiliar surroundings fail to ease my nerves.

As we walk up to the front door—Denny pauses to not reassure me at all: "Man, I bet Lloyd's freaked out that he's never seen your car before. I better wave to him, let him know it's me, before he thinks something's up." I start to worry about my glasses. Why did I wear them? Don't I want to give the impression that I'm good people, that I'm from here, that I can be trusted? After years of wanting to be something other than a Mattoon boy, I'm immediately crawling back, whimpering. I look like a squirrely English professor with my glasses, the kind of guy who would live in—insert the appropriate amount of disgust in the inflection here—*New York City*. I suddenly wish I were wearing a mesh cap and flannel while I flog myself internally for the offensive and demeaning stereotype the thought implies.

One of the first differences between Mattoon and the outside world I have noticed is how apathetic people here are about formal greetings. In New York, anytime you meet someone new, it's: "Will Leitch, pleasure to meet you," followed by a firm—gotta be firm, or you're weak, impotent—handshake and brief but clear eye contact. Here, I am introduced to no one. I just walk in, and immediately I'm part of the scenery.

Denny and Lloyd start talking shit, laughing to old jokes I don't understand, and I stand there, quiet, meek, surveying the atmosphere. Two boys, likely high school age and looking quite a bit like Lloyd, only smaller, lie prostrate on the couch. One is lying on his girlfriend, who appears to be paying more attention to *Con Air* than him, which just can't be a good sign. The trailer is barren. A couch, a TV, a table, a few empty cabinets. In the top left crevice of the room, where the ceiling meets the wall, there is an extravagantly designed cobweb, with the spider still there, spinning, spinning, delirious that it has built such an undisturbed home.

And then there is Lloyd. He's not as big as I imagined, but he's imposing in a Joe Pesci, live-wire-with-too-much-current-running-through-it type of way. The first thing you notice: his eyes. They're enormous. He appears to have no eyelids at all. They're the type of eyes that break your spirit, focused on the task of destroying you. The man needs no fists. I find myself suddenly very thirsty.

"Hey, anybody want a beer?" I blurt. Another thing about Mattoon: No matter where you are, there is always beer in the refrigerator, and it is always free game for anyone. It seems reasonable; you can buy a case of Natural Light for about nine bucks, which seems so cheap you almost feel obliged to tip the guy behind the counter. It's little wonder everyone looked so bloated at the class reunion. "Yeah, I'll have one," Lloyd says, acknowledging my presence for the first time. I tiptoe to the fridge and grab three MGDs. A seat is waiting for me next to Lloyd at the beaten kitchen table, which has a less impressive cobweb dangling from my chair.

Lloyd barely seems to notice I have sat down. He is, I now notice, about 95 sheets to the wind. I learn later that he has been drinking and smoking pot since about noon. He is a part-time plumber and a part-time farmhand, which is odd, considering the toilet doesn't seem to work right and the land outside his trailer looks barren.

I loosen up a bit, thanks to a few beers, and Lloyd begins to seem less threatening. His parents are both alcoholics—his dad, inevitably, works for the sheriff's department—and the two high schoolers, both seniors, mulling around the trailer are his brothers, left to his care until they graduate in June. They're nice enough kids, and Lloyd is too. What strikes me the most is how poor he is. This, friends, is dirt poor.

"You guys hungry?" he barks a couple hours later. "Want a pizza? Shit, they wouldn't deliver all the way out here, and I don't have any money for a pizza anyway." He ain't lying. He begins to talk about the beauty of "pretend sandwiches."

"You see, the best thing is a pretend sandwich. What you do is you take a piece of bread, right, and you fold it over and roll it up, and eat it like it's a sandwich. All you have to do is imagine what's in the sandwich." He takes a piece of old bread from the loaf. "This one here's a ham and cheese sandwich. Mmmm." You can almost taste the cheese, he says. He then points to a cabinet. "There's peanut butter in there, but I don't want to waste it."

I'm broke. A recent financial disaster of mine may end up costing me one of my closest friends. I haven't had any income in three months. But I am not starving. I have people who care for me, who will watch over me, who will bail me out when I've screwed up. I have a margin for error, a margin I've certainly used. Not Lloyd.

Denny is in the restroom. I'm drunk now. I get up the nerve. "So, Lloyd… I heard an old story about you." He interrupts me. "It's probably true, whatever it is. I used to be a pissed-off guy. I'm mellow now. I'm a big, fat adult." He then orders one of his brothers to grab him a beer out of the fridge, and off, off, off we go.

SCRAWNY LEAGUE FOOTBALL

When my group of friends from high school and I were about 14 years old, there was this kid named Lonnie. We all liked the guy; he was in all the advanced classes, always had a smile for you and was very, very funny. (After his girlfriend dumped him, he provided us with the immortal quip, "Well, love sucks. That's why I like ducks.") But in the back of our minds, we always wondered if there was something wrong with Lonnie. He'd been raised by an alcoholic father and had an absentee mother, and he'd shock you with unanticipated bursts of rage. We discovered this the hard way.

During Christmas break, or after school, or anytime it was in season, we would gather behind Bennett School, by Lytle Park, for a little thing we called Scrawny League Football. The concept was simple. A bunch of small, athletically disadvantaged kids, lacking speed, size or concept of strategy, would choose sides and play mammoth four-hour epics of tackle football. Nobody big or talented allowed. These were for the shrimps, the dorks, the mutts. The games were anything but complex; "one-Mississippi, two-Mississippi" passed for defensive alignment, and every play was mapped out intricately as "OK, you guys run downfield and I'll throw it to one of you."

But the games were ours, and they were pure. And competitive. Every game seemed to come down to the last decisive possession, or until my cousin Denny—the smallest of all of us—got hurt, which was often. Afterward, we'd adjourn to Jeff's hot tub and soak, ready to go again the next day, if our parents would let us.

We were careful about whom we invited to these games, because if anyone showed too much spirit, too much talent, it only would upset the delicate balance of the contest— which, after all, was founded on our equal uselessness. Once, the best player in town, a future Mattoon High School Green Wave star who would later play running back for a Division I-AA university, asked if he could join us. He was a great guy, and we all would have felt much cooler hanging out with him. But he was not for Scrawny League.

But Lonnie, we figured Lonnie would be fine. He wasn't much bigger than us, and other than the occasionally maniacal look in his eye, we didn't imagine he'd cause too much competitive disparity. Everyone shook hands beforehand, made fun of my hair as usual, then picked teams. The unproven Lonnie was opposite me, and we readied for the kickoff. Being a wimp, I never liked to field kickoffs, because then you, by definition, have six or seven people with the lone purpose of bashing you into the ground. But this one was kicked straight to me. I had no choice but to take off with it.

Two teammates were blocking for me, and I appeared to have some room. I juked left, spun around, and headed down the right sideline, following two lead blockers. Plenty of room. Might I take this all the way? Like Deion Sanders? Which dance would I do when I reached the end zone? Were any girls, by chance, watching?

Then, out of nowhere, my two blockers exploded. Poof... into smithereens, splintered in opposite directions. And there was Lonnie, arms flailing, eyes bulging, legs flapping wildly behind him, heading straight for me. I had a sudden urge to throw the ball out of bounds, dig a hole in the dirt and climb in it. But there was no time. With a primal "YARRRR!" and teeth a-gnashing, Lonnie lunged forward, Matrix-like, and deposited himself flat into my chest, knocking the ball loose, inserting me about 15 feet deep into the turf and inspiring me, for about 20 minutes, to forget about basic daily activities like breathing, talking, saying the name "Will Leitch" as if it were my own.

Unlike me—who was being pried off the ground by a complicated procedure involving a spatula, a ditch digger and a Dustbuster—Lonnie popped right back up, licked his lips and screamed, "FIRST DOWN, LET'S GO, PLAY SOME 'D!'"

We didn't invite Lonnie anymore. My breastplate, however, eventually popped back into place.

For whatever reason, even after we were all driving cars and growing hair in scary places, we always found time to play Scrawny League. As the years went on, and we approached college, we began to worry, as tends to happen, whether or not we'd be able to keep the gang together, all stay friends, keep up with one another. Jeff, the ringleader and resident troublemaker of the group, came up with the masterstroke.

"Day after Christmas. Mattoon High School football field. High noon. Let's play."

And so we have. Since a particularly rousing game in 1992, our senior year of high school, we have met every year, come rain or snow or sleet or 10-below temperatures, at Grimes Field, just outside Mattoon High School, while an annual girls' basketball tournament goes on inside the gymnasium, on the first weekday after Christmas for Scrawny League Football.

The lineups change somewhat from year to year, but the core group is always there. Jeff. Shad. Andy. Nick. Keith. Donnie. Denny. Rob. And me. Nothing is allowed to get in the way of the games. Two years ago, when I was working in St. Louis, two hours away, the blasted boss had me working from 4 p.m. to 2 a.m. on the day of Scrawny League. At 10 a.m., I left St. Louis, drove to Mattoon, played for two hours and then drove back to work. Missing Scrawny League was not an option.

With many of our crew scattered across the country or in the even more remote location of marriage, this is likely the only time all year we will see one another. But we don't bore each other with inane holiday patter: How's the family? What have you been doing with your life these days? How are the kids? Did that rash ever go away? We just warm up a bit, toss the ball around, stretch and then go at it. We'll figure out how everybody's doing the way we're supposed to, on the field.

Director Michael Apted has made a fascinating series of documentaries, called the *Up* films. The conceit: Every seven years, he revisits a group of 10 people he first filmed at the age of seven, in *7 Up*. He does not speak with them in between seven-year spans. He just shows up every seven years and says it's that time again. The films, watched back-to-back, are breathtaking. Anyone needing reassurance that the child is indeed the father of the man need look no further than those films. The kid you hated at seven is a jerk for much the same reasons at 28.

I think of those films every year we play Scrawny League. Everyone's pretty much the same as they were when they were 14. Jeff is still the smart, cocky, dominant one, making all the major decisions and egging everyone on. Keith is still the quiet, upstanding, straight-arrow, hard-working guy who always seems to be favoring some sort of injury. Shad is still the laconic one who always seems to be laughing at a joke none of us were let in on. And me? Well, I'm still the guy hoping the kickoff doesn't come in my direction.

The games themselves have changed, of course. We used to fear being hurt—the most notorious damages: Jeff chipped a tooth once, causing him to wear a mouthpiece for the next two games, and occasional Scrawny player Tim once gave me a black eye when I tried to tackle his legs and ended up with a shoe in my face—but not anymore. None of us can move fast enough to hurt anybody. Our four-hour epics, which were inevitably followed by more games that week, now last about two hours, tops, and we're all sore for weeks afterwards. Andy once quarterbacked with the ball in one hand and a cigarette in the other. From time to time, someone will have to beg out early to go check on the baby. And instead of the hot tub, we now adjourn to the bar.

Nothing stops these games, but we hit our first speed bump last year. For eight Christmases, we hadn't once been bothered for playing on the high school field. We doubt anyone had even ever noticed. Heck, we don't even wear cleats. It's our tradition. We've always played there.

But in 1999, the Green Wave football team, after years of struggle, went 9-0 and made the state playoffs under coach Gerald Temples. The achievement was most appreciated, to be sure, particularly by embarrassed alums, but Mr. Temples and his staff apparently became a bit power-crazed and prone to micromanagement. About an hour into our Scrawny League game last year, a school employee, presumably from the custodial staff, ran out to us, screaming obscenities and even using inappropriate sexual terms that disturbed our young and virginal ears. Something like: "Kind sirs, could you please exit the playing field?" except "Kind sirs" sounded a lot like "You cocksucking, motherfucking kids, get off the fucking field!"

Calmly, we met him at the sideline and tried to, in a clear-headed and composed way, explain to him our tradition and desire not to cause any trouble. He responded with more vulgar insults—he just kept saying such horrible, horrible things!—so, in the most moderated and even-tempered tone we could muster, we told him exactly what he could do with himself. At this point he made an obscene gesture with one of his fingers—lord have mercy!—and ran inside, vowing to do away with us meddling kids.

We continued playing, and an hour later, Gerald Temples himself showed up to give us a stern lecture. We explained to him that we wanted no discord, just to observe our tradition. He then, in a much nicer way than the custodian, told us what we could do with ourselves. We then, if just to finish our game, left the field and went somewhere else.

But that won't stop us this year. As always, we'll be there at high noon, the day after Christmas, Grimes Field. I am returning to New York City, my home, on December 27. I would have made it a day earlier... but I have a game to play.

FINDING AN OLD, NEW BEST FRIEND

About two weeks after I arrived home to Mattoon almost two months ago, ostensibly to write but also to straighten up the relentless mess my life had become, I borrowed money from my parents. A lot of money. Not a 20-spot so I didn't have to run to the ATM. Not 100 bucks to tide me over until a random freelancing check was deposited. I mean a shitload of money. I'll put it this way: I borrowed more money from my parents than you have ever borrowed from your parents.

I am 25 years old.

I had done my best to put off what should have been clearly inevitable. Once we were all laid off, I realized that, unlike others, I had not prepared. There was no nest egg to fall back on. I had no magic benefactor. I had been living check-to-check for quite some time, which is fine when you're sure each of those checks will come. It tends to bite you in the ass when it doesn't.

I had two choices. I could either pay all that I owed and likely not eat for a month or two... or I could skip rent. Just for one month, just this once, I'll get it back when I'm employed next week. I'm sure the landlord won't mind. I've been good about it up to this point. One month I skip... heck, it's not a big deal. I mean, I'm obviously employable and dependable, I've got my shit together. I'm the least of their problems, I'm sure. I'll make enough money in the next month to make up for it.

Then that month passed. I had made no more money. Zilch. Some freelance opportunities fell through. People were not lining up to buy my company, Ironminds, the way I thought they might. It was now obvious that I was officially unemployed. Rent came up again. This time, I'd spent most of the money that would have been earmarked for rent the month before. Sure, my editor at Ironminds had donated some cash from "the Ironminds fund," but since I was doing my best to prove to everyone that all was well, that I was not broke, no no, I was just fine, nothing to see here... that money evaporated quickly. Rent was not going to be paid this month either. Two months. Not a big deal. Just going through a rough spot. I'll catch up next month.

Then next month came, and by now, I couldn't lie. No money, no nothing. I was falling behind on my book as well. I came up with the solution: I would go home, finish my book and, to be entirely honest, hide from the rapidly increasing number of bills piling up at the

Greenwich Village apartment. My roommate had moved out, taking a new job in San Francisco, so he wouldn't know what was happening anyway. Who knows... maybe I would somehow make enough money in the next two months through freelancing to pay the whole thing off... maybe?...

And then two weeks in Mattoon passed, and my roommate caught wind of the whole deal, and he—he of the sweet Southern charm and firm Methodist faith—called me from San Francisco and was so angry he used words I'd never heard him use before. "We are three months behind on rent. They are going to evict us. I don't know about your credit—though I have my suspicions—but mine's fine, and I'm not going to let you [screw] it up. You find some way to pay it. I don't know how, but you find out a way."

My roommate was doing the right thing, of course, and when you broke it down, I had only one option. I swallowed every remaining bit of pride—and, truth be told, there wasn't much to swallow—and drove the six miles from my cousin Denny's to my parents' place. It was the only place I had to turn. They weren't home. I waited, and waited, and waited, and they never showed. Tired, I left them a note explaining the situation and dropped by the next morning. My mother was waiting: "We got your note." She looked sad, too forlorn for mere disappointment. My parents had always known I was flaky, and perhaps had my head in the clouds more than was good for me. But it had never come to this before. For the first time, it was obvious, she was seriously questioning everything she thought she knew about her son. "Oh my," her eyes said... "he might really be a screw-up."

"Let me talk to your father."

I am 25 years old.

The next weekend, after they had given me the money, I, feeling deeply depressed and more than a little worthless, decided to visit old friends at The Sporting News in St. Louis, about two hours away. I drove a beaten up old 1986 Chevy Caprice, the Green Mile, to see Matt and Chris and Brian and Liz and Benson and Jason and all the crew. Shortly after I left TSN, Paul Allen bought the magazine, and everyone who stayed earned bonuses that entered the five figures. But I didn't care. I had left for my fame and fortune and New York City, and I think, secretly, my friends at TSN thought I was going to find it. When I came back a year later, penniless, unshaven, despondent and depraved, Matt and Chris and Brian and Liz and Benson and Jason and all the crew couldn't mask their pity. I hadn't turned out how they had expected at all. It was wonderful to see everyone—I had missed them even more than I had remembered—but it was a miserable, humiliating trip.

About a half hour into the drive home, I noticed an unusually plentiful amount of smoke shooting out the exhaust pipe. I pulled to a gas station, lifted the hood and realized the car had overheated. It was fried. I was an hour-and-a-half from Mattoon. There was only one place to call. After smoking a pack of cigarettes and cursing God... oh the fucking timing... "Yeah, Dad? It's Will ..."

He arrived two hours later, and, as I'd feared, the car wasn't the only thing with steam coming out of it. We sat out in the cold for two hours, picking the car apart, putting this here, placing that there. At one point, the wrench my father was using slipped out of his hand and cut his left thumb. The blood oozed out, doing its best not to be noticed. The gash opened up further a few minutes later, and a large patch of skin was noticeably dangling perilously. Dad didn't pause in the slightest. He just kept working, as the oil and the grime and the soot mixed in, turning his thumb purple. He just kept working.

The car was continuing to leak, and it was obvious this problem would not be fixed tonight. Dad would have to take the next day off of work, just to help his failure son fix a goddamned car. We had an hour-and-a-half to drive home in his truck, just the two of us. We had yet to discuss, one on one, all the money I had borrowed just two days before. We both understood the ramifications of this drive. It could go one of two ways.

Dad walked inside the gas station and bought a six-pack of Natural Light. We hopped in the truck and were silent, motionless for about 15 minutes. He then handed me a beer. "So... did you hear about the Cardinals thinking about trading Tatis?" And so it was done. We talked for the next hour about the Cardinals, the Rams, the Illini, my friend Tim, my girlfriend... we were friends again. Dad knew—he could see it—how this situation had shaken me to my very foundation, and no matter how much he was questioning about his son, I was questioning more. He didn't yell, he didn't scold, he didn't even grimace. We just talked about what we'd always talked about, until I was ready, no longer too ashamed, to discuss the matter at hand.

"Dad... I screwed up. I'm so sorry." I told him how I felt what had happened over the last few months was in fact some sort of karmic punishment, my proper comeuppance for a summer where I was a financial and creative success, but a total asshole in life. I was so full of myself, invincible, that I stomped on everyone who even deigned for one second to care about me. I didn't know who was doing it, but some deity was mighty pissed about the way I'd acted since I arrived in New York, and they made sure I would pay for it. "You know, Dad... I really do think I had this coming."

It was the most meaningful conversation I'd ever had with my father. Not because of what was said, but what wasn't. For the first time since this whole mess had begun... he understood. I wasn't a fool and a deadbeat. I wasn't reckless. I'd just fallen into a hole, and I didn't pull myself out of it, not in time. My father, a man of whom I'd lived in fear for the first 18 years of my life, was fatherly. Somehow, listening to me, talking to me, actually hearing his son and hearing himself, it dawned on him... Will's going to be OK. And for the first time in a long time, it dawned on me too.

The rest of my time in Mattoon was a joy. Any time the Illini played, I would head down to my father's new basement, his pride and joy, and we would watch the game, and drink beer, and high five, and scream at the TV. He would show off how many points he'd won on his video poker machine, and I would beam at his muffled excitement when he opened up my Christmas present to him, the "Sopranos" first season videocassettes, a gift I could not afford but bought anyway. For the first time, my father had become my best friend.

On New Year's Eve, from the party I was at in Long Island, I called my father two hours before the ball dropped. He was at the neighbors' house, one house over. He'd brought the phone with him.

"Happy New Year, Dad. You watching the game on Wednesday?"

"Yeah, of course. Bar's open! You gotta come on by."

I'll never be able to spend a month and a half with my father again. I'll never be able to just come on by. I'm back to my life now. But I'll always have the last month and a half. If I never appreciated him before, I certainly do now. After all, no matter what happens, we'll always have the Illini, and the bar, and the video poker. If not each other.

LOOKING THE CITY IN THE EYE

This city is hard. I don't know why I thought, when I left St. Louis in December 1999, that I was going to take over New York, that I was going to a place where my alleged genius would be embraced, that I was going to achieve fame and fortune and the trappings of literary stardom… but, well, that's what I thought.

In St. Louis, I saw myself as that proverbial big fish in that proverbial small pond. I started out just logging agate text, editing incomprehensible team reports, cropping photos, writing 100-word blurbs about the Clippers' upset win over the Timberwolves. But as I spent more time there, I started to gain confidence in my writing and my presence, thanks not in small part to a Web site, where I was allowed to publish my most private and self-indulgent inclinations, a freedom I appreciated at first, then took for granted. After a while, I felt entitled to the freedom. That was a freedom that is perhaps not healthy for a 23-year-old kid who, when you broke it down, really never had to work very hard for anything before in his life.

After a while, I was known as the artsy literary guy of *The Sporting News*, which, in retrospect, was a title probably built more out of my own self-promotion than any actual merit. I was the one always championing the plight of the writer, blasting the corporate higher-ups for not realizing the artist they had on staff, the brilliance that resided in their midst. I worked there long enough to earn a little bit of clout, and I parlayed that into a successful lobbying effort for two columns. The conceit of these columns was that they were columns for the common man, the guy who had more to do than obsess about the minutiae of sports statistics. The average sports fan, I argued, doesn't care about how many yards Trent Dilfer threw for in Week 13 against Green Bay; they just wanted to be entertained by columns with a sense of fun. To anyone who would listen, I would describe the "vision" behind these columns: *They're not about sports; they're about me writing about sports.* They were filled with self-referential humor and relentless digressions.

The whole thing was a scam. I just wanted to be heard, wanted to feel special, wanted to feel like I was good enough to get away with something. When the columns started to be read a bit, as the page views inched up infinitesimally, I took it as validation: I was bigger than my job, I was onto something that the corporate schmoes were too square to understand. The columns always meant more to me than they did to the readers, but that's because I was *important*. I deserved those columns.

I began to feel that St. Louis was a waste of my time. I would never be able to realize my full potential in the Midwest. Goddammit, didn't they realize who I was? And sports... true artists could not be shackled to something as trivial as sports. I had larger fish to gut, clean and fry.

I was invincible. A woman I worked with, engaged to another man, happy with her life, caught my eye. A lesser man would have recognized this and stayed away. But I was different. I was special. There were no rules for me. I pursued her relentlessly until a moment of weakness, when she caved. I then made her feel guilty, lacking vision, for returning to him.

I then met a sweet, loyal, beautiful blonde who, for whatever reason, thought I was worth hanging around. I fell for her... until I realized she was a St. Louis girl—more shackles. I was offered a job in New York. I was about to conquer. I accepted the job without even a second thought as to her. Later, she would follow me to New York, where I would break her heart because she stood in the way of my destiny. Because New York was mine. I left St. Louis and vowed never to look back.

And here I sit, more than a year later, confused, humbled, crumbled.

Eric, one of my closer friends, lives on the just outside of Chinatown. He pays too much for his apartment, like everyone here does, but it's a great one, homey, quiet enough, conveniently located. I have spent many hours at Eric's apartment. Anytime I show up there, it's only a matter of minutes before I swipe a beer from the fridge and head to his roof.

In New York, there is nothing better than a roof. Eric has a great one. When you step up there, you have a breathtaking view of the city. To your left, the awesome Twin Towers looming, imposing, solid, comforting in their invincibility. They are not architectural wonders; they are just enormous and dominating. And then, to your right, the rest of the city... the Empire State Building, the Chrysler Building, all of midtown and uptown, shining luminously. What always amazes me about this view of Manhattan is how colorful it is; even though we're dealing with just massive amounts of concrete, stacked end to end to unthinkable heights, the color never fades. It's always beaming red, or green, or blue, or just bright. It's always shining, like the city itself is a pilot light that will extinguish only long after the rest of us are gone.

In the film *The Cruise*, Timothy Levitch talks of the city being alive, a breathing entity with mood swings and fits of anger that ebb and flow like anybody else's. You feel this looking at downtown New York from a distance. New York is like the kid in school that got all the girls, the guy you want to be friends with, the guy who kinda likes you and maybe will give you the chance to hang with him, but who ultimately doesn't care one way or the other.

He'll be there no matter what, impenetrable, the guy the girls love, the girl with the most cake.

And there's something about roofs here... a roof makes you big. A roof makes you feel as if you can see the city at a distance, see what you're doing here. It grants you a perspective you lose when you're another anonymous drone bustling around aimlessly on the ground floor. You feel like, for once, you can talk to the city on its own level, look it in the eye, try to make it understand.

I have been talking to the city a lot lately. I'm staying at a place in Brooklyn with a roof that's not quite as nice as Eric's, but close. You can see the Statue of Liberty, positioned strategically away from all the chaos, laughing at us all insignificant idiots inflated with self-importance. But most of all, you can see *the city*. You feel like you can put your arms around it and grab it, for once, get a handle on the damn place. For a few minutes, you find peace and can see the whole picture.

It makes you feel larger. It makes you feel that New York has a place for you. And, at times that you really need it, in a weird way, it does a favor... it makes you feel smaller.

There is one problem I will not have the rest of my time in New York, however long that will be. I will always feel smaller. This city has done many things to me, and it has beaten me in ways I hadn't thought possible, but it is New York that I have to thank for being humbled and crumbled.

I think back on St. Louis. The Missouri city has an underrated downtown view; the Arch swoops over nondescript buildings and lends the place an awe it wouldn't otherwise have. But it is small. It makes you feel big.

New York has made me feel small. Which city is correct is a question yet to be answered.

BACK TO WORK

T he other day I realized, with a twinge of panic, that I had forgotten how to ride an elevator.

Over the last few months of pathetic scrambling-for-a-meal unemployment, I'd ridden in an elevator maybe three or four times. I'd been with friends, who had more experience in the practice, each time, and I was able to blend in. But I was among only strangers last Thursday.

There were three people in the elevator with me. One was an elderly woman, older than she wanted to be perceived, with eye shadow dripping off her eyelids and leggings so tight you could see the veins in her thigh. An African-American messenger was there too, clearly annoyed with this particular transaction; he had to go all the way to the top floor and tapped the pointless "door close" button incessantly. And, like in all elevators in New York, there was a hot girl, distant and dispassionate, aware of every glance she received, returning none of them.

And then me. As I zipped up to the 16th floor, I found myself, at first, hopping. I was standing entirely in the wrong place: Right in the middle. Right in everyone's way. Then I turned around and looked around aimlessly, catching the eye of the messenger, which, as most of us know, is the cardinal sin of elevators. (This theorem also applies at men's urinals.) I then coughed and said something like, "Boy... getting cold out there!" No one even blinked. You know how Beavis and Butt-Head used to look at each other blankly when they'd see a Winger video or something? That's how they were looking at me. I clearly had no idea what I was doing.

You see... Ladies and gentlemen... believe it or not... hold onto your hats... holy moly... heavens to murgatroid... yes, it's true... it just can't be... I have a job.

It changes everything. Before, back when I was unemployed (so, so long ago), the days stretched out lazily, without any particular reason. You find yourself structuring your days in the most wretched ways: 9 a.m., "SportsCenter;" 10 a.m., "The Daily Show;" 10:30, "Whose Line Is It Anyway?" By 11 a.m., it's time for the first cigarette of the day. Noon, check e-mail. No job leads. Shit.

Then comes a pivotal moment: masturbation or a nap? This decision affects everything that comes afterwards. For example, if you masturbate first, then the nap comes later. If you nap first, you masturbate after that. The whole framework of the afternoon is shaped by this value judgment, and believe you me, I've mucked up the procedure too many times to count.

But now, I have to be at work—at work! At work! Say it with me now... WORK!—at 8 a.m. It gives you something to look forward to at night. It's a reason for being. Tomorrow, you have to be somewhere. Someone will be upset if you don't show. People are actually aware of your existence.

When you've worked all day, everything that comes afterwards improves. The beer tastes sharper, the music sounds better, the women look hotter, the guys look less intimidating, the whole evening just opens itself up to you, full of promise and vitality and hope and hope and hope. When you meet people at parties, you can say, "Hi, I'm Will, I work for XXXXX XXXXX." As opposed to, say, "Hi, I'm Will, I'm a complete worthless human being without a single thing to possibly contribute to this conversation. In fact, I don't even deserve to be in the same room with you, which is saying something, considering I've only known you for 30 seconds and I already don't like you. If you could possibly shoot me in the face on your way out tonight, the gesture would be greatly appreciated."

I'm not sure if I'll ultimately like this job (it seems just fine so far) or if it's beneficial for my career, or if it will win me the respect of my peers. At this point, I really don't care. I'm just happy I'm out there, working again. Do you realize how many times my father has had to stumble when his buddies at the electric company ask how Will's doing? There really isn't a worse answer he could give than the one he's forced to.

"In jail."
"Gay."
"Following the Chicago Cubs around."
"Dead."

Nope. "Unemployed, and supposedly looking for work." Nothing more demoralizing, for me or my father.

Now he doesn't have to do that. He can say the name of a magazine he doesn't know, that they don't know, and then they can all nod and say, "We knew he'd amount to something." Then they'll go home and tell their 35-year-old son to get his feet off the couch.

So I'm back. Part of my job involves running a section of a magazine's Web site. I'm the editor, actually. I think it's a nice little site, but I'm planning on making it better. My name is listed on the site as "Editor."

I had been there three days when I received the following e-mail:

Dear Not-So-Good Will Leitch:

I thought I noticed a sudden dip in quality of XXXXX XXXXX. Sure enough, you're [cq] name has been added where XXXX XXXX's was previously. Please resign now, and ask the estimable Mr. XXXX to resume his former duties.

To remind: resign now.

Waiting for XXXX,

XXXX XXXXX

And, ladies and gentleman... we are OFF! It's great to be back.

WE ARE FUCKING OLD

D o you realize that high-school kids today—the ones shaping our culture, for cripes sake—think of Guns N' Roses the way we in our mid-20s think of the Rolling Stones?

We are so fucking old. I know a large percentage of you are older than me, so, lest you think I'm a kid who's just whining, let me reassure you that you're fucking old too. I recognize that if I eventually quit smoking, I could live another 50 years, maybe more. But the fun part is over. I already missed it. I'm not sure what I was doing when I was supposed to be having fun. That's frustrating. I know I wasn't studying, or working, or preparing myself for world domination. I was frittering away time, drinking, goofing off. I should have been having more fun. I think I just wasn't sure where the fun was. I think the fun was avoiding me. I think the fun saw me heading in its direction, then turned and walked the other way, pausing only to push my grandmother in front of traffic and flip me off.

Do you realize that *Appetite For Destruction*, only the cultural landmark for our generation, the first album we ever heard that made smoking, drinking, drugging, cursing and whoring sound, hell, like a whole lot of fun... that album came out in 1987? 1987! That was 16 years ago. Babies born when *Appetite For Destruction* came out are having sex already. (In Iowa, they're getting married, and in Kentucky, they're getting divorced and fighting over custody of the six-year-old.) If you were old enough to be driving when *Appetite* came out, you're over 30. Guns N' Roses is now classic rock on the station where your parents used to listen to Lynyrd Skynyrd and Bob Seger.

1991 was a groundbreaking year for music. Look at all the albums that came out that year: REM's *Out of Time*, Metallica's self-titled black album, Pearl Jam's *Ten*, the *Use Your Illusion* albums, Matthew Sweet's *Girlfriend*, U2's *Achtung Baby* and, of course, Nirvana's *Nevermind*. Those albums laid the foundation for all the music I listened to from then on, and if you look at my CDs, probably about a third of my collection is made up by those artists (hardly a week goes by when I don't put in *Nevermind* or *Achtung Baby* at least once). These albums came out 12 years ago. Twelve years.

The first great experience I had in a movie theater was Oliver Stone's *JFK*. I was with my friend Tim and a couple of other nerdy Mattoon kids, and we were absolutely entranced. Sure, I went to the movies all the time, but that was mainly just to get out of the house, or, if the stars were aligned perfectly, to find a dark place to make out. But *JFK* sucked me in.

For three hours, I forgot who I was, where I was, what I was... I was only living in the land of Oliver Stone, a place I was too young to realize that probably was not psychologically healthy to dwell. With about five minutes left in the film, right when they're about to announce the verdict of the Clay Shaw trial, the projector broke, and I snapped back to reality with a jolt. I looked over at Tim and barely recognized him. It took a good 20 minutes to readjust to the world around me. I had been transported, and there was no going back. I devoted almost every waking minute from then on to going to movies. I discovered Woody Allen and found my muse. That was also 12 years ago.

Last year, my childhood hero, Ozzie Smith, the guy who did the back flips on Opening Day, who made the gravity-defying diving lunges at shortstop, who hit the ninth-inning, game-winning home run off Tom Neidenfuer in Game 5 of the 1985 National League Championship Series and inspired broadcaster Jack Buck's legendary "Go Crazy, Folks!" radio call (a moment that remains my most beloved in Cardinals history)... Ozzie Smith was elected to the Hall of Fame.

When I was a kid, my father and I made a deal. When Ozzie Smith was inducted into the Hall, we would make a pilgrimage to Cooperstown on the sacred day. We surely wouldn't be able to get in the actual ceremony—not unless we were willing to offer up our firstborns for tickets, and I was against that, considering I'm his firstborn—but we had to be there to see Ozzie, the guy whose batting stance I had memorized, the guy who was just below (and sometimes above) my parents on my worship scale for many, many years.

Our family vacations every year revolved around where the Cardinals were playing, and one year, in Cincinnati, we stayed in the same hotel as the team. My dad rode down an elevator with Ozzie and his son, Osborne Jr., and Ozzie was cordial, welcoming and accommodating. My father smiled for a week. Ozzie is about to go to the Hall of Fame. He is now a legend. Ozzie Smith, my favorite baseball player ever, is 50 years old. I discovered him in 1982, when the Cardinals won their last World Series. That was 21 years ago. Twenty-one years.

It was my old friend Andy's birthday last week. I don't get to talk to Andy as much anymore. He's married, lives in Illinois, and is in graduate school. We don't share a lot of common interests these days. I'll talk to him from New York like it's Mars, and he'll talk to me from wedded bliss like it's Pluto. But he was my closest friend from the ages 13 to 16, and those are critical years. We went through That Awkward Stage together (Andy, unlike me, eventually pulled himself out of it), and we would stay up all night sometimes, talking about girls and wondering what, exactly, we were expected to do with them if we ever happened to find ourselves alone with them. Andy knows me as well as anyone, which might be a reason I always feel nervous talking to him. We went everywhere together, which was why I dragged him to my church youth group's trip to Six Flags on Friday the 13th, 1990.

I was trying to set him up with my girlfriend Barbara's best friend. Kyla was sweet and funny, and, girlfriend be damned, I found her pretty cute myself. (I would later spend a good four years of my life trying to court her, failing miserably.) Barbara and I thought they'd be just darling together, but it rained the entire day at Six Flags, and even though Kyla was interested, Andy decidedly wasn't, telling me in an aside that "she looked like a drowned rat." Five years ago, I told this exact story at Andy and Kyla's wedding. Thirteen years. Five years. Jesus Christ.

Just got laid off again, and I'm on the job hunt once more. There's one I found that, if I do say so myself, I'd be awesome at, and I think they would hire me. It's outside of this crazy media world, but it's still in my comfort zone, my sweet spot, right down the middle, I'd smack it into the left-field bleachers. I applied immediately, and then I remembered...

There was this girl. I won't get into the particulars, but I had known her for a long time and admired her from afar. Then she announced she was moving to a different city. Almost accidentally, one drunken night, we confessed feelings for each other. Then she was gone, and I never saw her again. I was broken up for a while, but life went on, and I found a whole new set of problems and women to vex me. I left her well enough alone, kept my distance, never contacted her, figured she could go on with her life.

Then I applied for this job. And I realized, with a heavy sigh, that she now works there, a senior staff member, the type of person who looks at all the resumes, and there ain't a damn way that she'd ever work in the same office with me. I'm a black mark, a tumor. The chaos with her happened almost four years ago, but with all that's occurred since then, it might as well have been 20. We are old, and we know that we are old when four years is a lifetime. Four years is always a lifetime. It's a wonder we live long enough to string so many four-year spans together.

Because it just gets worse. They add up, and next thing you know, it's over. It's all history, and it never stops, and we leave trails of mud and pus and blood and shit, dragging our entrails behind us, slugs of time. Ozzie Smith retires; Andy and Kyla get older; Kurt Cobain gets dead. And we all move along, decaying, never making sense of a bit of it, wondering how and when, exactly, "Paradise City" ended up sandwiched between "Stairway to Heaven" and "Hotel California" on the radio.

SPRING CLEANING

A friend called at about 4 p.m. Sunday afternoon. "Will, isn't it beautiful outside? It's summer! Have you been to the park yet? And have you seen the women that are out? The breastometric pressure today is way high."

I slipped off my latex gloves, wiped my sweaty brow with a soiled, swarthy towel and sighed. "No, sorry, I haven't. I've been inside all day. Fuck this guy, man."

About a month ago, when matters were cruising along at my new job and my life was just a few steps away from normal again, I let it be known to associates that I was on the search for an apartment. I was almost whole. After six months of living in a state of either joblessness or homelessness (and sometimes both), my life was to be put back together again. I scoured through apartment listings, just trying to find a room, somewhere, anywhere. One day, I received an e-mail from my friend Heather, alerting me to a suspiciously cheap apartment on Manhattan's Upper East Side. My ears perked, I fired off a witty, charming, *don't-you-just-love-me?* e-mail to the guy with the apartment. He called me within 20 minutes and asked if I wanted to come over and see the place.

The guy's name was Vin. He was about 35 years old, with stringy, long and strategically unkempt black hair, a week's worth of stubble and a Genesis T-shirt (he would later attempt to explain to me, with varying degrees of success, how Phil Collins ruined the group and that Peter Gabriel was a true visionary on the scale of Bob Dylan, Gandhi and Christ). He began to show me around the apartment. It's a one-bedroom with a huge front room that served as his bedroom as well as a living room (big wooden screens separated his bed area from the rest of the apartment). The one bedroom, which I would be renting, was down the hall and set off from the rest of the place. It had two windows, a spacious closet and, perhaps most important, its own door for privacy, a luxury I didn't have at my twice-the-rent apartment in the West Village. It was clean, nice, and perfect.

The front room, however, was a whole other ball of wax. Vin had somehow, for some reason, done everything in his power to shut out all the light in the apartment, hanging odd shawls from the ceiling and draping curtains over the windows. It looked like the section of the zoo that caged the lizards, and though I lack olfactory nerves, I suspect it smelled like it too. It was dirty, dank and repulsive. But I didn't care. That was his room. I would just be spending time in mine. He could do whatever he wanted out there.

We sat down in the front room for a get-to-know-you session. I told him I was a writer and was looking forward to having a boring life again—New York always seems to find a way to drag you into its drama—heading for work, going home, locking myself in my room to write and leaving everyone well enough alone. He said that was cool. I told him I had a cat. He was down with that too. I had noticed a pack of cigarettes on the table in the kitchen. I told him I smoked too. His face turned to curiosity.

"I should let you know, I smoke pot. I hope that's OK."
Hey, man, it's the '90s. (Well, close enough.) No problemo.
"Do you want to smoke now?" he asked.

Now, at best, I'm a recreational pot smoker/paranoia purveyor, which is another way of saying that when I'm hanging out with a bunch of people smoking pot, I'll join in and spend the rest of night wondering if their heated conversations about old Scooby-Doo episodes are veiled references to how much they despise me. Ordinarily, the last place in the world I'd want a bong hit would be in the apartment of a guy I'm trying to impress. But I needed this apartment, and he was looking at me as if this were some sort of test.

"Uh... sure, yeah, I guess, if you're going to." And so it was. He fired one up, and I did my darndest to inhale as little as possible. (I have become an expert at this tactic, if just because I am wont to begin violent coughing jags.) And then we started "conversing."

"You seem like a nice guy. I think you might be my first choice. A friend of mine was wanting the room too, but he's kind of unreliable. He pretty much just plays Magic with me."
Magic: The Gathering?
"Yeah, that's it. Do you play?"
Uh, no.
"Shame. It's an incredible game."

And...

"I know people will find this strange, but I think you can learn more from one episode of *Star Trek: Voyager* than from any philosophy book. There's some serious shit going on there."

And...

"I just decided about three years ago that I didn't have to play the game anymore. I realized, man, that I can be Jim Morrison, yeah!"
Right.
"Ride the snake."

He asked me the name of the magazine I was working for at the time, and then he paused.

"I'm in publishing too."
Really?
"Yeah. In fact, you should know this. If you move in here, there are going to be a lot of people who look like this hanging around."

He handed me a folder. I opened it and, to my shock, saw stacks of black-and-white glossy photos of women. They were like headshots for a casting call. Except the women were naked. And probably about 15.

"Yeah, I work in porn."
Oh. That's something. What kind of porn?
"I work for a magazine group. We publish *Cheri, High Society, Playgirl* and various niche publications."
Various niche publications?
"Yeah, you know, midgets on tricycles, that type of thing." (He actually said this.)

We both had a cigarette, and then he said he had to meet his girlfriend—this man dates!—and needed to go. He smiled and said he'd let me know if I got the place in the next couple of days. That night, he called me and said it was mine if I wanted it. Two days later, he dropped by my office, and I handed him a deposit. I was to move in in three weeks. And then he vanished.

No matter what I did, I couldn't track him down. I called his cell phone, I left notes at his apartment, I e-mailed him. Nothing. Finally, the day before I was to move in, he called me, said he'd been in England and invited me to come over to his office (gulp) and hand him the first month's rent. I left work early and headed over, where I was greeted by him and an odd-looking British woman with fingernails the length of No. 2 pencils.

He cleared his throat uncomfortably. "Listen, Will, I've been thinking. There's this leak in the apartment, and I don't want to have to deal with it. So I'm moving out."

Ahem. Um, sir, that could be a problem. You see, I have all my stuff ready to move in right now. And I don't have anywhere else to live. I thought I was going to pick up the keys today.

"Yeah, what do you think we should do about that?"

It dawned on me what he was doing. He wanted out of the apartment but couldn't wiggle out of his lease until October. What to do, what to do? Ah, yes, we'll put the Midwestern kid with the center part and big cheeks in a position where he has to take over the lease, so I can bolt and leave him responsible for everything. His plan worked beautifully.

Sigh.

"I guess I could take over the lease," I told him. I had no choice.
He smiled. "That would be great, Will."

I called him the next morning, trying to organize a time to move my stuff in. He didn't call back for two hours, and when he did, he sounded haggard.

"You'll have to excuse me, Will. It's been a busy day. I got married this morning."
You what?
"Yeah, we decided to go ahead and get it done. We're moving to England."
You know I'm moving in today, right?
"Sure, no problem, we can swing that. Just drop by my work and pick up the keys, and we'll all go up there together."
By the way, where are you right now?
"Oh, I had to go back to work. The wife's at home. We may go out tonight, I'm not sure."

The next time Casanova saw his new wife was while holding the door for me as I dragged in two suitcases. We went downstairs and spoke with the landlord, who clearly didn't like or trust Vin, but he took a shine to me because he's also from Southern Illinois. The lease was signed in my name, and I paid the full April rent, with the assumption that Vin and his wife would be out in a few days so I could find a new roommate.

Three weeks later, Vin left. I only knew he left because he wasn't there anymore. I received no clue from the apartment, because everything he owned was still there.

Vin had told me he would leave some things for me, in case I wanted to keep them once he was gone. I recognized immediately this was code for, "Listen, I don't feel like throwing all this shit out, so could you do it?" He had left everything. Some stuff was labeled with "Please Leave." Everything else was just lying there. He hadn't cleaned the place, he hadn't even bothered to take the socks and stained copies of *Barely Legal* out from under his bed.

I mean, the place was a disaster. I don't know, you tell me: It's common courtesy to clean your apartment before you leave it, right? Or at least get rid of all your shit? But no, instead, it was on my shoulders. So I've been cleaning.

I tell you, readers, I have seen things you cannot unsee. An unspooled condom lying under a stack of Batman comic books. A *Hustler* video called *101 Horny Nurses (And One Lucky Guy),* complete with some doofus with a dipshit grin on his face wearing a doctor's overcoat. A notebook full of musings on the unlimited depths of the lyrics of Yes. (Yes!) All of these items were covered in about three feet of dirt and grime.

I'm still on the roommate hunt, and it's difficult to explain to prospective renters why the entire apartment is surrounded in a cloud of dust. Sure, it's a nice place, roomy, quite a steal at the price, if I say so myself. But it certainly doesn't look it now. And I have to have the place cleaned up and spotless by May 1, whenever the new roommate moves in. This asshole dropped all this shit in my lap. Good thing I have this to occupy all my time too, considering I don't have anything more important to do, like, say, look for a job.

I don't know what the weather's like right now in England, but I hope it's rainy and gloomy and awful, because it's gorgeous in New York, and I'm not seeing a second of it. Instead, I'm peeling Trojans off the floor and earning valuable practice at fighting off the vomit reflex. All for a room I won't even be living in.

Isn't spring the most wonderful time of the year?

GO V.F.W.!

My Lord, is it ever beautiful outside. It's almost too much to take. I forget this every year. Spring seems to come out of nowhere. The season is even more beautiful in New York, as if the universe is finally smiling on us, spreading sunshine over even the most dirty, deserted alleys. Not even Gotham can escape spring.

And, of course, spring is time for baseball. I've mentioned this before, but it bears repeating: The largest tragedy of my adult existence is that I no longer play baseball. Softball won't cut it. I'm talking about real baseball.

Until the age of 18, all I ever did was play baseball, and this time of year fills me with both wonder and deep regret. Save for occasional Wiffleball games in the park, my ball-playing days are over. Next year—every year at this time, I say I will do this next year—I would like to coach a Little League team. Nothing serious, just some kids running around, playing. My years devoting every waking moment to playing on such teams have laid the groundwork. I think I would be a wonderful coach. The world could certainly use one.

There was one coach, in particular, that current overbearing kids' league coaches would be wise to emulate. I played for many, many teams and even more coaches, even people being paid simply to coach, and no one ever came close to the guy who coached our V.F.W. team in the Jaycee League, ages 8-10.

We all knew he wouldn't be like other coaches when he showed up at our first practice with my cousin Denny in tow. Denny, despite being in the same grade as me at school, was a year above me in the baseball leagues, so he was a one-year Jaycee veteran when I came into the league. He'd played for Pepsi-Cola the year before, under the eye of Coach Diamond, a loud, abrasive, and entirely awful woman whose son, Dustin, was renowned for running out of the batter's box in fear every time the pitcher started his windup.

After witnessing Denny's first season with Coach Diamond, it wasn't difficult to understand why. Denny didn't really like baseball very much in the first place, but under Coach Diamond, he quickly grew to loath it. You see, Denny was (and still is) very small. The smallest eight-year-old you ever did see. He barely even registered. The bat was almost as tall as he was. He was scared anyway, and Coach Diamond made it far worse. She would typically refuse to play him, but when his father complained, she would stick him in late in the game with explicit instructions, whispering in his delicate, underdeveloped ears, not to swing.

"Just stand up there. If you swing, you won't play next game." Denny was so little, it was darned near impossible to throw him a strike, and he would inevitably walk every time he came up. He would then be replaced with a pinch-runner, followed by a nasty glance from Coach Diamond in his father's direction, as if to say, "There's your goddamned at-bat!" Once, Denny, if just out of boredom, swung three times, struck out and was promptly screamed at by Coach Diamond. He quietly cried on the bench.

Thanks to a quirk in the Jaycee League rules—which typically did not allow you to switch teams until your three-year sentence was up—our new VFW coach signed on Denny's dad, whom he knew socially, to be an assistant coach. That meant Denny could play for us now. And from the looks of this first practice, there was clearly a new sheriff in town.

"Denny is going to be our catcher. Put the gear on, Denny." Now, Denny did own a glove, but under Coach Diamond, he was rarely called upon to use it, and then only as a harmless right fielder. Denny? As catcher? Any pitched ball would surely knock him over. Denny looked up at the coach with a look that somehow combined confusion, horror and, strangely, absurdly, excitement. Ricky Frey, a classy, smart 10-year-old with a firebrand younger brother who ended up in the Coles County Jail, was our best pitcher, and Coach directed him to warm up with Denny. Ricky was nervous himself; he certainly didn't want to hurt the puckish imp. But he fired his best heater in there anyway. Denny, to his surprise, snatched it out of the air with his virgin catcher's mitt. Through the mask you could see a huge smile. He popped back up and winged it back to Ricky. And we had our catcher, and V.F.W. had found itself an All-Star (Denny was perhaps too enthusiastic; he walked only twice the rest of the season). And baseball found itself a fan.

The fever swept through the team. There was this chubby eight-year-old named Jacob Hawkins. He was so obese he could barely swing the bat, and when he did, it was with no extension, like a top spinning aimlessly. He also couldn't catch with his undersized glove jammed uncomfortably over his plump fingers. Once, when "patrolling" right field during batting practice, he was smacked in the face with a pop-up because he'd been chewing on his glove and watching a nearby train pass. Coach was undaunted.

The first game of the season, John was the leadoff batter. In a moment that couldn't have been scripted more beautifully, he was hit with the first pitch and was given the steal sign by Coach on the very next pitch. He waddled recklessly toward second and belly-flopped into the base safely. That the catcher's throw had sailed into center field was irrelevant. He was safe. His grin could be seen three states over.

Then there was John Miller. A gangly, shy kid from a dirt-poor Mattoon family, raised by a single mother, he would cry every time she dropped him off at practice. He would often refuse to step into the batter's box, then scramble to sit in the car with his mother, who, anticipating a moment like this, would always stay for the first half-hour. Coach would have an assistant run practice, then sit in the car with John and his mother as John tried to explain, through sobs, why he didn't want to play baseball. Coach talked him into coming out, and, a couple of practices later, started calling John "Bulldog," which, obviously, was the exact opposite of what he was. His mother even took Coach aside one practice and chided him for applying such a snide nickname.

Funny thing was, John started to look a little less scared when he came to the plate, and about two weeks later, he showed up for a game with the name "BULLDOG" blazoned across his uniform. By his final year, he made the city all-star game, and years later, he hit a home run off me in the 13-year-old league that cost us the game. His family remains close with Coach's.

Then there was me. By the age of eight, I had already begun my torrid love affair with baseball, memorizing Stan Musial's statistics and rattling them off to my parents' friends' amazement. When I would later play high school baseball, my devotion to the game was unable to eclipse my lack of talent, and I sat on the bench. But at eight, if you loved the game, you were already better than three-quarters of the kids out there, who were plopped in the league just so their parents could have a few hours of peace each week. I was one of the best players on the team and, to me, practice and games were just more organized versions of what I did in the backyard every day. And I was a throwback. I refused to use aluminum bats, finding them vulgar and against what baseball was all about. Besides, Ozzie Smith didn't use an aluminum bat. What was good for Ozzie was good for me.

Problem was, Coach kept batting me near the bottom of the order, behind Jacob Hawkins and Denny and Bulldog. My batting average was far higher than theirs, and I could play any position on the field (although I preferred catcher, which Denny unfortunately occupied, straining our friendship daily). I was good, dammit. Back in tee-ball, before I'd discovered the infinite wonders of baseball, I was horrible, often running to the wrong base whenever I'd happen to make contact with the ball. It had been awful, but now, now I was a force. I had earned this. I'd paid my dues. I deserved to be batting fourth, and pitching, and catching, and playing every damn position on the field if I had to. Why were those shrimps who were so obviously terrible batting above me?

Coach didn't see it that way. I would complain to him regularly, whine about all the attention he gave to the other players, moan about receiving the least batting practice of anyone on the team. Everyone on the team loved Coach instantly, but I didn't see it. Why? All he did was let crappy players on the field when it hurt us the most. I mean, we could have totally beaten the Elks Club if I'd have been batting fifth instead of Kevin Thomas.

Yet Coach persevered. He would often drive out of town to pick up players whose parents couldn't make the trip. If a kid wanted his name on the back of his jersey but couldn't afford it, Coach would pick up the tab. He would even encourage me, one of the more popular players, to make friends with the ones the other kids rarely talked to. It seriously decreased my cool cachet.

Coach also developed this weird habit, inspired by one of Jacob Hawkins' at-bats. Despite Coach's repeated attempts to change the laws of physics and motion, Hawkins' girth made it tremendously difficult to get the bat around on even the weakest of fastballs. Most of his at-bats were strikeouts, walks or a hit-by-pitch. (Another of Coach's impressive accomplishments was coaxing Hawkins—or "Hawk," as he was inevitably known by the end of the season—to resist the temptation to cry every time he was hit.) But one time, Hawkins happened to time his lunge at just the right moment, and POW! The ball had all of Hawk's weight behind it and went soaring over the left fielder's head. Hawk stood there in wonder. *I did that?*

Coach noticed the delay, stifled a laugh and screamed "GO!" Hawk snapped out of his daze and took off, and I'll be damned if the sonuvagun didn't end up on third base. Coach, patrolling the third base coaching spot, hugged him as he stood, panting, on the base. From then on, any time any player would hit the ball, Coach would yell "GO!" I'm sure it annoyed the other coaches, but man, those kids, they ate it up. (The best was when Bulldog drilled one down the first-base line and ended up on third, where he scolded Coach for forgetting. "Hey, you didn't yell GO!" Coach apologized and smiled broadly.) And, eventually, I ate it up too. It was impossible not to get caught up in the euphoria. We were just kids, playing baseball, just for fun. And we always got milkshakes after the game, whether we won or lost.

Coach led the V.F.W. charge for three years, all three years I played for the team. We never won a league title, only made the playoffs once, though we ended up a respectable .500 during his tenure. At the end of the third season, the entire team went out to Coach's house for an end-of-the-year picnic. They shocked him with a trophy with the names of every player, with the inscription, "Presented to Coach for a wonderful year. Thank you, and go V.F.W.!" It remains on the wall of Coach's home, having survived years of moving and chaos and upheaval and all the curveballs growing up and growing old throws you.

To this day, anytime I'm back in Mattoon and run into one of the old V.F.W. kids, they always mention that team and how much fun it was. Many of them played only one more year of organized baseball and learned right quick that most grownups weren't like Coach, that most cared too much about winning and losing and not about making sure that kids— kids, after all—have fun and get to feel important and part of something, part of a team. Many of them have kids of their own now. Many of them have faced so much of the tragedy and the heartache and the disappointment and the sorrow that adulthood brings, it's a wonder they can remember childhood at all. But they all remember V.F.W., and they all remember Coach.

If it isn't obvious to you at this point that Coach is my father, you've simply never met him.

ROUGH DAY

W hile conducting an exhausting, maddening and ultimately futile search for a misplaced and beloved photo album the other day, I came across a box full of old videotapes. (It has been a long time since I've had a stable place to live, and I feel like I'm constantly unpacking.) Because I haven't had a television and VCR for many months now, I'd almost forgotten I had the tapes.

The selection was fairly standard-issue. The *Star Wars* trilogy, Orson Welles' *Touch of Evil, Hoop Dreams*, a letterboxed version of Woody Allen's *Husbands and Wives*, Mark McGwire's 62nd-homer game, that sort of thing. Then I saw it. The little sticker thing on the front of the tape—is there a name for such contraptions? I humbly submit "sticker thing" for the linguistic court's approval—was faded and falling off, and appeared to carrying a stain I can only hope is butter, but I could still read it.

89 Enrichment Plays. Good Lord.

When I was in the eighth grade, there was this special class for the "gifted" students called Enrichment. There were only 15 kids in the class, and they were my entire world. (Side note: Parents of the world, if there's one piece of advice I can give you in this crazy world of child-rearing, it's this: If your kid does well on stupid standardized tests when he/she is very young, if the teachers call him/her "gifted," if they want to put him/her in special classes and accelerated learning programs... don't you dare let them do it. The last thing a 13-year-old wants is to be considered different. But that, friends, is a longer, more depraved story.)

We had this dingbat teacher named Mrs. Patterson, who was renowned for losing her glasses on top of her head, forgetting to show up for class, and giving writing assignments that lent themselves beautifully to pubescent sex-obsessed comedy larks. (My friend Andy's haiku about masturbation, delivered to the class while Mrs. Patterson chased him around the room, begging him to stop, was a particular standout.) My favorite Mrs. Patterson story: She wore this necklace that was the shape of a bottle opener. She was telling the class once that it was a family artifact, passed down from ancestors in Greece. Ever the smart-ass, I cracked to the class that she was lying, that it was just a can opener. She paused, looked down and said, with a tone of exhausted resignation, "Well, actually, yes, it is a can opener." She then left the room, forlorn, where we sat in stunned silence. She was a damned loon, and we loved her.

In retrospect, I remember the class being awfully touchy-feely for Mattoon. We were always working on projects that would "stimulate our creativity," which basically meant they were open-ended and free. We were supposed to express ourselves, nurture our "gifted" minds. (I once wrote a six-page short story called "Wet Dream," which was about, well, you can probably figure out what it was about.) But we were in the eighth grade. The only thing we wanted to nurture was Andrea Blair's boobs. Mrs. Patterson, to her eternal credit, never stopped trying to enrich us.

The entire school year built up to one major endeavor. Every May, the Enrichment class put together three plays to be performed to the entire school. Everyone in class had to team up with partners and write one, and then an independent panel of teachers would vote on the best ones. We looked forward to it all year. After a year of being the nerdy smart kids who couldn't get girls, we would have a chance to show our stuff to the whole junior high, which to us was, of course, the entire planet. Everyone wanted their play to be picked.

There were four major contenders. Two were lame fairy-tale knockoffs, one based on "Goldilocks and the Three Bears" and the other on "The Wizard of Oz." The third was a funny, typically raunchy mock talk show, written by two classmates who now both happen to be screenwriters in Los Angeles. (The panel, sadly, didn't pick this one, because the teachers thought it was too ribald, which pissed us off, since we had no idea what ribald meant.) And then there was mine.

It was called "Rough Day." The plot is pretty complicated, so stick with me here. There's this kid, named Dan Andrews, played by me, obviously, who had a perfect weekend. His baseball team won the sectional final. He earned an A on a paper in his Enrichment class. And, most important, he went with Jenny Johnson to the school dance, kissed her at the end of the night and is now "going out with her." The play opens Monday morning, when Dan wakes up and speaks directly to the audience—the entire play is performed, *Garry Shandling's Show*-style, with the main character commenting to the crowd on all the action—about how wonderful the weekend was and how the first day back at school can only be better.

His life then quickly falls apart. He breaks a family heirloom lamp while trying to shut his alarm off. His parents humiliate him at breakfast, then ground him until he's 35. He misses the bus to school, then gets detention for coming into class late. (True to form, there was a Mrs. Patterson-like character who keeps forgetting the names of her students.) His locker, messy and packed with too many books and baseball magazines, is jammed, and a peculiar janitor won't help him, causing him to be late for another class and his mother to be called by the principal. He receives a zero on a class assignment for writing the word "shucks," which one teacher interprets as a profanity. He is falsely accused of writing "Mr. Barreto Is Gay" on the bathroom wall and is forced to run 50 laps around the football field. Jenny Johnson is told by rival Shane Palmer that Dan has been cheating on her, so she slaps him and breaks up with him. Shane enters, punches Dan and carries Jenny away on his shoulders. Shane later pours milk over Dan's head in the lunchroom, and Dan receives another detention for it. On the way home, Dan misses the bus again and is grounded until he's 45 by his angry father. Dan collapses on the floor, and every character in the play looms over him, screaming at him, until he wakes up and realizes it was all a dream. He then actually breaks his lamp when the alarm goes off. *Fin.*

This was, of course, based on a true story, a point I made sure to emphasize at the beginning of the performance, after the play was chosen by the teachers and the roles were cast. The entire school was there, as were my parents and family friends.

And of course, they all got mad at me.

My parents were mad because I'd publicly humiliated them in front of half the town. (Donnie Shepard did a particularly cruel impersonation of my father, wearing a Cardinals jacket and screaming at me to mow the lawn, clean the garage, straighten up my sister's room and put a new roof on the house.) Emily Averitt was mad because I'd emphasized that Jenny Johnson was in my third, fourth, fifth and sixth period classes, just like Emily was, and that Jenny Johnson had jilted me after a dance, just like Emily had. And Mrs. Patterson was mad because I hadn't told her I would be inserting a line about her loony daughter, an addition made right before the show started. But it didn't matter to me in the slightest. I wanted the world to know my pain, be able to laugh along with me, make chicken salad out of chicken shit. I was using that public forum, casting classmates as my family and friends, bit players in the Will Leitch life story, to try to make people listen to me. For attention, of course.

Watching this the other day, right before I sat down to write, it became clear how much I've changed over the years.

For example, um... I'm taller now.

TEMPORARY INSANITY

A woman named Hillary meets me at the reception desk. She is probably about 30 years old but looks older, haggard, helplessly distracted. She asks me what time it is, and before I have a chance to answer, she asks me what day it is. It's Thursday. That, for sure, I know.

She takes me through an inexplicably locked metal door to a back room that is clearly in the midst of a chaotic move. There are half-opened boxes, computers that aren't hooked up to their monitors and a cubicle strewn with seven stacks of paper covering any open space.

Hillary sighs, pats me on the back and says, "OK, this is yours."

I was to take a sheet from each of the seven stacks, place them together and stuff them into a pre-addressed envelope. I would then place the envelopes in yet another stack, and then repeat the process about, oh, 700 times. Sheet, sheet, sheet, sheet, sheet, sheet, sheet, shuffle, straighten, open flap, slip sheets in, close flap, stack. Seven hundred times. When I finished, I was to cart the envelopes to a postage machine, where I would run them through and place them in another box.

I am almost 26 years old, college-educated, with work experience at two of the oldest, most respected publications in the United States. I have helped start and sustain a moderately successful, reasonably well-regarded Web magazine, where I write a weekly column that has a smattering of loyal readers. I have a book agent and a publishing company interested in my manuscript, lest it ever be completed. I once made more than $50,000 a year. I was writing for the *St. Louis Post-Dispatch* my senior year of college. I have interviewed Ewan McGregor, Sen. Dick Durbin, Hunter S. Thompson, Whitey Herzog, Reese Witherspoon, Bob Knight and former presidential candidate Paul Simon. Um... I'm taller than the average person, am considered by some to be a good kisser and typically beat my friends in computer Jeopardy! I got a goddamn 34 on my ACTs. And I am stuffing envelopes for six hours, all to earn $54 (before taxes), sitting in a nondescript office with people I don't know who will not say a word to me all afternoon. And I am loving it.

I am temping. I am not doing this as a lark, or as some sort of self-indulgent journalistic exercise. I am doing it because I am broke and I need the money. That's the simple fact of the matter. Thing is... six hours of dreary, lonely busy work provided me the most satisfying weekday I've had in months. I was one mean envelope-packing motherfucker, I tell you. I flew through those things, didn't mislabel or mispostage a single package and even received a compliment from Hillary. ("You're much faster than the last temp," she said, watching me beam with pride.) It was a most fulfilling six hours; I just worked. I'd missed it. I worked so hard, in fact, that the job, which was supposed to take two days, was done in just those six hours. That's good because it speaks well for a generations-tested Midwestern work ethic; it's bad because it meant they didn't need me to come in on Friday, which meant I wouldn't get paid that day. But it was work, and it made me feel needed for the first time in a while.

The real question: How, exactly, did I get here? Which is worse: being forced to temp because of severe financial constraints and an apparent inability to find a job even remotely related to my field of expertise... or finding that a day of temping is the highlight of my week?

I have no problem with temping, or people who temp, please don't get me wrong. It's honest work, and in wintry economic climates, it's a way to make quick money, which, of course, is why I'm doing it. But it's hard not to get hung up on the fact that temping is something you're supposed to do when you're just starting out, when you're trying to meet people and get your foot in the door. I'm a bit old for it now.

OK, fine. I've made some mistakes here, and I've been wasteful and irresponsible, and I've done a few things that probably didn't score positive karma points, if you believe in that crap. But... jeez. Uncle. Mercy. I give. What has happened in the last nine months—the shriveled job market, the constant layoffs, the demoralizing indifference to the fact that I live and walk and breathe—is enough to break a man's spirit. And how long am I willing to take it?

While I've spent a year-and-a-half idling here in New York, just trying to keep my head above water, everyone out there is still going, moving on with their lives. There's so much living going on. Two of my closest friends from St. Louis, since I've left, have met people they might very well end up spending the rest of their lives with. I've met each of these significant others once, and to be honest, I'm not sure I could pick either out of a lineup. I feel like I've missed so much out here, chasing something, I don't even know what anymore.

What am I bashing my head against the wall for, anyway? Currently, I'm basing my immediate future on the possibility of a two-month job doing lousy work for a magazine I would have never even thought of working for a year ago. If I end up catching a break and getting that, who's to say I won't be going through this exact same thing in two months? And for what? The right to pay too much for rent? The constant harmony of car alarms? One of my best friends when I moved to New York now no longer speaks to me. Is it because of me? Him? Did the city do something to one or both of us when we moved here? Has it changed me irrevocably? Does it matter?

Maybe it just didn't work. It was worth a shot; everyone always says you should live in New York at some point in your life, and then you should leave. When will the point hit that I just give it up? I never could have predicted this would be where I was a year-and-a-half into this journey. Will it get worse or better a year-and-a-half from now? And where the hell else would I go anyway? What would I do? Could I swallow my pride and go work in PR or advertising? And why would they hire someone with such obvious contempt for their industries anyway? Maybe I could teach. I don't even think you need a certificate to do that anymore.

I just don't know what the next step is. Perhaps that's what temping really is for. For people who have no idea, not a goddamned clue, what they're doing with their lives. People for whom a weeklong job is a huge commitment. People in limbo, between two phases in their life, neither all that appealing, treading water, waiting for life to tell them what to do next. Never thought I was one of those people, but, well, hey, I also never thought I'd be so damned good at stuffing envelopes, either.

(Note: The author finally found gainful employment and pretty much stopped writing about how low your self-esteem is when you're unemployed...

You're welcome.)

THIS COLUMN IS ABOUT SEX

I've covered a lot of topics in this meandering mess of a series, but I've found one aspect of the human condition near impossible for me to write about: sex. I just can't write a sentence about it without cracking a lame, backpedaling joke or hitting delete immediately before anyone has a chance to make fun of me.

I'm not sure why that is. I enjoy sex. Quite a bit, actually. I might even say, if I dare, that sex is somewhat of a driving force behind many of my decisions in life. Certainly more so than my cat, and I've sure written a lot about him. I don't consider myself a prude, far from it. It's just... I dunno... it's hard writing about sex. What seems majestic and earth-shaking at the time comes across ridiculous in print. I can't fathom how people write those dime-store novels with a shirtless Fabio on the cover, with titles like *To Tame a Texan*. I mean, could you type "His brawny, sweating chest glistened as he ripped off her blouse and caressed her supple, ripe breasts. She found herself flush with desire..." with a straight face? I sure can't.

A couple of months ago, as a practice session intended to help correct this writing deficiency, I sat down to write a 2,000-word piece about my most recent intense, powerful sexual experience. To make sure I got in the groove, I drank about a quart of Dewar's, shut off all the lights and cranked up Motley Crue's "Dr. Feelgood." (When writing about love, try Miles Davis; when tackling sex, nothing but the Crue will do.) Adequately drunk, I tore in and tapped away for about three hours straight, pausing only for three cigarettes and to restart the CD. I didn't read what I wrote until I woke up the next morning. It could not have been more embarrassing if it had been written by one of my former partners with an ax to grind. It read like Garrison Keillor being anally raped by David Foster Wallace. Here's a tip: When trying to write sexy, avoid the words *labyrinthine, perpendicular, snorkel,* and *mayonnaiseish.* I beg you to trust me on this one.

A market has sprung in recent years for sex columnists. We've actually had a few on my Web site. People love reading sex columns, but I'm not sure I ever believe them. It's one thing to be frank and matter-of-fact about sex; it's another entirely to confess the weird shit you do in print, with your name attached. If most of these women (and, of course, they're almost always women; a straight guy's columns about sex would always have the same predictable, abrupt end, and they'd all run about 150 words) had sex as often as they claimed, I don't know how they'd even have time to write their columns. And how real can it be when everyone you're having sex with knows you're a sex columnist? I would suspect, knowing most guys, that would be more of a detriment to finding willing subjects than a benefit.

Sex is such a mystery it's a wonder anyone even knows how to do it. You never know who will be into what. Who would have guessed Marv Albert was a biter? I'm reminded of Woody Allen's *Manhattan*, when Diane Keaton's character tells Woody about her last lover, a ferocious hellion in bed who sent her to heights she'd never imagined. When we meet him, he's played by Wallace Shawn, the short "inconceivable" bald guy from *The Princess Bride*. I suspect that's always the way it works. The hottest girl is often the coldest fish, and the guy who boasts about sex all the time can't get it up.

But two play this game, and it's strange sometimes how two people simply cannot click. I've been with people in the past who have surely considered themselves skillful at intercourse, and they appear to know all the right moves. But for whatever reason, we were never quite on the same page. It wasn't her fault; it wasn't mine. (No! It wasn't! Couldn't be!) That thing just wasn't there. Barry Bonds is one of the greatest hitters in baseball history, but he couldn't hit it out of the infield against journeyman lefthander Tony Fossas if he placed it on a tee. Sometimes it just doesn't work, no matter how perfectly matched people seem to be. And, as we all know, when the physical attraction goes, it's all over. We can fake smiles at cocktail parties... but we can't fake that (though we can't help ourselves from trying). On the flipside, we've all had that person that we have crazy chemistry with even though they drive us nuts. Sex has a tendency to goad us into abandoning all reason and self-preservation. It's either a not-that-funny joke played by the cosmos or God punishing us for having sex before marriage.

It's nerve-wracking writing this, you know? It makes me uncomfortable just putting it into words. Once, I had a brief fling with an associate of a few close friends of mine. The Monday after we went out, my friends cornered me and demanded some locker-room talk. I couldn't do it. They peppered me with questions, digging for details, intricacies—they were just friends of hers, but she *was* pretty, and they had to have wondered—and I gave them nothing. Just stammered, babbled, changed the subject. "Uh, guys, did you see Pedro Martinez struck out 16 yesterday? Um... did you see that bill that Clinton signed? Man, that weather... how about that weather?"

It didn't feel right, reporting back details. It never does. People look at the sex other people have far more dispassionately than they do their own. Personally, we have this notion that sex is supposed to be this sacred, two-become-one experience that is deeply profound, and we hold out for that ideal, but when we imagine others having sex, it's either repulsive or just a manipulation of genitals. And both views are right, of course. We never truly and irrationally surrender ourselves to sex—I submit the condom as Exhibit A—but it's supremely important to us nevertheless. Sex does change everything; it's just that none of us are sure why.

After all, it's only natural, right? Birds do it, bees do it. (I'm thinking of the way the parents of a friend of mine explained sex to him. "It's like a hug, only it takes longer and you're tired afterwards." Ladies, you have to agree... sometimes, that sums it up entirely.) That sex affects us the way it does is a uniquely human thought process, and sometimes I wonder if the rest of the animal kingdom has it right. I witnessed two flies having sex the other day. It went on for about five minutes, which in a fly's lifespan is about four years. I doubt the male fly was bragging to his larvae friends the next day, and I seriously doubt the female fly was upset the male fly didn't call her. (I, naturally, swatted them both. Hey, why do they get to get some?)

Think of it this way: If you and your current mate had never had sex, had never even considered it, how would your relationship be? Is what you learn about your mate during sex worth knowing? I've tried to foster an image as a cultured, witty, subtle member of the intelligentsia, but I'm a sweaty, hulking mess when I have sex. It is us at our most open, unguarded, completely bare for another person—an entirely different person! A whole other person!—to witness and comprehend. There is nowhere to hide. That we continue to have sex is a triumph of nature, not our brains. It is safer not to be close. It's more comfortable keeping it inside.

But look at me... I'm saying too much. I knew this would happen. I'm giving away my secrets.

It occurs to me... what is the "sexiest" thing I've done? Lemme think... hmmm... mulling... well, there was...

oh, jeez, Will, you can't write that... no... seriously, don't... you wouldn't dare... what if your parents read this?... your readers will lose all respect for you... people will mock you forever...

OK, fine, fuck it: One of my old lovers and I once filmed ourselves. We were both drunk, there was a camcorder in the room, we figured what the hell, we're young, footloose, fancy-free, all that. Besides, with me, there wouldn't be any worry about running out of tape. It was a sexy, dangerous thing to do at the time, and whenever we talked about it afterwards—only with each other, of course—it never failed to titillate us both. It was exciting and reckless, and certainly worth the trouble. So we thought.

We eventually broke up, but the tape remained in my possession. Choose to believe me or don't, I could care less, but I swear, I never thought about putting it in the VCR again. OK, that's not quite true; I did once... but I had no choice.

Two lifelong friends came to visit me in St. Louis once. They stayed a day later than I thought they would, so on the last day of their sojourn, I had to work. They grabbed a case of beer and hung out at my place while I was gone. I thought nothing of it. They returned for New Year's Eve about three months later, and at the end of the night, the three of us went in my room to artificially scramble our cerebral cortexes. We were giggling through the smoke when one of them stopped abruptly.

"Hey, Will, we gotta tell you something. You're going to be pissed," he coughed, still laughing maniacally. "Uh, remember when we were here a few months ago? Well, we got pretty drunk and started watching some of your old tapes. We found this one..."

The next morning, when I finally came out from under the bed, I took a tennis racket and destroyed the tape, admittedly, a bit late. When your friends have witnessed something that inspires the comment, "um, interesting technique there, Will," it's best to destroy the evidence, and violently.

Hey, check it out... I think I'm finally writing frankly about sex.

Ahhh... about that story I just told... I made it all up. Not true. Don't believe it. Just kidding!

HANDS IN POCKET, WHISTLING AIMLESSLY

At my job, we are sporadically required to attend these fancy, high-end functions. Do not got me wrong. We are not suits. (No! Really!) On a daily basis, I throw on my headphones, crank Faith No More, drink Diet Coke straight out of the bottle and, when the feeling strikes me, occasionally wear a shirt.

We have a small staff, and even though we don't drink in the office like my old Web startup, it's a fairly informal place. But we do sometimes host these functions, and since our target audience is rather upscale, we are obligated to dress up for them.

The other day, we had this breakfast at the storied Harvard Club in midtown Manhattan. Now, I'll forsake any jokes about what a University of Illinois club would be like—OK, I'll make a couple: there'd be a keg in the middle of the banquet hall with half-empty Dixie cups scattered about, we'd all be wearing cutoff jean shorts and inevitably one of our members would be in the corner embracing a nitrous tank—and simply point out that this place is *nice*. Paintings of storied alumni surrounding the table, waiters and busboys wearing tuxes and a coat-check room the size of my parents' home, with a better kitchen. We all had to be there at 7:30 decked out in our finest suits and ready to promote our startup magazine to an audience that, when it's freezing outside, tosses a couple logs of hundred-dollar bills on the fire to keep warm.

I sat down at an end table, looking as sharp as a guy in a suit that his uncles were going to throw away anyway possibly can, and delicately placed a cloth napkin—a napkin that's made of cloth! Seriously! No joke!—over my lap. To my left was one of those middle-aged white men whose toupee probably cost more than my winter wardrobe, and he started asking me about our magazine. He looked me dead in the eye, like he respected me, like he thought I belonged.

I won't lie; it was awesome. After months of unemployment and scraping together pennies just so I could catch a subway downtown, here I was, in the freaking Harvard Club, wearing a suit, talking about the venture capital industry, and the storage infrastructure sector, and business plans, and the future of our long-term fiscal securities. I made a pithy little Inside Venture Capital joke; we shared a hearty chuckle and he patted me on the back with a mixture of respect and knowingness. All I was missing was a copy of *Crain's Business Journal* in my leather briefcase, a tasteful handkerchief positioned strategically in my breast pocket, and a cigar dipped in Cognac. Dammit … I did belong!

I then felt a tap on my shoulder. It was my boss. "Hey, listen Will ... I think we overbooked this thing. We don't have enough chairs. We, uh, need you to give up your seat." Some other middle-aged white guy loomed behind him ominously. I sighed, buttoned my jacket, excused myself and went out to the hallway, hands in pockets, swaying aimlessly, looking around, whistling silently to myself.

The transition from devil-may-care free spirit to proud, upstanding member of the capitalist community our culture revolves around, with 401k plans, two-car garages and matching linens is not something that is coming all that easily to me, and I think maybe I should stop trying. My idea of a schnazzy wardrobe, in the past, has been a pair of khakis with no visible stains and a T-shirt without a sports team logo on it. With the assistance of a now-ex-girlfriend, I tried to look nicer, even spending a solid two hours in this H&M store that's apparently popular. I would try on clothes, I would see if this matched that, I even started putting this goopy crap in my hair. I tried. For a while there, I was even starting to look kind of nice, like one of those people who knows where all the sample sales are and can tell you whether or not it's acceptable to wear light green turtlenecks with dark black pants. I even attempted putting on cologne, no small feat for a guy with no sense of smell.

But I was only fooling myself, striving to be something I wasn't. When I visited St. Louis for an old friend's wedding, she remarked that I looked downright sharp in my tight-skin Banana Republic shirt and DKNY jeans. Then she paused. "You look like you're dressed up like somebody else."

Looking and acting and feeling like a grownup is such a difficult endeavor, requiring focus, discipline, and restraint that would test the patience of monks, that it's a wonder anyone even bothers. We all sit in meetings with colleagues, and we go to parties where there are people we don't know, and we make polite small talk with various acquaintances in order to put across a positive, secure, wholly sane image... and I'm not sure any of us believe a moment of it. We're all crazy and insecure and happy and sad and laughing and crying, and we spend most of our time trying to hide those very things, the parts that make us human. It seems that there's rarely a moment where we simply *be*; we're too busy trying to impress everyone all the time.

I'm reminded of when I was laid off from one of my magazine jobs. It hadn't been announced by the higher-ups, but everybody knew it was going to happen, including me. Half the staff was out at a bar, and I happened into a conversation with my boss. She knew it. I knew it. So I just told her. I said it was OK, that she was going to have to cut me loose, that I knew it wasn't her fault, that we were just simple human beings thrust into these managerial/employee roles by society and circumstance, that we should merely talk to each other as people, that I didn't hold it against her, how could I? She looked at me like I'd beamed in from Neptune. The frank discussion had upset her notions of middle management and proper employee relations, and as far as she was concerned, I was this crazed Guevera-esque revolutionary who didn't know his proper place in the capitalist food chain.

After all this employment strife and a girlfriend who would rather not date a guy who wore shoes with holes in them, I decided it was time to change. I tried to become a grownup. I studied *Esquire* pages about "How a Man Should Dress," I learned how to tie a tie and I started talking about the weather and other banal, boring topics that always go over in non-threatening, conventional way in crowds. Working in public relations or studying the stock market started seeming like legitimate, honorable ways to live my life. Shit, I even stopped hitting on women I worked with, because that's wrong, that's not the way it works, bad, bad, bad. I wanted to play ball. There is a point where you're just too old to be the wacky, goofy guy. I thought I'd reached that point.

And, I'm realizing, that point is a delusion. I think I was, for once, actually right. I yam who I yam. I think we're all just stupid people who have absolutely no idea what we're doing, scrambling around, trying to move from one point to another while causing as little damage to ourselves or others as possible, hoping our illusion earns the respect and affection we all desperately need. Some of us are better at hiding this than others. Some, like me, aren't. When you start believing you have to put up this facade to people, that there's this act you have to put across, well, in my experience, you end up sitting alone in the hallway while someone bigger, and smarter, and richer, and better at playing the game than you are … they're sitting in your chair.

I'm beginning to realize my place in this world, which is to say, I don't really have one. When I go to parties, I will continue to make a spectacle of myself, calling people "sir" and "ma'am," bowing incessantly, making silly jokes for a cheap laugh, ignoring the regular protocol of such matters, doing what I do. That is who I am. I am not a guy who wears snappy suits, or tasteful turtlenecks, or appropriately-tucked scarves. I'm just a dude out there, trying to be happy, hoping others are happy, crossing my fingers that I don't step on anybody's toes while I'm shambling about with no real guiding force by myself. Dammit, I am not a venture capitalist, and I never will be, and that's just fine with me. No need to pretend anymore.

Unless of course you're a hot girl I run into at a party. In that case, I'm whatever you want me to be, baby.

MY ANTI-DRUG IS PARANOIA

W hen I lived in Los Angeles, I did a lot of drugs. This is for a variety of reasons. First, my fiancée had left me on national television. Also, I had been dating this girl, then asked her to marry me, and she'd said yes, but then she decided she didn't want to and told me just hours before I was on a cable game show. Another reason: I had a wedding planned, but the person I was going to marry changed her mind and moved away with no explanation. These were the main motivations, but I'm sure there were others. Like how my engagement ended and I was left alone in a strange city I didn't know, or how I almost got married but then didn't. Those are a couple more.

These were not crazy drugs. On only four experiences have I tried anything more extreme than marijuana. Three of them involved hallucinogenic mushrooms. Now, I'm not saying I'm too maladjusted to do mushrooms, but the last time I did them I started crying, stripped down to my boxer shorts and tried to jump in the ocean—not easy to do when you live in St. Louis. The other was an ill-advised evening where I inhaled about four individual grains of cocaine off the top of a key, which did nothing more than make me fairly certain I had accelerated the physics of puberty and suddenly grown about four feet of nose hair.

The first time I did drugs was in college. It was the summer after my sophomore year, and I stayed in Champaign rather than go through all the work of procuring an internship. I'd just started drinking a few months before, and one night, when my roommate and I were downing a couple bottles of MadDog 20/20, a guy from the newspaper named Mike came by. Mike was the type of guy who was constantly extolling the virtues of hemp as a cultural savior and had named his fantasy baseball team the Leesville Leafsmokers. (We all know a guy like Mike. Perhaps you are a guy like Mike. Yes, yes, we know, you can make rope with it. Yes, yes, George Washington and Thomas Jefferson grew it. Got it.) He was carrying a satchel you could store skis in. He opened it up and took out a film container and this glass tube that stood about four-and-a-half feet tall. He spoke. "Will … it's time you became an official staff member of the *Daily Illini*." He left me little choice.

Forty-five minutes later, after I'd coughed up my colon, I decided to head to the kitchen where I found, to my surprise, someone was hiding the cabinets from me. I'd lived there for a month and thought I had a fairly strong grasp of their location. But whoever was in charge of this deception kept shifting them around; it was like watching my father search for the "T" on a keyboard. Move 45 degrees, no, 15, no, behind you *behind you.* Wait … where are the cups usually? That has to be where the cabinet is. I shall catch the cabinet by surprise. FLIP AROUND! Shit. Not there either. They couldn't have gotten too far. THERE they are! Shit. Not there either. I noticed laughter in the corner. The culprit! Bring back my cabinets, you rat bastard! Mike was there, tittering madly as I spun in circles, looking at my feet.

This state of oblivion appealed to me instantly, and I began smoking quite regularly. It was such a novel way to meet new people. You'd see someone across the room, you'd look them in the eye, and you just knew: He smoked. Let's find a room. Got a hookah? By the time I moved to St. Louis, I found myself hanging out with Phish phans and having serious discussions as to whether or not the government had hidden aliens in John Gotti's basement and whether or not the NBA had rigged the 1985 draft to make sure Patrick Ewing played for the Knicks. Working a 4-12 night shift, this was my daily schedule: See a movie at noon, work eight hours, go home, smoke two bowls, read a sports magazine and pass out watching ER reruns. Man, those EKG machines are some serious shit. Fuck. Wow. Serious. Shit.

But somewhere down the line, the tide turned. It was around the time that I started developing real, meaningful relationships with beings other than my cat. The notion of plugging in and tuning out lost its appeal. The grownup world kept sneaking up on me. I wasn't able to concentrate on, um, not concentrating. It's not all fun and games. Whenever I smoked, I stopped thinking about having long, circular conversations with friends and started thinking about my bank account, or my broken relationships, or my lack of success in my chosen field. It didn't give me insight or just a happy time away from life; it just made me … oh … *paranoid.*

I think it's very possible that I might be getting too old. Don't laugh. I know you want to laugh. Fuddy duddy Will, just not *down.* Can't you just relax, Will? I get it. Will's too uptight. Fine. Understood. But hear me out. In college, when our major concerns revolved around securing a believable fake ID, it was easy to just numb our brain cells without suffering any major repercussions. But when you're in the grownup world, a lot more stuff bubbles up when you're high. It's not just a pleasant diversion anymore. One minute, you're just loafing around, blithely floating through life with little awareness of the ramifications of every action, and then you smoke a bowl, and suddenly your mind is afire. I start thinking about everything. It starts small, and snowballs.

Do these shoes make me look gay? Man, I think I'm gaining weight. Did I remember to feed the cat? Man, I gotta pay that phone bill before the 15th. Do my roommates like me? I hope they don't make me move out just because I occasionally leave socks lying around. I gotta make sure to finish that project at work by the time my boss gets back from California. I don't want to get laid off again. Nothing is worse than unemployment. Is this job doing me any good in the first place? Where exactly is my career going? That column I wrote last week, I just half-assed it. I had a busy week, but that's no excuse. If I don't start devoting myself, I'm never going to break out of my little online niche. Do I even have *a niche? What made me decide to become a writer? I don't think I'm all that good. Why did I even come to New York? Am I just a stupid Midwestern kid who thinks he's more important than he is? Man, I really broke that one girl's heart. What's my problem? Am I an asshole? Are my parents disappointed in me? Do my parents love me less than they love my sister? Are people always laughing at me behind my back? Am I just a big joke? Is my father embarrassed to talk about me to his friends? And so what? It doesn't matter, regardless, because eventually we all just die and rot. We're worm food. Dammit, my life is so pointless. I'm a waste of air. Why are any of us here, anyway? We're just a bunch of randomly constructed cells somehow simulating a living, conscious being. Fuck all this. I should just jump off this roof right now and end the whole charade. Whom am I trying to kid? Fuck all this. Fuck. Fuck, fuck, fuck, fuck, fuck, fuck, fuck. Fuck. Fuck, fuck. Fuck.*

And now… shit, I just don't smoke anymore.

Check this out: The other evening, I caught myself hanging out with two friends of mine, watching boxing. I'm recently single, so, by definition, I should be out going crazy with my boys, causing trouble, raising a ruckus. They had the right idea. They bought 40s and took bong hits all evening. I sat in the corner, sipping a Diet Coke, hoping nobody noticed. I just didn't have it in me.

I just don't think I can take it anymore. Life has too much going on now. Drugs do nothing but upset my delicate balance. Life's hard enough. When they make you uneasy and anxious and off-kilter and you start to agonize over something as simple as a conversation with a friend (*he thinks I'm an idiot. I am an idiot. What am I doing, trying to talk about David Foster Wallace? I can't finish that book. I'm not very smart. Smart people like that book. I'm trying to fake it. I'm trying to fake everything. God I hate myself.*) … maybe it's time to stop.

How bad did it get? Fairly recently, I dated a woman who felt, as many women do, I've found, that marijuana relaxed her. She would smoke pot for the same reason many of us take off our shoes after a long day at work. Nothing is wrong with this, of course. Whatever works. But I am not emotionally sound enough to be so flippant about something that plays little games with my brain. After one experience with her, when I became convinced that every time she said, "Could you hand me your lighter?" she actually meant "I think your penis is too small," I decided to try to head this off at the pass. When she brought out a bowl, I stopped her.

"OK, I need you to help me out here. I have a pen. Do you have any paper?"
"Uh, sure?"

"All right. Now, do you like me?"
"Um … yeah? Er, yeah, yes I do. Sure."

"Close enough. I need you to do something for me. See these five sheets of paper? I need you to write little messages to me on each of these five sheets of paper. You need to remind me that you actually like me, that I'm not too fat, that I'm not too stupid, that I'm not horrible in bed. They don't have to be sweet or fawning. A simple 'Will is not a bad person' or 'Will is not a complete moron' will suffice."

"What?"

"Yeah, yeah, so then, when I start to get that funny look in my eye, when I start to stutter and stammer and clench my hands together and then clam up, just show me one of the signs. Because I'll forget."

"Uh-huh."

To her credit, she did. It must have taken much patience. Particularly when I asked her to go over her writing in black magic marker so I could see it when I was hiding under a table about 50 feet away. So readers, can I get a witness? I heretofore secede from the weed union. I just can't handle it anymore. It is causing me too much trouble. I am psychologically fragile. I am weak. I want not to crack. I want to be normal. I quit. I cry uncle.

You know, it's a shame, too. I was really starting to get into the Cartoon Network.

YOU WANT AN ALPHA MALE? YOU GOT HIM

I t has been brought to my attention that women want *confidence*. My lack of it is why they're always leaving me. Women want a man with his act together, someone who knows what he brings to the table, who isn't asking a woman to take care of him or fill a void, someone *male*. Preferably with big, ripped abs.

I suppose they're right. They *should* want those things. They *should* want a confident alpha male. Who wants a sniveling girly-man who needs constant reassurance? They want *men*, dammit!

So I am putting together my resume. I will attach this to my back at all times, right next to the "DORK" sign. In this day of constant advertising, it just seems natural, like a boxer with a casino ad in temporary tattoo on his back. This will take the form of a list: My alpha male accomplishments, year-by-year, since birth. Think I'm a pantywaist, too much of a sensitive pony-tailed man? Think I can't make a relationship work because I don't feel good enough about myself? Ha! I snort at your shortsightedness. I guffaw at your inability to look past my lack of facial hair. I chortle at your continued insistence that you don't want a man who pees sitting down.

You don't know me. I'm all man. I am a Midwestern John Wayne, a tall Humphrey Bogart, an albino Wesley Snipes. And don't you forget it. Or I'll do that thing where I clinch my hands together and move my arm toward you really quickly, where it then hits your face! Yeah! Take that! Your pain shall be immense, and incapacitating. Feel my wrath. And then, before you even had a chance to think about attacking me in return, I will be long gone … poof! like that.

You don't think I'm enough of a typical male? I'm too self-loathing and feeble? That I'm too sensitive? You just wait, punk. I've got Full-Scale Male Credentials. I can prove it. Because evidently, this is what women want.

My resume will look like this:

1975—Upon exiting my mother's womb, doctors were stunned to find I had stenciled lyrics to the Rolling Stones' "Under My Thumb" in the birth canal. Also, they found circumcision near impossible because of my massive, almost elephantine testicles. Overheard in the delivery room: "This kid's gonna be one hell of a baby maker someday."

1976—I share a nursery with a blond-haired nymph named Nicole. By withholding a rattle until just the right moment, refusing to poo while Nicole is in the room, and being generally uncommunicative, I drive young Nicole wild. There are other babies who share their plush toys and do not fling their feces at her, but Nicole finds them dull and too easy. The year ends with Nicole heartbroken when I decide it's not working out and that I'd rather spend more time drinking my own drool.

1977—I bite the head off a toy bat. It was an aluminum bat.

1978—I learn how to read, years earlier than my family expected. I use this newfound power to write letters to girls in my preschool, telling them they should really lose some weight.

1979—My family buys me a toy phone for Christmas. I tell Shannon, the five-year-old next-door neighbor, that I'll call her… then I don't.

1980—My little sister is born. I make a vow to be exemplary in every aspect of my schoolwork and social life, so that she will feel inferior and grow up with self-esteem issues. My dad and I conspire secretly to never tell her we her love her.

1981—My mother, as our family struggles to make ends meet, says she needs to find a job. I tell her that if she were a real mom, she'd stay home and take care of her children. To make sure I am successful, I urinate on all her cover letters and then blame it on a mysterious bed-wetting problem.

1982—Next-door neighbor Shannon comes over to play. I tell her I'm watching the Cardinals in the World Series. And to shut her damn trap.

1983—I learn that flatulence not only disgusts people, but, in fact, is quite funny. I commence to pass gas every time I'm in mixed company. Years later, I will refine this process, adding open flame.

1984—A new girl moves into the neighborhood, named Tonya. She makes many friends, but I am her favorite because I am unresponsive and mysterious. One night, with parental approval, I spend the night at her house. She asks me to come over the next night as well, but I refuse, because I'm sleeping with all her friends.

1985—While showering after a basketball game, I see my cousin naked. I beat the crap out of him, because, shit, man, he was looking at me. You know… in that way.

1988—I score my only lifetime goal in youth league soccer when the goalie is distracted by an asthma attack and I trip on the ball, sending it spiraling toward the net. In years, this story will be told as so: "Well, I was being chased by wolves, see, that had been released onto the field by Nazi sympathizers. Meanwhile, a janitor with Down's Syndrome was plugging a semiautomatic at me while I ran. Fortunately, I avoided them all and made the winning goal, which was huge, since the Libyans had kidnapped my family and had threatened to anally rape our cat had we not won. It was right after this that I stopped the bullet meant for the President."

1989—I start junior high a week late because I refuse to ask directions to school.

1990—To try out for my high school baseball team, I am required to take a physical. The female doctor asks me how I'm feeling. I look down, grunt, and act like I didn't hear her. When she asks again, I exclaim, "Jesus, I'm fine! Christ! Enough with the questions already! That's all I get from you! Nag, nag, nag, nag, NAG!"

1991—I persuade my girlfriend to give me her virginity by explaining that "everyone's gonna think we did it anyway, so we might as well. Besides, uh, I, like, love you or something." I tell her I don't want to use a condom because "I want to be as close to you as possible."

1992—I break up with my girlfriend and sleep with all her friends.

1993—My first week of college, I participate in fraternity rush. When asked why I would make a great Pike, I hand them a then-up-to-date version of this resume. I am immediately selected rush chair.

1994—I drink my first beer. Upon finishing it, I exclaim, "Wow! This really does make fat chicks less repulsive! This stuff rules!"

1995—I buy my first Dave Matthews Band record. It, like, really speaks to me, like, on a really deep level. Dude.

1996—After an unfortunate three-week stretch without intercourse, I discover roofies, and the sky is the limit.

1997—Over spring break, I have sex with seven females in six days, with a combined age of 85.

1998—I get Amy Chen really drunk and lay her, thereby completing my goal of promoting diversity by boffing a girl from every major ethnic group.

1999—I set a personal record in January by waking up in my own piss and/or vomit six times in one month. This record is broken five times by September.

2000—I set an Alley Katzzzzzz club record by filling out my 17th Frequent Diner card, punched each time I order the $11.99 all-you-can-eat buffet. I receive a free "rubdown" from Candi and Staci, twins originally from Omaha, now studying to get their Masters in kinesology.

2001—In October, I buy a firefighters' uniform from a Salvation Army store and wear it to New York City bars while sitting alone in a corner, pretending to weep while looking at an empty pint glass. I break another record by having sex 57 times in a week.

2002—I am selected one of the Upper West Side's "20 Most Eligible Bachelors" by New York magazine. I am lauded for my "burning mystery," "quiet sensitivity," and "virile masculinity."

OK, ladies… this is what you wanted… it is now time to take a number. Step right up. The line, as always, forms in the back.

HONKEYTONKIN'

My father drinks and drives.

That sounds worse than it is. Many people out here on the East Coast don't understand this, but in the Midwest, particularly in Southern Illinois, where there's little more than unnamed roads and cornfields, beers are essentially permanently fused to your hand. I recently returned from a week and a half at home, and I don't remember a moment past 5 p.m. that I didn't have a beer in my hand. It's just part of the fabric; you go to a friend or neighbor's home, and without anyone even pausing to blink, you immediately head for their fridge and pop open a Budweiser. People aren't drinking to get drunk, not necessarily. You just drink because that's what you do.

I mean, beer is everywhere. I went to a post-service "mixer" at my mother's Catholic church, and they had a keg. I visited my cousin, and there was a car accident outside his house. We were both drinking a beer, and we sauntered outside, curious, beers in hand. I was downing an MGD when I went up to the police officer who responded and asked what happened. I was moderately surprised he didn't ask me for a sip. On the Fourth of July, we all had a Bud in one hand and a lighter to set off the borderline illegal explosives in the other.

In a society like this, where beer is less a troublemaker than an appendage, it's no surprise that, while teaching me to drive, my father once told me, half-jokingly (I think), "you gotta learn to drive with your knees so you can open your beer." (My mother smacked him on the head after he said this. Then, from the backseat, she opened a beer for herself.) To be entirely honest, I think I'd feel less comfortable with my father driving without a beer in his hand than when he does, which is often. It's just part of the driving process. We live outside of Mattoon, and it takes us 15-20 minutes just to go to the supermarket. That's one or two beers, right there.

It's not like my father is an alcoholic or anything; I've hardly ever seen him drunk, and I've seen that man consume many beers in my lifetime. (The highlight: an 18-pack of Natural Light, the only beer he'll drink, during a 10-inning baseball game. The only result, as far as I could tell, was a particularly violent belch.) That's just what you do when you're driving through the middle of nowhere. When you have to pee, you pull over to the side of the road. My father was pulled over once by a Mattoon cop; Dad got out of the car with his beer in hand. He did receive a ticket… for speeding. It's not encouraged, mind you… just accepted.

When I was home, my father drove the two-plus hours to St. Louis to see a Cardinals game, my third in a week and a half. (It had been more than three years since I'd been to Busch Stadium; my father and I estimated that's the longest I'd gone since birth.) Despite a late night up talking with my equally tormented sister the night before, I was ready to rock, and Dad and I each had three or four large beers at the game. We talked about Jack Buck, and Darryl Kile, and the important stuff, like whether they were going to trade for another pitcher, and then Ryan Klesko grounded out to second, and the Cardinals had another victory.

It was time to drive home, but once we hopped in the car and crossed back into Illinois, we realized with alarm that we were woefully short on beer. To wit, there were only four Natural Lights left in the cooler. With a two-hour drive home, not to mention an empty fridge back in Mattoon—I'd already made my presence felt—this just simply wouldn't do. We made it to Vandalia, about halfway home, when we both finished up our stash. (At this point, our conversation had hopped from baseball to girls to our sick dog to pool to 9/11 to suicide to mortgage payments to whether one of my cousins was gay. Nothing beats a late-night drive with your dad when beer's involved. I highly suggest it.) And we were rapidly approaching midnight, the drop-dead time when gas stations and supermarkets stop selling beer. We pulled off the interstate and into Vandalia… but we were too late. They'd already locked up the freezers. I hate locked freezers.

This left us only one option: a bar. One of the more unique aspects of Midwestern bars is the "To Go" option. Essentially, you can sit in a bar, usually sparsely populated, and drink all night; then, when you're ready to leave, slap another seven bucks on the table and get a 12-pack to take home. It's true genius; I can't believe there are bars in this country that *don't* do this.

But one downside—you often have interlopers popping in, with no intention of actually drinking at your bar or soaking in your atmosphere. They come in, grab the 12-pack, and bolt. Like the bar is some kind of drive-through. I know when I am at one of these bars and see people do that, I sneer at them like the rest of the people in the bar, and then I talk bad about them when they leave. Dad and I didn't want to be one of these hops tourists, but with no beer back at home, we had little choice. Another obstacle: We were in Southern Illinois, and the only bars you'll find open past midnight sneak up on you. You'll be on a deserted road, and all of a sudden you'll see a sign that says "Dietrich(Pop: 1423," and they'll have one bar, which looks like a trailer home, with a Hamm's sign out front and a couple pickup trucks out front. And after that, there will be nothing for 30 miles.

But we were undaunted. "I think I know a place in Sigel," Dad said. This is not a comforting statement to hear. Sigel is essentially a suburb of Effingham, which is essentially a suburb of Mattoon, which has 15,000 people. Sigel has a population of 150. It is certainly possible that they all have the last name "Sigel." It has one stop sign, about 40 houses, a post office, and a bar. The types of people who populate Sigel's one bar at 1 a.m., they likely guzzle motor oil, devour lit cigars, and have food stuck in their beards from 1983.

And we were hardly dressed the part. We, as is expected at Busch Stadium, were decked out in all bright red Cardinal T-shirts and white shorts. Dad had binoculars around his neck. I was carrying a scorebook. We were strangers straight from Central Casting, and we had a sneaking suspicion that Sigel's finest wouldn't take too kindly to our popping in for package liquor. There would be nothing left of us but a pair of Oakleys and a few strands of hair.

We arrived in Sigel. The exterior of the "bar" was not comforting. First off, it was called "BAR," which, while truthful, does not inspire much confidence in the reasonable nature of the clientele. It had a sign on the door for "Chicken Fried Steak." There was a huge crack in the glass. A flag waved out front with "Don't Tread on Me" blazoned across it. And there were four vehicles out front: three pickup trucks and a Harley. One truck had a bumper sticker: "I Got Your Jihad Right Here." We were clearly toast. But we needed that beer.

We exited the car. Dad looked at me and tried to make a joke. "You got your fighting clothes on?" I looked back at him. "Dad, I have a picture of J.D. Drew on my chest. What do you think?"

A deep sigh. I made Dad go first. He pushed the door open, which rang a loud bell. I cringed. Here we go.

Four people were sitting at the bar, big dudes, and a bartender, even bigger, and every single one of them darted his head immediately toward the door. We had clearly interrupted something, and we were about to pay. They registered our faces, blinked, and then turned their heads directly back toward the television. They were entranced. The room was silent, except for the TV.

They were watching *Mr. Holland's Opus*.

More specifically, they were watching the end of *Mr. Holland's Opus*, when Richard Dreyfuss' character sums up his entire career during a rousing concerto as an entire town weeps. The music rises, the crowd swells, everyone's crying. That Mr. Holland sure did touch a lot of lives.

Dad and I stood at the front door, not wanting to interrupt. I looked at him. He looked at me. I attempted to stifle a giant, all-encompassing guffaw, and succeeded, until Dad whispered in my ear, "I bet we could kick the ass of every single person in this room."

We waited until the film ended, tiptoed to the bar, asked for a 12-pack of Natural from the moist-eyed bartender, and drank all the way home. I love Southern Illinois.

LEAVING IT ALL AT THE ALTAR

Did any of you ever go to summer camp when you were a kid? Could anything beat summer camp? For anywhere from one week to two months, whomever you were at home—whether you were the youngest squirt in a family of eight, a baseball-card-collecting dork with no friends, or just a regular kid looking for a change of pace—none of that mattered. You could completely reinvent yourself because you were with people who didn't know you from Adam.

Your friends at camp weren't the type of people you usually hung out with; they were just the guys who happened to be staying in your cabin, or the guys you were assigned to activities with. As far as they knew, you were the most popular guy at your grade school. You could actually be cool, for a week or so.

My friend Matt got married about a month ago, and his wedding was about as close to summer camp as this adult's gonna get. On the grownup hand, everything was gorgeous, the bride looked ravishing, the food was fantastic, the reception was at this vineyard with a stunning, picturesque vista, or something. On the other hand, it was one big huge tequila-soaked party. That's my kind of wedding.

Bill is in some sort of sales. He went into greater detail about what exactly he does the night of the rehearsal dinner, but it was loud in the bar and I couldn't really understand him. He spent a lot of time on his cell phone, though, talking about accounts payable and end-of-the-month sales goals and quotas and dammit, JoAnn, just file the papers, file the freaking papers. Bill is an excellent golfer, nearly bald, and lives in Philadelphia.

Tyson is about to get engaged, I think. I'm told he's in a serious relationship, and it's only a matter of time. I couldn't tell you what he does for a living. Something with computers, maybe. Tyson is a terrible golfer, even worse than me, is rather tall, and lives in Washington, D.C.

That pretty much sums up all the personal information I have on each. Oh, and Bill has this really wacky father who wears plaid sports jackets, writes books on the Kennedy wives, and actually tells knock-knock jokes with a straight face. And I know both Bill and Tyson went to Davidson College, a small school in North Carolina, with my friend Matt.

And for four days, Bill and Tyson were as close of friends as I've ever had.

Bill and Tyson were the other two groomsmen. Matt's brother was the best man. (Isn't meeting lifelong friends' siblings a fascinating experience? If my friend Matt had chucked the corporate life and became a long-haired schoolteacher in Austin, he'd be his brother. It was like Bizarro Matt.) But he brought a date, and, as tends to be the case, he was preoccupied with her most of the weekend. Bill and Tyson were dateless, like me. So, essentially, it was summer camp. Three dudes, with everything paid for, with endless fountains of alcohol, dressed up real nice and ready to stir up some shit.

Whatever you do when you're home, when you're thrust into the decadently formal chaos of being a groomsman at an out-of-town wedding, the normal rules of engagement no longer apply. It's a world of free booze, attractive women in tight, sparkly dresses, and everyone in a raucous, joyous mood. The outside world doesn't matter anymore.

And it was basically the three of us. Matt was busy, you know, getting married, so we were on our own. Almost immediately, it was us against the world. There was a wedding going on around us, but we were in our own world: three guys, drinkin', talking girls, sharing old stories about the groom like we'd known each other forever.

We picked enemies, whether they deserved it or not. The ushers at the wedding were the bride's friends, not the groom's, and we, not to put too fine a point on it, found them insufferable weenies, total snot-nosed wimpy kids whom we ultimately labeled "The Yahoos." We joked about which bridesmaids were the hottest. We sucked tequila shots off the table. We sat in the corner and snidely mocked anyone, really, who wasn't us. Because we were the only cool ones.

It had the feel of a locker room. To be honest, it was a lot like a sports team, actually, to the point where we even started using sports clichés to describe what made us such excellent groomsmen. We talked about "giving 110 percent, 'cause that's all you can give" and "leaving it all out there on the altar." We stayed up late and yammered every night. All we were missing was towel snapping.

Hanging out with Bill and Tyson helped me to understand why people join fraternities. Just a bunch of dudes, causing trouble, being guys.

The night before the wedding, after the rehearsal dinner, the entire wedding party shambled over to a nearby watering hole and commenced more heavy drinking. Bill and Tyson settled in with a group of attractive women, of course, and I caught my friend Matt's eye. After a few shots of tequila, we decided to go upstairs and play Golden Tee, that video golf game popular among balding white men. But it was taken. So we sat down, grabbed a beer, and, the night before his wedding, talked for about two hours, man to man. When we both lived in St. Louis, we were the two single dorks, with no girls around, ever. And here he was, almost a married man.

You know that point when your friends make that leap into true happiness? When they put themselves in a position where you know they've got it, they have it all figured out? When they become a man? That was Matt that night. I'd never seen a guy just beam like that. It was all he could do not to start jumping up and down, twirling about, hollering, "I'm getting married tomorrow! To her! Me! Woooo!"

It was really something to see. I felt honored to have the opportunity.

Ultimately, the wedding came and went; we all drank; I had a strange experience with a female tennis player, and we folded into the hotel room. I was quite intoxicated and, thanks to my recent breakup, rather depressed.

OK, a lot depressed. By the end of the night, with Tyson, Bill, Bill's wedding hookup, and another friend in the room, I had decided to lie down on the floor between the air conditioner and the bed because "I didn't deserve to be anywhere but on the floor, like the pathetic worm I am." Many of my friends would have left me there, or tried to reason with me, or told me about how they'd had troubles with women too. Not Tyson. He walked over, blurted, "Jeezus, Will, get up. Christ." And I did, and we talked for three hours, and he pulled me out of it, and the Groomsmen reigned triumphant again.

The next day, everybody left to go back to their lives. I shook Bill's hand, then Tyson's. I made them promise to invite me to their weddings, eventually. I'm sure they won't. I'd be surprised if I ever see either of them again, to be honest. But, for one weekend, we were the Three Groomsmen. We left it all out there at the altar. We pushed ourselves to be the best. And we drank. Oh, how we drank.

Perhaps this whole column has the feel of a postcard, a note containing nothing but in-jokes that only those involved would understand. That's fine. That's the way it should be. That's summer camp.

See you next summer! Make sure to write! Good luck in homeroom!

HIGH PAINS DRIFTER

A lmost two years ago, I was interviewed by *The Village Voice*. The story was about dotcom kids—who had become accustomed to ludicrous salaries and affluent lifestyles—being thrown onto the street with little to show for their efforts when their respective dotcoms crashed.

The *VV* story, like just about everything written about the dotcom era, is hilariously dated, full of angst-filled twenty-somethings fretting about how they can't believe their new offices don't have private masseuses. But there's a little quote at the end that continues to resonate.

"I really don't know where I'll go," Leitch said. "I might stay here with some friends in the city. I have uncles in Philadelphia, so I might head there."

According to Webster's, a drifter is defined as, "One who drifts, especially a person who moves aimlessly from place to place or from job to job."

Well, for a substantial number of months, friends, I was a full-fledged drifter. I don't mean someone who moved around a lot on some sort of voyage of self-discovery. I mean someone who had no money, no place to go, nothing to do, absolutely zero worldly possessions. I'll put it this way: You're reading a former homeless guy.

I had nothing to my name but two suitcases full of clothes and books, and a cat carrier. Let's track those months.

October 2000—Months behind on rent, I cry mercy and take a two-month sojourn to my cousin Denny's home in Mattoon. There, I eat his food, drink his beer, tie up his phone line, and sleep in his guest bed. I contribute nothing but tens of thousands of words for a book that will likely never be finished. Income during this period: $0.

December 2000—Fearing that if I do not head back to New York when I had initially intended, I never would, I spend my last $65 to hop a Greyhound bus from Effingham, Illinois, to the Port Authority in New York City. It is a 25-hour trip, with stops in Cincinnati, Cleveland, Pittsburgh, and some other condemned properties I mercifully slept through. I do this even though I'm fully aware that when I get to the city, I have no money, no job, and nowhere to live. Income during this period: $0.

January 2001—Out of options only a week after arriving, I finagle my way into my girlfriend's apartment in Brooklyn. Even though we hadn't been dating long and didn't know each other well enough to survive a drive uptown together, let alone sharing quarters, we convince ourselves it will work out because, heck, she can't just kick me to the street, can she? There, I eat her food, drink her beer, tie up her phone line, and sleep in her bed—well, for a week anyway, when I am then kicked to the couch, justifiably. Income during this period: $0.

Early February 2001—She kicks me to the street, because, yes, she can. Scrambling, I plan to stay on a friend's couch for two weeks. I last a week, because "it's getting crowded in here. You understand, Will, right?" Before I leave, I swipe some stray beer and food. Income during this period: $35, thanks to a used bookstore.

Mid February 2001—A friend is invited to stay in a SoHo loft for two weeks that is manned with 36 cameras sending a live feed to a Website. (Will people in 10 years really believe what it was like here during the dotcom craze? It's hard for me to fathom, and I was *here*.) This is a fascinating sociological experiment, worth documenting for the raw audacity of it, but this is lost on me. I'm just ecstatic that it has a full bar, a shower, and, most joyous, a washing machine. I contact my uncles in Philadelphia and tell them I have nowhere to go and that I may need to move in with them for a while. An hour later, I am interviewed by *The Village Voice*. I then speak to a friend in New Jersey about staying with him for a week before heading to Philadelphia, and he agrees. Months later, I will borrow a sizable amount of money from him, which, to this day, I have not paid back. Income during this period: $5, in change, swiped from the Webcam house owner's dresser. I make a mental note to pay him back. I have not.

Late February 2001 — The day before I am to leave for New Jersey, fate intervenes. Not only do I learn I have been offered a job, but, upon a visit to a friend's house, I learn a neighbor has a spare room for a month that I can rent, and she doesn't even want the money upfront. I call off my friend in New Jersey and my uncles in Philadelphia, gleefully plop my suitcase and cat carrier on her couch, and declare myself home.

April 2001 — I find an apartment on the Upper East Side. A week after I move in, I am laid off. At my housewarming party, a friend points out that when she went through her datebook, she found four different addresses and three different phone numbers for me. Various temp jobs bring me to a new apartment, which brings me to my new job, which brings me to now.

I have lived in Inwood, a nifty residential neighborhood at the northwestern-most tip of Manhattan, for two years months now. I have a stable home, awesome roommates, a bed, a desk, a computer (which doesn't work, but no matter), and even a litter box. I am as stable as I have been since I moved to New York in January 2000. But I'm still finding it difficult to shake the habits of a drifter.

To wit:

Over the last two months, I have slept in my office four times. This is not because I have been working all that diligently; I just wanted the air conditioning. I lay my head on my briefcase and crawl under my desk. My daily meal typically consists of the complimentary cereal my employers graciously provide.

My room has no decorations on the wall. My books are stacked on top of one another against the bed, as are my CDs. The room's only light is a desk lamp borrowed from my roommates. I have a closet, but the majority of my clothes are folded neatly in a suitcase. If I feel a night has gone too late and I don't feel like catching the long subway ride home, I simply pass out on a friend's floor.

Recently, I had a busy day. I had work until 2 p.m., a job interview at three, and a softball game at six. This required three different sets of clothes. Rather than plan accordingly, perhaps making sure the outfits were where I needed them ahead of time, I simply folded a suit jacket, tie, pants, dress shoes, a T-shirt, sweatpants, and cap into a suitcase. I then dragged it across the city from point to point. This led to the inevitable moment when I had to explain to the woman I was trying to convince to give me a job why, exactly, I had brought carry-on luggage into her office.

This is being written at work, simply because it's where I happened to be when I came up with this idea. The last six pieces I wrote have been written on my roommate's computer, a friend's computer, a Kinko's, a hotel's "Business Center," here at work, and on a notepad. That one was then read over the phone to a loyal friend, who graciously typed it for me. It is logical for a writer to, lo, have a ready-made area where he produces his work, but a drifter has neither the time nor the resources for logic.

In this economy, one never knows how long any job can last or when we'll be tossed out with no severance and no parachute. I cannot say that financially I have prepared myself for this possibility … but I assure you, I know that I can handle it. I am quite resourceful. That's one way to look at it, I guess.

Hey… that's a nice couch you have there.

MELTDOWN

My family is in town. I can tell my family is in town because I'm drenched in my own sweat, I've yelled at the cat five times in the last 20 minutes and I'm so tired I can't find the blasted "jee" button on this frijjin' computer.

My family hates New York. I do not mean that they are charmingly adrift in this unfamiliar urban world, the innocents abroad. I mean they despise it, the way cats despise dogs, the way the Goldman family despises O.J., the way vampires despise sunlight.

This is the Leitches' second trip to New York. The first was two years ago, during the height of the dotcom boom, back when I was a surreal (and, of course, completely fake) success story making too much money for pretending to edit a Website that none of my bosses even knew existed. My life was so different then. I made about three times as much money then as I do know, and I lived that way. We went out drinking every night, stayed in fancy hotels, took cabs four blocks uptown and bought rounds of drinks for complete strangers simply because we thought they might, possibly, perhaps, be from somewhere near the Midwest, maybe Nevada.

I grew up in a small town, 16,000 people, tops, and my family has lived there for more than 50 years. It is all that they know, and all they really care to. The 2000 Leitch family visit was our first real family vacation, just the four of us, alone together, for a week, in nearly six years. My family has always gotten along very well; we are not a dysfunctional clan full of hidden secrets and buried resentments. But after about 36 hours in New York City, we were dangerously close to killing one another.

I don't remember the circumstances of it, but on day three of that first trip, the Leitches went to Shea Stadium to see the Cardinals play (and lose to) the Mets. It started out fine. We joked that my nose-ring-wearing, armpit-hair-bearing, Ani DiFranco- and Phish-loving sister should find a good Christian guy like the Cardinals' J.D. Drew, and we drank seven-dollar lukewarm ballpark beer. Then the game ended, and we hopped on the subway. It was packed, and soul-crushingly hot. My sister started complaining, I snapped at her, my dad snapped at me, my mom snapped at my dad, and we were off. To try to lighten the mood, I convinced them to stop by a Chevy's restaurant in Times Square for a margarita.

All hell broke loose. My sister started yelling, my dad started yelling, my mom started crying, and I hid under the table. I don't even recollect what it was about. It was like the seedy, nasty, angry underbelly of New York had slipped under our skin, and everything each of us did made us want to strangle everyone else. My sister eventually stomped off, then came back to yell at us some more. My mom (like her son, a non-conflict-oriented person) left the table and stood on Eighth Avenue, trying not to weep as her family disintegrated around her. We stayed in the bar and screamed at one another while the waiters kept their distance. Not content to let my mother escape the chaos, we took it to the street, where the Leitches yelled and hollered insults at each other as the respectable denizens of the Port Authority passed by and gaped. (That's how serious our fight was. New Yorkers took notice.)

It was awful. Everyone was vicious, holding nothing back. I was trying to keep peace, pausing only to make war. It was a public Leitch family meltdown, with the wretched city bearing full witness, right there on the street. Right about the time I started to worry if any of us had a gun, I noticed someone walking past us. While my sister was cursing, I stopped her, and everyone else.

"Hey, guys, check it out. It's J.D. Drew."

It was. He and two Cardinals teammates were passing by. We all halted, looked at him, then each other, and did a collective "Well, I'll be darned." And then the screaming conference reconvened.

My family left two days early. Until today, they had not returned. New York truly brought out the worst in all of us; I did not expect them to come again.

And now they're back. It's funny, really. The initial intent of their visit was to see my uncles' new apartment in Philadelphia, and to catch a couple of Cardinals-Phillies games at Veterans Stadium. They arrived in Philly on Friday, and we drank and were merry. We sat in the swelter for Saturday's game, then went home and drank some more. Sunday was another game of Leitch Liquefy, this time in the 100-plus-degree upper tier. We laughed and cheered and smiled and bonded.

Originally, this was all the visit was to be. They'd head back after the game, and I'd go back to New York, and none would be any the poorer. But about a month ago, while going over details for the trip, my dad paused.

"You know, I wouldn't mind seeing the Ground Zero." (I love the way my father says that term like he invented it.) Ignoring the inherent crassness of treating the site of a nightmare made alive as some sort of tourist attraction, I was ecstatic; I never thought they'd want to come back. Much has changed in two years, and I couldn't wait to show them how far I'd come. Whatever got them here was fine with me. So it was. After the game, we were to drive back to New York, and they'd spend the night at my place before heading downtown Monday morning.

I don't know what I was thinking, honestly.

What was a glorious, celebratory Leitch reunion turned sour fast. It's like they could smell New York coming; as soon as we waded through traffic to enter the George Washington Bridge, Dad started yelling at Mom, which made my sister yell at him, which made me yell at her, which made people behind us start honking because we were sitting in the middle of the highway. By the time we made it into the city, Dad was grousing about the lack of parking spaces and the smell, my sister was screeching about how she couldn't understand why anyone would want to live here, and my Mom was trying to get them to relax, which just made them be grouchy to her.

And, oh yes, the heat. After two days at the ballpark, we are all brutally sunburned. (I look like a butch Sacagawea.) New York, and most of the East Coast, has been stricken with a historic heat wave. I have the greatest apartment, and I couldn't wait to show it off to them. (My old apartment was the size of a cell phone case, with worse ventilation.) But I hadn't accounted for the heat. It is so hot. And we do not have air conditioning. We have a fan, powered by a paraplegic gerbil.

The heat only added to our dour nature. We ended up ordering food delivered to the air-conditioned bar downstairs, while Dad grumbled about the bartender and the loud music, and my sister yelled at him for not being nicer to my mother, and my mother hollered at me for not being better organized. And then we decided to go to bed. With our sunburns. In the apartment with no air conditioning on the hottest New York City night of the year.

I write this while my parents try to sleep. My sister just came out and asked if we had ice, or if "they don't have ice in this godforsaken city." My roommates are looking on helplessly as my family melts down, again.

It is as if New York City is lemon juice to my family's invisible ink. All that is ugly and underneath, typically unseen, emerges when the combustible elements are introduced.

They go back tomorrow. I will miss them. I cannot wait to see them over Christmas. But next time... we're staying in Philadelphia. Even if they do boo J.D. Drew there.

NULL SET

T his is how it starts, I think.

One of my biggest curiosities about myself, along with my biggest fears, is wondering when I will just drop this whole writing thing and move on. Do I think this is going to happen anytime soon? Not at all. I can't fathom such a thing; it would be like living without oxygen, or nicotine, or masturbation.

So why is it so difficult right now? I mean, I'm sitting here, staring at a screen, and nothing is happening. And I can concentrate on nothing for more than seven minutes. Five if I've been drinking.

Hey, I haven't listened to that entire White Stripes show I downloaded off Kazaa in a while. God, there's so much good stuff on Kazaa. Did you know you can download movies that aren't even out yet off Kazaa? Friend of mine watched Punch Drunk Love the other day. Can you believe that shit? I mean, that's no way to watch a movie, but you can get it on your computer ... fucking nuts. Hey, look, it's the original CNN broadcast of 9-11. It's perversely amusing to watch the opening minutes now. There's almost a whimsical quality to the newscasters' voices, before they realized what was going on. "Get this, folks! A plane! World Trade Center! Seriously! Well, the U.S. Open was last weekend ..." There's a reason they never rebroadcast that live. Paula Zahn looks like she'd rather be interviewing Wolfgang Puck.

To be honest, I haven't produced anything of value in about two weeks. I can't even write a letter to a friend who just left for the Peace Corps in the depths of Africa. How hard can it be to come with something to say there? "So, is it true that they all talk in clicking sounds?" "Do they really not wear clothes in the village? If so, is it true what they say about the men of Mali?" "Do you have a cheek ring yet?" Yet I can't even do that. The lady moves halfway around the world to do good deeds, and I can't even write her a letter. This is new. This is different. This is trouble.

Ever hear of Budd Dwyer? He's that politician who, about to be indicted for bribery, shot himself at a news conference. Absolutely insane. You can get that on Kazaa too. It's an exhilarating feeling, to be honest, to watch someone about to shoot themselves. Look at his face. He knows what he's going to do. It's the craziest thing; he's telling the audience to be careful, he has a gun. Then ... BLAM. If only Kazaa had slow motion. Maybe I can run it through my Real Player. In other news, have you seen that original Spider-Man trailer, the one where the bank robbers get caught in the web Spider-Man spins between the WTC towers? Creepy.

Is there anything more useless than a writer who can't write? I mean, in just about any practice, you can half-ass your way through something, doing the minimum effort for a day or two, and no one can really tell. But one uninspired column, and it's obvious to everyone. If only I could be so lucky to write an uninspired one. It is 5 p.m. on Sunday. I began this Saturday morning. This is the first sentence I wrote. No, wait, it's this one. No, this one. It's pathetic, really. It's not that writing is the most essential trade in the first place, and here I am, too flaccid to avoid complaining how I can't even do something so trivial. I mean, I highly doubt handymen sit there whining, "You know, I just can't put together this shelf today."

But nevertheless, here I am, telling you: I cannot produce this shelf today. Not that you care anyway. Not that you really should.

Some woman just got her leg bit off by a shark. I didn't think that's what it would really be when I clicked on the title, but sure enough, there it was. I am learning not to underestimate Kazaa. She's swimming, leisurely, carefree. It's sunny. I like her breasts. And then ... there goes the leg. Everyone's screaming, the camera's shaking, people are jumping in the water. Then the tape stops. That shark came from out of nowhere. I should watch that again; maybe I can catch him coming this time. Slow ... slow ... nope. Still didn't see him. Let's see, what else ... oh, man, people jumping from the WTC. They never showed that on TV. No wonder. When I heard about people jumping from the top floors, I imagined one final decision, that's it, let's go, a graceful, soothing, swan-like glide, a final act of defiant peace. That's not what it was, though. One man [woman? figure?] violently twists, turns, flips, gyrates, no control, here, there, before, then, the strangely dull thud. Another hits the side of the building and splits in half. Do not underestimate Kazaa.

When did this start happening? I cannot move. I believe this is called atrophy. I can feel my bones decaying. Am I going bald? I suspect I haven't moved from the couch in two weeks, except to go to work, where I stare blankly at a screen and wait for my company to dissolve. It'll happen. Has to. They always do. There is a football game tonight. Maybe I'll watch it. I should write. Maybe I'll sleep through it. But I should write! Maybe I'll just sit here and meld with the computer a while longer. Inspiration has to strike eventually, right?

There's police helicopter video. They're above the North Tower. The South Tower has already gone down. I don't know how the pilot and cameraman aren't gagging. They're directly above it now. Then the rumble. Then down it goes. They must feel so helpless. They must want to hang upside down from the helicopter, grab the needle and just pull, goddammit, pull. How the cameraman had the wherewithal to keep filming this is beyond me. Maybe it's an automatic camera, like, attached to the side or something. How did this video get leaked anyway? Why would the police give this up? Because once you give it to anyone, it's gonna end up on Kazaa, everything does, and then some guy is watching in the silent dark on a Saturday night, wondering why he doesn't feel worse, wondering why it isn't bothering him more than it is.

I am numb. There is nothing there. Believe you me, I'm looking, and I'm telling you, there's nothing. It is not affecting me. I want to bash my face into the wall. I want to set my leg hair on fire. I want to scream until my throat turns raw and bleeds. Something has to really hurt, right?

This is how it happens. That fire, that spunk, that let's go get 'em, that hey, what are we all here for but to CREATE... one day, it just vanishes. It'll come back, sure, in spurts, here or there, but it's never been gone before, so who knows when it'll go again? Without it, everything is grayer, dull, obtuse. Nothing feels good, nothing hurts. Everything just is, uninspiring, trudging forward into powder. It is, of course, meaningless. You know that, right?

This is how it happens; this is why people stop.

ATROPHY, DECAY AND ROT

An associate of mine is running in a marathon this weekend. Let me say that again. She is running in a marathon. She is not driving it. She is not taking a cab. She isn't even riding a bike. She's running it. Like, with her feet.

This is unfathomable. People who run in marathons are outside of my frame of reference. I live in a world of alcohol, nicotine, order-in burritos, and free downloads. A few of my friends belong to gyms, but few go that often, and the ones who do partake under a strange code of silence, sneaking it in on occasional mornings, brought up sparingly, lest those snotty pseudo-intellectuals among us, those rotting away, scoff or scowl. You're the type of person who *exercises*? Good for you. Tell us how your latte is, or how chipper Matt and Katie were this morning. How's your Ikea furniture treating you, anyway?

I have helped foster this mindset, I admit. My mind is always balancing so many issues and difficulties and fears and worries that it seems strange that self-preservation, actually *taking care of myself*, never seems to enter the picture. It occurs to me, during rare moments of introspection, that I am on the fast track to death. My eating habits are horrendous, still at one meal a day, usually a slice of pizza or a couple cheap hot dogs from the stand across the street. I drink a glass of chocolate milk in the morning, I guzzle Diet Coke all day, and it's either beer or Scotch in the evening, depending on whether I'm writing. I smoke a pack of Marlboro Reds a day. And physical exertion is limited to masturbation and running to catch a leaving subway train, sometimes simultaneously. And vitamins? Please. Next thing you know, you'll want me to start eating carrots or something. A friend once pointed out to me that the only aspect of medical prevention I explored were condoms.

And it's not like I have some sort of superhuman fortitude. My family history is not good. The Leitch men are notorious for dying young; no Leitch male in direct lineage has ever lived past 65. Think about that: *65*. I think Congo and Afghanistan have better life expectancies. My father was on blood pressure medication in his early thirties. My grandfather had four heart attacks and lung cancer. The Leitches are, essentially, toast. My life insurance policy, I suspect, will have a New York Lottery logo on it.

A few months ago, when my job's insurance kicked in, under the suggestion of a girlfriend in the medical industry, I decided to visit the doctor for a routine physical. I hadn't been in more than two years.

I will confess to having a problem with doctors. If there's something seriously wrong with me, to be honest, I'd rather just not know. Whenever I've scraped my knee or something, and there's blood running down, I'd prefer just to wipe it off with a napkin and worry about cleaning it when I'm in the shower the next day. (True, I swear. I recently seriously banged up my left knee sliding into first base—which you should never do—while playing softball. I finished the game with blood pouring down into my sock, dyeing it completely. I put nothing on my leg, not even a Band-Aid, and it of course became infected. I was limping for a week afterward.)

So, the doctor knew I was trouble from the outset. He asked all the right questions: Did I smoke, did I have any history of heart trouble, do I take drugs, so on, what not. He then took my blood pressure, listened to my lungs, and even made me drop my pants and cough. (I did find it strange, actually, that he had his wife do that, and that he filmed it. But, I dunno, I guess that's normal in New York.) He left the room for a while and came back with this big chart. He pointed to this number, and this number, and this number. I was hung over, so I was having difficulty paying attention. He finally laid it out for me.

"William, you have the blood pressure of a moderately healthy man. A moderately healthy 65-year-old man."

He then explained how I should quit smoking, and eat more fruit, and try to leave the house a bit more. I chuckled. A 65-year-old man? Sucker. I'm not even going to *make it* to 65. You'd think he would have recognized that from my family history. Freaking quack.

He sent me on my way, and I have paid his advisements little mind. And since I've been single, without anyone to get on my case about only eating raisins over a two-day span, I can't imagine I'm any healthier. But, really, that's fine. I mean, I'm not obscenely obese, I don't do heroin, and I don't play with guns. That's about as health-conscious as I'm going to get.

Whenever I get down on myself, when everything just seems wrong and helplessly muddled and soiled, when it appears I will never be able to do anything right, I can just step back and take a deep breath and gain that precious perspective. After all, this life, inevitably, won't last too long.

So, bottoms up!

VERSE CHORUS VERSE

W hen you add it all up, the Cardinals, and the Woody Allen, and the penis insecurity, and the fear of ex-girlfriends, and the whole I'm-from-Southern-Illinois-so-bear-with-me thing that I fall back on when I get scared, none of it matters… the only thing that ever really made an impact was Nirvana. Everything else, put together, isn't close.

It's easy to forget this. It has been a long time since Nirvana first seared that *thing* deep into our brain, made us feel like there was this whole other planet out there, good lord, what is out there, could there be more people like this, there couldn't be, no way …

You see… we have grown old. We have changed. We are working 9-to-5 jobs now. We are worrying about the economy. We wonder where we're going in our careers. We don't want someone to release the plague in Times Square. We wonder if we're missing out on the primes of our lives. We wonder if anyone will ever love us. That *thing*, that part of us that once flared up, previously undiscovered, where did that come from? We try to muffle it.

We discover new things. We find our new obsession. Some of us get married. Some of us devote ourselves to making money. Some of us snicker when we see our company's commercial come on television. We forget. We forget what happened.

We rationalize it. We were young and stupid, we didn't know shit. Man, that was *college*, or that was *high school*, or that was *my 20s, man.* Yeah, that was a great song and all… but a song's a song. We were just kids.

Don't you remember? It hasn't been that long, has it? Come on, man … *you remember*. I know you do.

Everybody remembers when they first heard "Smells Like Teen Spirit." Laugh if you will, mock us for being stupid twenty-somethings who never had to fight for anything in our lives, we get it, and we agree. But you ask any of us, we still know where we were when we saw the video for the first time.

You have to keep in mind, we were listening to Warrant at the time. We were listening to Slaughter. We were telling ourselves that Axl Rose was Mick Jagger. We were looking for something, and, unable to find it, we just figured we'd take what we could. You have to cut us some slack here. We didn't know they were coming.

So when that happened, the experience bore such a deep hole in us, we can all tell you when we first saw it. All of a sudden, some other force showed up. All of a sudden, something new happened, something we never could have anticipated. Where did they come from?

This scruffy little guy, not singing, not really, but not just screaming either. He was like a bent garden hose finally straightened, a spring uncoiled, a live wire with too much current running through it, as Jimi Hendrix was famously described. Sure, the song rocked, which was what caught our attention in the first place, but there was something else, something authentic, something afraid and pained and sardonic and intelligent and hopeful… and *furious*.

This sound was so unusual, we had no idea what to make of it. Who were these guys? You heard rumors. They were bisexuals. They were Satanists. I hear Axl hates them. One of them had a baby born addicted to cocaine. An associate of mine from high school, still confused, sold his CD after seeing Krist Novoselic and Dave Grohl kiss on *Saturday Night Live* and became convinced Kurt Cobain's garbled lyrics were going to make him gay.

But man, did it hit us. Everything changed… like *that*. Suddenly everything we'd been doing up to that point was ridiculous. We ditched our Skid Row albums, we dumped our parachute pants, we put down the hair gel. Authenticity was suddenly what mattered. Really believing, really *caring*. Sure, like everything eventually, what Nirvana meant was warped over time, and you could buy pre-ripped jeans at the Gap and "Grunge!" compilation CDs. But you can't deny that it was there, and it was pure. Suddenly, something was important. We just wanted to eat something that wasn't spoon-fed to us; we wanted that fire. It really was a revolution, however brief and fleeting it was. And it was all started by one song, one verse, one chord, one man.

Sure, we've changed. Nirvana is classic rock now. But Kurt is as woven into the fabric of our lives as our first date, or our first love, or our first death in the family, or our first broken heart. Or did you forget?

You remember standing in line at midnight, with a line around the block, to pick up *In Utero*. You remember hearing "Heart-Shaped Box" on the radio. You remember explaining to skeptics that "Rape Me" wasn't really about rape. You remember the *MTV Unplugged*, back when there was an *MTV Unplugged*, where we were shocked to learn that not only was Kurt *not* incapacitated by heroin, but also that he could also produce 70 minutes of utter beauty that people would still talk about eight years later in awe. And you remember the pain, the worry, the fear, those hidden parts of you that sprung up when you listened, even if you weren't sure why.

Admit it. You do remember now… don't you? God, you have to.

I remember a controversy that bubbled up when *In Utero* came out. The album's original back cover art was a collage of fetuses that Kurt had insanely patched together. Because of that image, still weirdly gorgeous, and the song title "Rape Me," K-Mart and Wal-Mart stores refused to sell the CD. Nirvana, predictably, was the target of intensely boring "underground" fans who were perpetually accusing the band of "selling out" after *Nevermind* hit big. They were apoplectic, then, when Kurt said he would alter the art and change the name of the song to "Waif Me."

Kurt explained that when he was growing up in Aberdeen, Wash., there were no record stores or underground shops. The only place you could buy music was Wal-Mart. Therefore, he made a Wal-Mart-only version, cleaned up. Urban hipsters screamed corporate sellout. The rest of us knew better. After all, Wal-Mart was the only place I could buy CDs growing up, too.

When Kurt died, when he'd had enough, I sat in my dormitory, alone, listened to *In Utero*, and cried for hours. I don't care what you think about that fact. It's true.

The new song is called "You Know You're Right." I'd heard it before, actually; no Nirvana freak worth his salt hasn't searched and found a version from a 1994 concert. It's a terrible mix, though. You can hear two idiots who happened to be sitting next to the bootlegger loudly complaining, "Man, I don't know this song," and then blabbering through the whole thing.

A friend of mine sent me a link to the "lost Nirvana song" that was supposedly leaked to the Web. I scoffed at him. I'd heard everything.

Wrong. I mean, I was just sitting at work, writing a brainless story about nothing of particular significance, tap-tap-tapping away, wondering about my fantasy football team, and whether this check would clear by Monday, and so on, and so on. My headphones were on. I hit play. A heavy bass line. *"I would never bother you … I would never promise to … I will never follow you … I will never bother you …"* And then … BAM.

The guitar comes in like a buzzsaw to the skull. I mean, it has been so long. You don't remember what it's like to listen to a Nirvana song for the first time. Then, from the grave, from the pit of that acrid stomach … *there* it is. *"Never speak a word again … I will crawl away for good."* It knocked me out of my chair. I'm not kidding. Then that chorus, that *pain*, that *living*… that thing that made Kurt different, that thing that made him one of us. It's all right there. God, how could we have forgotten?

Sure. It doesn't sound like a mix that Kurt would have signed off on. It's too clean, it's too produced, it's too *convenient*. It doesn't matter. It captures exactly what made Nirvana matter, what we've missed, what he could have done. And Jesus … it was a *new Nirvana song*.

I couldn't work the rest of the day. I was legitimately afraid to listen to it again. I, myself, had forgotten.

Some of us follow foggy tracks, full of faith that, if we stay true to what brought us here, they will lead us right. Some of us have lost our way all together. Some of us can't remember what it was like to have believed. Some of us are too busy to notice much of anything anymore.

But, remember, damn you. Remember what that was like. It's as close to something real and binding as we had. Don't rationalize it away.

Just listen. That is, after all, why they recorded everything in the first place. To remember, to document, to celebrate.

And don't forget to play it loud. *Real* loud.

FROM MATTOON TO METHADONE

In two weeks, I will be starting yet another new job. I will not attempt to hide my excitement about it; it's always important to capture and bottle initial enthusiasm for a new job, because eventually, no matter how much you love it, you'll find plenty of stuff to whine and bitch about. Nothing against my current job (the people are nice, it's been surprisingly stable, and, uh, they let me download shit from Kazaa all day), but I suspect I won't miss it all that much. What I will miss: the neighborhood.

Ever since I moved to New York, people from home have asked me if it's dangerous here, if I feel uncomfortable walking the streets late at night. You can tell they're just begging me for sordid tales of back-alley raping and pillaging to justify all their established notions. I'm inevitably a disappointment to them. Allotting for my status as a post-Guiliani, cops-everywhere NYC immigrant, I haven't noticed a single area of town, including outer boroughs, that's any scarier than, say, East St. Louis, or Gary, Indiana.

New York has a distinct safety advantage; there are people everywhere. True, they might not actually help you if you're being attacked, but it at least feels better knowing they're there. Sure, Bushwick, Brooklyn is shadier than the Upper East Side of Manhattan, but on the whole, I don't really know of a "bad" part of town. Except for maybe the block on which I work.

Our offices are on 36th Street and Eighth Avenue in Manhattan. This is about six, seven blocks south and a block west of Times Square. The closest landmark is the Empire State Building, just over a bit east, off Sixth Avenue. But in Midtown, the dividing line is Eighth Avenue. East of there, you have Macy's, and Fashion Avenue, and Bryant Park, and Broadway. West of there, you have New Jersey, the Port Authority… and my block.

You see, there are two methadone clinics in my building. Two. There are no other methadone clinics in the general vicinity. In fact, I might accurately say that our building is the place for all your methadone needs. Your one-stop shop. We will not be undersold. Step right up.

Now I am not trying to trivialize drug addiction. It's a disease, not a choice, it's a horrible affliction for those gripped in its clutches. I have genuine sympathy for these poor souls, and I hope that methadone helps them escape the horrors of heroin. It's awful. It is. Really.

But it still sucks that every smoke break I take turns into a journey into the heart of darkness.

Over the last few months here, while I was just trying to have a cigarette, I have seen things on the street that words cannot do justice:

✓ A shirtless man walked up to where I was smoking. He had been looking directly in front of him, intent on some point in the distance, moving swiftly. He stepped to where I was, stopped, pivoted 90 degrees, and faced me, eye to eye. He then burped, and smiled. He then pivoted back, focused again on the spot in the distance, and continued onward. I resisted the urge to salute him.

✓ A man a few feet away, leaning on an invisible stepladder. I can only assume it was a stepladder; he had the silhouette of a high school senior posing for a class picture, elbow resting comfortably on one of the steps. I watched him try to stay awake. Occasionally he would close his eyes and slip. His arm would hit an imaginary step below the one on which he had been resting, and he would imagine catching himself and readjust. It was fascinating. After three minutes of this, repeated, I was fairly certain that, if he wanted to, he could actually climb this imaginary stepladder. It was lunchtime, so I scurried past him to grab a hot dog. He saw me, stopped, and moved the imaginary stepladder, so I wouldn't bump into it, which I thought was quite considerate.

✓ A drag queen (I hope), struggling with her own smoke break. She asked me for a match, and, having "accidentally" swiped a lighter from my roommates that morning, I gave her a whole book. She thanked me, honey, and then lit the wrong end of the cigarette. It took her about 20 seconds to realize this. She muttered "Shit!" threw the cigarette to the ground, and lit another one. From the wrong end. I watched, riveted, as she did this three times.

✓ Three ashen, shivering gentlemen huddled in a corner, desperate to keep warm, even though it was mid-August and I wasn't even wearing a jacket. They looked gaunt and sickly. They looked kind of like that guy in *RoboCop* after he falls in the vat of toxic waste. Baseball was the topic of discussion, specifically Texas Rangers shortstop Alex Rodriguez. From there, the conversation segued to former Texas Rangers owner George W. Bush, and then a weirdly lucid discussion of a possible war with Iraq. Well, two of the men were discussing Iraq. The other one had his finger so far up his nose I thought I'd be able to see it poking out the top of his head. He was also looking away from the conversation, staring at a wall display for a store that sells zippers, and only zippers. He was wearing jeans, though I lacked the intestinal fortitude to check and see if the zipper was functional.

✓   A man in a full suit and tie, but betrayed by a face ghastly pale and lined with scars, sprinting up Eighth Avenue, screaming, "I HAVE A BIG DICK! LISTEN TO ME! I HAVE AN ENORMOUS DICK! MY DICK IS SO LARGE!" I heard his voice trailing off as he approached 40th Street, but he must have turned around when he hit the crowd of Port Authority, because I heard the voice coming closer before he passed by my street again. "I HAVE AN ENORMOUS DICK! IT IS HUGE!"

My new job is further downtown, about halfway between Chelsea and Greenwich Village. This is a fine area, with trendy bars and a prep school nearby. When I went on my interviews there, I noticed three different sushi restaurants. It is clean and nice. I'm sure I will love it.

But it won't be the same. I mean, after all, his dick is so large. Listen to him. It is huge.

I miss this place already.

DECADE OF DECADENCE

November 3, 1992.

I t's important to remember that it was election night, the big election night, the night we switched from a boring, Republican country to a shit-kickin', skirt-chasin' tornado of absurdity. My friend Gary was having our whole nerd crew from high school over to his place to watch the election returns—I was looking forward to rubbing it in my right-wing friend James' face when Clinton inevitably won—and I was supposed to come by afterwards.

It was my girlfriend's birthday. My first relationship, really, the first one that meant anything, was with Betty. She had worked at the movie theater, the Cinema 1-2-3, in downtown Mattoon. She'd been there for two years, going to the community college during the day, tearing tickets at night, and then drinking and cruising until dawn. She was blond, sweet, smart, and funny. She was turning 22.

I was 17. I had just recently started dating Betty. When I met her, she was engaged, and I was, well, I was a 16-year-old dweeb who was the captain of his scholastic bowl team, wore a feathered mullet, and had kissed two girls. For whatever reason, we started hanging out when we screened the new movies after work, and we would subtly flirt, knowing it would never happen, what, with the age difference and all. (What, she would pick me up from lunch at the high school?) Then one night, she had a bit too much to drink, and I drove her home, and she kissed me in front of her place, and the floodgates were open. That had been two weeks before November 3. On Halloween, I saw my first pair of exposed breasts. She did not know this. I had told her I'd had sex before, because I surmised (correctly, I later found out) that if she knew I was a virgin, she'd be freaked out and not let me kiss her anymore.

She felt more comfortable about the age difference than you might suspect. In a nice twist, her father had been close friends with my grandfather, and she remembered having schoolgirl crushes on my uncles, who, not surprisingly, look exactly like my father, who looks exactly like me. In Betty's eyes, I was a lucky coincidence, a nice, smart, innocent, harmless guy whom she could train in the ways of the world before I inevitably bolted for college. Betty would be my water wings before I left to swim in the big pool.

Ultimately, I would prove anything but nice, smart, innocent or harmless for Betty, but that is not the story we are telling here.

The day after Betty kissed me for the first time, I spoke with my mother. Mom had heard me talk about Betty for a while and was keeping a close, skeptical eye on the situation. (I didn't know it at the time, but Mom had decided there was no way her only son was going to gallivant around with some 22-year-old floozy.) I had never sipped alcohol before, so I asked my mom, while she was ironing, what it meant, exactly, if someone kissed you after they'd been drinking. Did it mean anything? Was it an accident? Was it indicative of larger feelings, or a fluke? Would she even remember it the next day?

I underestimated my mother's resolve against Betty. She put down the iron, looked me in the eye, and said, "She was drunk. She didn't mean it. She won't remember it, and she doesn't even like you. Stay away from her." It was the first of many battles I would have with my mother over Betty, and, to be honest, I have never been as open with my family about what's going on in my life since. (Ironically, years later, when I'd graduated from college and lived in Los Angeles, Betty ended up working with my mother. They put the past behind them and became close friends. Betty even taught my mother how to tie a tie. At this point, however, Betty had long since stopped talking to me. But, again, another story.)

Let's get back to the timeframe here. I apologize. I have not thought of these days in a long, long time, and I find myself wanting to toss in every detail as I remember them. That makes for a convoluted storyline. Ten years is a long time. It's funny how the details return.

So I told Gary that I was taking Betty out for her birthday, but I planned on stopping by in time to see Clinton's acceptance speech. I picked her up at her house in my father's 1967 Chevy Camaro, the car he and I had rebuilt into his crowning achievement. I don't remember how I talked him into letting me take it. She was wearing a black jumpsuit-type thing with blue jeans on over it, and a black jean jacket. The jumpsuit has a little snap at the crotch, she said with a giggle. I couldn't imagine what kind of outfit would have a snap at the crotch.

We were heading to Arcola, about 15 minutes north of Mattoon, up Route 45, a two-lane thoroughfare through cornfields and barren, silenced dirt roads. The restaurant was called the French Embassy, and it was the world's only four-star French restaurant that was also a bowling alley. That's not a gag. It was a real place. To the left was a bowling alley, and to the right was the finest French restaurant in Illinois, from actual French guy Chef Jean-Louis. It's odd how it didn't seem all that strange to me, at the time, that the fanciest restaurant I knew was also a bowling alley. I don't think Betty found it that strange either. She was just impressed that I'd saved up enough from my minimum-wage usher salary to take her to a nice birthday dinner, and that I wasn't wearing a Wayne's World T-shirt, which was my style at the time.

We headed up Route 45, with Nirvana's *Bleach*—Betty's birthday present, on cassette, which is what people listened to before they downloaded MP3s—providing the soundtrack. She smiled from the passenger seat, looking fantastic, her large breasts firm, the snap intact. She had recently stopped calling me "Skippy," which was the older girls' nickname for me at the movie theater, apparently because of my boundless energy and enthusiasm. I had never liked being called "Skippy," and now that I had seen Betty topless, I definitely didn't like it. She rolled down the window, laughed and said, "Well, Skippy, thanks for taking me out tonight." I made a pouty face, which, at 17, was as close to a frown as I could come. She smiled again—lord, that smile—put her hand on my leg, bit my ear, and said she was just kidding, *William Franklin Leitch the Third.*

The restaurant was not crowded. It was a Tuesday. I ordered something I couldn't pronounce and a Coke, and Betty had a glass of wine. We talked. She took her shoe off and playfully snuck her foot up my pants leg. I acted like that happened to me all the time.

I paid the bill. It was 9 p.m. I think Florida had been called for Bill Clinton. We hopped in the car and drove back down Route 45. We were just outside the Donnelley's publishing plant where, two summers later, I would work a temp job on an assembly line with my Uncle Ron. Betty leaned over, unzipped my pants, and took me in her mouth. She bobbed down, then up, then down, then up again. A whisper. Pull over.

I turned left, over the railroad tracks on which I had never seen a train, drove about half a mile and eased to the side of the dirt road, leaving my parking lights on, lest a drunken teenager come barreling through. Betty took off my jeans, and then hers, and then my boxer shorts, and then, snap, snap, up went the jumpsuit. She reached in her purse and pulled out a condom, a strange ring-shaped contraption which, up to this point, I had never seen. It was different than I'd imagined. I was hardly the epitome of manly dimensions, but, still, it seemed unlikely that I could fit that thing on. It seemed small.

Betty bit off the wrapping and tore. She grabbed my penis, tightly, and then unspooled the green latex—*green? I hadn't imagined it being green*—onto me. I worried, instantly, that the tightness of it would make me lose my erection; I had never worn one before, after all. She licked my ear. Does that feel OK? I nodded like a retarded basset hound. *Yup-yup-yup.* And then she hopped over the stick shift and straddled me.

The seats in a 1967 Chevrolet Camaro do not recline, and the steering wheel is far too close to the driver. This makes for discomfort. Betty tried to move, but could not. Move to my seat. I did, scraping my bare ass on the stick. *That's better.* She then began to move, slowly, slowly, slowly, so slowly. She lifted up her jumpsuit so that her breasts were exposed. The windows steamed up, instantaneously, it seemed.

I cannot say I was enjoying what was happening. Sure, I enjoyed the view, and I suppose, had I been able to separate myself from the experience, it might have even felt OK. But I was panicked that I would lose my erection, and we wouldn't be able to finish, and she would be embarrassed for me, the teenager, and then she'd start dating a burly farmer named Hank, and she'd tell all my friends I couldn't perform, and they would laugh and laugh and laugh and laugh.

Amazingly, I was able to keep going. She sped up. I was surprised it was still happening. How long had it been now? Thirty seconds? Four hours? A week? Faster now. A moan. A grunt. A misstep … *get back in there*. Another moan. A strange whistling sound. Faster. And then, and then, and then… it was over. Betty made an unhinged, insane smile I'd never seen before   her lips appeared to be pursed, yet above her eyeballs—and kissed me. That was good. She then raised, and lowered herself off me, took off my soiled cover, opened the side door and threw it into the ditch. For some reason, I had an urge to go grab it and put it in a Ziploc baggy.

Thanks, she said.
No, thank you, I said.

I drove her home in silence. I didn't even turn *Bleach* back on. It had suddenly become very cold, and Dad and I hadn't fixed the heater yet. I saw her shiver. I put my arm around her shoulders and pulled her next to me. She kissed my ear again. She was always kissing my ear.

She opened the door, looked at me and sighed. "So, I'll see you at work tomorrow?" I said yes, yes she would. And happy birthday.

I never made it over to Gary's. But Bill Clinton did win the election, a fact that a young Illinois kid, just off a dirt road, in a Camaro, with a mullet didn't learn until the next morning.

FROZEN TUNDRA

I got the bright idea to try out for my high school football team sometime in July 1990. Save for occasional backyard tussles with fellow kitten-armed pre-pubescents after grade school, I had never played football before. I'd never worn shoulder pads or a helmet, and to me, a mouthpiece was something you wore to apply the polish to your teeth after a cleaning.

The main reason to play football, to my 14-year-old mind, was to get in shape for baseball tryouts, which would be in the spring. Baseball was the only sport I'd ever played, and it had been a dream of mine to star for the high school team as the scrappy, spunky catcher. (I was entering my freshman year and was still allowed to dream big.) But I felt like I might need to add some muscle. I weighed about 105 pounds.

Something about being a football player appealed to me. Just the uniform was compelling. It was like wearing catcher's gear, all the time. And real men played football. I imagined it was like football on television, caked in mud or snow, and blood, and sweat, and pain. It was a brotherhood of men, and this was a time of life where I was eager to be considered a man. After all, I'd be driving in two years.

My mother was not pleased. She made me promise I would not "get yourself paralyzed." Also, she had just started her career as a nurse and was none-too-eager to start carting my bruised carcass back and forth to two-a-day practices. I made her a deal. We lived about 15 miles from the high school, so Dad would pack my bicycle in the back seat of his work truck and drive me in for the 8 a.m. practice. I'd head to my godfather's house, just by the high school, at 11 a.m., have lunch, douse myself in ice, then head back at 2 p.m., practice for two more hours, then ride my bike the 15 miles home afterwards. This seemed like a perfectly logical plan at the time.

I showed up for my first practice to the shock of my former junior high classmates. I was not the type of guy who played football. I was in all the smart classes, played scholastic bowl, and recited baseball statistics. I had never played youth-league football, like everyone else, nor had I attended any of the football camps. I showed up with a backpack, a water bottle, and a bunch of baseball cards, wearing an Ozzie Smith T-shirt and a pair of shorts with a zipper. I introduced myself to Coach Timlin, who was moonlighting to keep himself interested before basketball season started. (He was the varsity head coach.)

He asked me what position I wanted to play. I had no idea. I hadn't thought about that.

"I don't know. Wide receiver, maybe?"
He looked at my tiny bones and non-existent deltoids. "Can you kick?"

I could not. But we were off. Before we started learning plays, it was time to run. Sprints. Many, many sprints. My first lesson of my first football practice: Football practice makes you, and all those around you, vomit. I think half the team left half their innards on the sidelines that day. We ran until our hair fell out; we ran until our pores bled. We ran for three straight hours, then Timlin blew his whistle and said, "OK, that's it. I'll see you all in three hours. 2 p.m. Don't be late." I then crawled to my bike and found I could not lift it.

Somehow, I survived, and even made it to the third day of two-a-days. We were assigned pads. One of the key pieces of football equipment is the pants pads—I am sure there is a real name for them, but I cannot remember it; I was tackled a lot and have many fewer brain cells as a result. I looked at them like it was a chicken with four beaks. I couldn't even imagine how to put them on. I discovered one pad that was in the shape of a protective cup. I took this as my cue as to how to put them on. It was uncomfortable, but since when is wearing football equipment comfortable? I waddled onto the field. Coach Timlin noticed me immediately.

"Jesus, Leitch. What in the hell are you doing?"
"Playing football, sir!"
"Your goddamn pads are on backwards. Christ. Look at you. You've got your ass pad over your wiener. What happens when you get knocked on your ass? You're gonna break in half, kid."

He then made me change right there on the practice field. I suppose I deserved that.

I somehow survived the brutal three weeks of practice and excruciating bike rides home. I even found a position: fourth-string strong safety. This was notable not only because I was the weakest strong safety since the inception of the pigskin, but also because we only had enough players for two strings. School started, and our team won its first four games. I played in none of them.

Meanwhile, I was acing all my classes. I liked high school. All you really had to do was turn your assignments in on time and not openly mock the teachers, and you'd get A's. There was one important exception: biology. Mrs. Tudor was in her mid-30s and had just started at MHS. We had to do a bug collection. I have never been able to stand bugs, and when they assigned us to capture a wasp, which is as unfair a class assignment as I can imagine—as if Mrs. Tudor did not know they had stingers—I became a conscientious objector. I would not be going after a wasp. I was in enough pain from football as it was.

We had a game scheduled against Effingham, about 20 miles away. We jumped out to a huge lead, and when the fourth quarter came around, all the scrubs were playing. Finally, when even the scrubs were tired, Timlin turned to me. "Leitch, get in there. And do try to stay out of everyone's way."

I was assigned to the tight end. The Effingham quarterback must have noticed immediately how scrawny I was, because he threw it to the tight end immediately. There he was. *He was coming toward me.* What now? I hadn't tackled anyone who wasn't a blood relative before. What to do? On instinct, I ran toward him and POP! I just drilled him. He went down in a flash. The trainer came on the field. I had knocked the wind out of him. I jumped up, stunned. I didn't even know how to celebrate.

Timlin called me off the field, "Christ, son, one HELL of a hit! You taking steroids or something?"

The next Monday's practice, I was fired up and ready to go. I hit the blocking sleds extra hard, and Timlin took special notice of me. He even promoted me to second string. I was breaking through. Screw baseball. Who needed baseball? I was Dick Butkus.

I rode my bike home after practice. My mother was waiting for me, with that look that parents give when they're silently reminding themselves that murdering their children is illegal and would likely cause them some trouble down the road.

"I got a letter from the school today. You're getting a D in biology." The bugs. The wasp. Fuck Mrs. Tudor. "It's that football. You're spending too much time playing football. You're off the team until your grades get up."

I didn't dare argue. After all, I'd just rode my bike 15 miles and could barely breathe.

I turned in my pads to Timlin the next day. He shook his head and sighed. "You were getting better, Leitch. I thought you were smart. How are you getting a D in anything?" I had not the nerve to tell him about the wasp. I'm not sure he would have understood.

I ended up acing biology once we no longer had to capture hostile insects, and when

baseball came around, I, out of shape already, didn't make that team either. I never played football again.

I do like to wear the butt pad from time to time, however.

ONE MORE CUP OF COFFEE FOR THE ROAD

I made a financial mistake.

I'm still not sure exactly what it was, but I think I subtracted one from the tens side rather than a two, or a three, or a nine, and it plunged me into a week of chaos.

I realized it right before I left to visit family in Philadelphia last weekend. I did the math in my head and, to my horror, discovered that not only had I just bounced a check to my roommate, but that until Friday morning, I had not a penny to my name. Actually, that's not quite true. The change cup by my bed had about $1.74 in it.

This seems fitting. For the last year, I have worked for a struggling publication that barely paid me above minimum wage. This is good because it has taught me how to live in New York City on what is essentially an ox's salary. It's bad because, well, cigarettes are expensive. There have been times of such intense poverty that my breakfast, lunch, and dinner have consisted of the free apples at work.

But I just took a new job, and even though I'm hardly rich, it's certainly a welcome step up in salary. I will be able to start living like a normal human being. It is something I have been looking forward to for three years: a job with a living wage. I am so close.

My first paycheck was to be Friday. I somehow had to make it four days until then. One last week of being an unwashed mass.

I did an inventory of what I had to survive one week:

$1.74 in change.
14 cigarettes. (Marlboro Lights... not even my brand!)
Half a box of cat food.
Endless cups of hot chocolate (courtesy of work).
One package of Ritz crackers.

That's it. I had no money left on my subway card, so after work Monday, I headed out into the cold New York night and walked from 17th Street to 207th Street, where I live. That is 190 blocks. I have always been curious how long it would take me to walk that far. This was as good a time as any to find out.

One of my favorite books when I was younger was *The Long Walk*. It was written by Stephen King under his Richard Bachman pseudonym, published decades after it was written (when King was a freshman in college, which is just depressing). It concerns a competition in the "not-so-distant" future in which 100 young men simply begin walking. They are required to walk a minimum of four miles an hour. If they go under four miles an hour, they are given a warning. They have an hour to walk off the warning. If they receive a fourth warning, they are shot.

There are stilted political implications in the story, though I can't for the life of me remember what they are. But the story fascinates me still. I mean, it's simply walking. Anybody can do that, right?

From my office in Chelsea to my apartment in Inwood, it is, according to Yahoo! Maps, 10.7 miles. It's a walk I've been curious to take since I moved to Inwood, which, after all, is halfway to Canada. This final week of poverty seemed like an ideal time to finally go forward with the experiment. So, after a hard day of work—we are finishing up an issue of our magazine, traditionally the most exhausting, aggravating time in the whole cycle—I packed up my briefcase and turned right onto Eighth Avenue at 6:02 p.m.

I walked fast. It was exciting, really. Why don't people do this all the time? Up, up, I went, past Madison Square Garden, past my old office with the methadone junkies, past Port Authority, past Columbus Circle and through the Upper West Side. I moved at a steady pace, passing all pokey tourists and meandering shoppers. It was *I* who could not be stopped; it was *I* who was on a savage journey. Four miles an hour? Please. I'd double that, backwards, blindfolded, walking on my hands.

The Upper West Side is an area of town where I have spent much time, but I have never really understood it. An old girlfriend lives up there, and, like her, everything on the Upper West Side is a little too precious. There are little Italian-only bookstores, and ceramics bars, and stores selling only novelty strollers. I had barely been back to the Upper West Side since we broke up, and I was reminded why; the Upper West Side makes you feel like you don't bathe often enough, like you're this swarthy minion swooping up from the city's underbelly, lurking in to sully their happy, lily-white pseudo-suburbia. The Upper West Side is a strip mall designed by *The New Yorker*, where people pat themselves on the back for "getting" the new Todd Haynes movie and hypothesize about the city's homeless "problem." The whole area makes me want to drink six cans of Pabst Blue Ribbon, and then fart. Preferably in a crowded Starbucks.

That said, when I reached 77th Street, next to the Evelyn Lounge, where we had our first date, the pangs of envy were overpowering. Nobody here eats hot dogs for lunch simply because they're only a buck-fifty.

Plus, my feet were starting to hurt. I noticed it about 86th Street, which, all considered, isn't bad. But I was only 70 blocks into my journey and had another 120 to go. It was 6:54. Not bad time, I thought, but a pace I was unlikely to keep.

When I lived on the Upper East Side, most of my favorite take-out/delivery places wouldn't deliver to me because I lived on 97th Street. "We only go to 96th," they'd say. That might sound patently ridiculous, but the change when you cross 96th is obvious. The quaint little organic mom-and-pop shops start turning into liquor stores and check-cashing joints. Strangely, the streets become quieter, and there is far less evidence of the "homeless problem." It makes sense. It's not a dangerous neighborhood, really, but not a particularly affluent one either. It makes no sense to ask for spare change on a street where no one has any to spare.

On 100th Street, I felt the blister. I walk on the backs of my feet, something you'd think would help my posture but doesn't. Right there, on the base, right under my ankle, it started to swell. I kept wondering if it would burst as I moved forward, soaking my sock. But it wouldn't. Just a *squersh, squersh, squersh,* as it shifted with each step. But, nevertheless, on I walked. I had declared to my roommates that I would make it back to the apartment by 9 p.m., and time was a-wasting.

Through Harlem (much, much nicer than people realize), up to 137th Street (7:45... good pace still), up to Washington Heights. I never realized how many McDonald's there are in this city. New York seems like the least conducive city for a McDonald's; fast food seems archaic here. Everything is fast food. If you have a choice between a processed hamburger and a fresh-from-the-oven slice of pizza, at comparable prices, why would you get the same thing you get in Kansas? Yet a lifetime habit remains; I order from McDonald's, usually to reward myself after a busy week. Not only do I go to McDonald's, I consider it a reward. You can take the boy out of Southern Illinois, but...

Speaking of which, at about 170th Street, it occurred to me that I was starving. I hadn't eaten all day, which, sad as it is to say, isn't that highly unusual a situation for me as it probably should be. But I was expending energy now, starting to slow perilously toward that 4 mph threshold, and it was beginning to look like calories might not be as wretched as I'd always believed. But the compiled change (up to three bucks now!) in my pocket was to be used for tomorrow's subway rides. No food could be had.

It dawned on me that I was a moron. When people heard that I was broke for the week, I received a surprisingly high number of offers to help, *here, Will, let me order you a pizza, hey, do you have a Paypal account?* These entreaties were kind, warm-hearted, and downright touching. But, to me, they missed the point. This was a test for myself, one last week of struggle, something to never forget, something to put in the pocket of an old coat and discovered years from now with a fond smile. This was a project. This was life as art.

As I trudged up Broadway toward the George Washington Bridge, 158 blocks into my journey, "life as art" was starting to look like a tremendous load of horseshit. I was hungry, cold, and, to my alarm, my calves were starting to cramp up. But, at this point, what choice did I have? I couldn't exactly waste the whole trip by hopping on a subway now and wasting a valuable token. I had to make it home. Wait... is that a hill? Jesus. When did Manhattan get hills?

If I had been in the Bachman contest, I would have been shot somewhere around 190th Street.

But past the Cloisters I went, almost home now, so close. In the distance, my apartment building. I glanced down at my right shoe. The sole of it was flapping aimlessly. "Come on, buddy... hang in... almost there."

I crawled up the stairs and put my key in the lock. I heard a "Wow!" from one of my roommates. "We weren't expecting you until 10, at least!" It was 8:51.

Weary, I forced a weak grin. I wanted to lie on the couch, watch Monday Night Football, and not think about how hungry I was. I shuffled to my room, peeled my shoes off, crow-barred my socks onto the floor, and shuffled back. My roommate, to whom I had accidentally bounced the check that had started this whole mess in the first place, smiled.

"Will, do you want some food? We made you a pizza."

They had. It was most wonderful.

This week wasn't even half over. And all it took to wear down my "I don't need help, this is for me, I must prove myself and remember and make it last" was an oven pizza, John Madden, and two warm roommates on the couch, administering the *Cosmo* quiz ("What Kind of Lover Are You?"), huddling up in blankets, staying safe.

Because your friends, the ones who are there for you, they would have no place in the long walk. If you slow down, they don't shoot you. They crouch besides you, take your arm gently, rub your back, and tell you, "I'm here." Then, once you're up, you carry on down the road, together, scarred but stronger for larger, fiercer battles ahead.

THE B-TO-G RATIO

Two Christmases ago, my then-girlfriend gave me a planner. It was a nice one. It was leather-bound, with a guide to Manhattan restaurants, a nationwide area-code identifier, and a detailed, if already outdated, subway map. (This was Christmas 2001, and the map included trains that went under the World Trade Center.) I'd never had a weekly planner before.

"You see, Will, you can organize your life. When you have a wedding to go to in May, you can write it in there months ahead of time, so you don't forget." I always forget dates, and phone numbers, and pretty much everything, actually. It was a well-thought-out gift.

But she had no idea the monster she had created.

Within two days of receiving the gift, I had filled in almost half the days of 2002. Somehow, a date with nothing written in it became a day wasted. I researched the last four years of my life and found every possible anniversary, relevant or irrelevant. I listed the one-year anniversary of living in a Webcam house, the four-year anniversary of the day I received the first e-mail from a woman I later dated, and the birthdays of just about anyone I ran into on the street. I scoured through the schedules of my favorite sports team, marking every game, even if it wasn't until November.

The planner never left my side. To this day, I take my 2003 planner into every work meeting, even if we're just discussing what we have planned for after the meeting. Nothing is too minuscule or frivolous for my planner; flipping through the other day, I discovered that August 15 is the one-year anniversary of seeing the White Stripes in concert. That information will undoubtedly come in handy somewhere.

Of course, now the whole situation is out of control. I've been dating a girl recently, and she asked me last night if I'd like to see a movie with her next week. Before she'd even finished the question, the planner was in my hand.

Let's see … Wednesday, the Illini play Purdue, along with the new edition of ESPN's Hot Stove Heaters about the St. Louis Cardinals. Tuesday is the five-year anniversary of interviewing Reese Witherspoon in Los Angeles. Monday is the third episode of *Joe Millionaire*. And Thursday is out too. Hmm. I can pencil you in for Tuesday, February 11, between 8 p.m. and 10:30. Wait, check that: The Oscar nominations come out that morning. Make that 9 and 10:30.

For years, I had sleepwalked through life, not knowing or caring what happened the next day, just hopping from one stone to another. But my planner, this newfound elixir, gave me the ability to see into the future. What am I doing on May 29? Well, I'll be sending Kathie Fries a birthday e-mail and lamenting that the Cardinals don't play that day. And it fits in my breast pocket!

With my control-freak tendencies already running rampant, this just pushed them over the edge. Nothing in the world exists that cannot be grist for my incessant planning mill.

Last year was the perfect Super Bowl to have a party. True, my beloved Arizona Cardinals weren't playing, but considering my likely crowd, it didn't matter. The New England Patriots were on one side, and about half my friends, it seems, have signed up for the life-long Sisyphus-like task of rooting for sports teams from Boston. On the other: the St. Louis Rams, who not only reminded me of home, but also were the favored team of the woman I was helplessly agog over at the time. We had just begun dating, and it was essential that she not just have a good time, but that she have a mind-boggling unbelievable time, that she levitated from her chair and spun around in ecstasy, that she bowed to the heavens above that she was so fortunate to have such a brilliant, charming, astonishingly handsome and, most important, well-organized host.

Because my apartment is too far away to expect anyone to travel there, I decided to hold the festivities at a bar where we'd watched various games during the season. They had an area in the back, ideal for a group of about 20 people, the amount I anticipated. Everyone just shows up, watches the game, easy peasy. No problems.

But then my mind took over. What if she doesn't know anyone there? What if my friends are too crass for her? What if we don't have enough seats, and she has to stand through the whole game? What if there aren't enough girls there? What if she thinks we're all just a bunch of stupid guys screaming at men wearing butt pads running into one another? What if I ruin the whole thing? What if she thinks I'm a misogynist? What if I blow the whole thing?

More girls. There had to be more girls. I began contacting every girl I knew in the tri-state area, or at least the ones who still spoke to me. I asked every male friend to encourage every woman they knew to show up. I became obsessed with the B-to-G ratio. Male friends who couldn't wait to watch the game were left off the invite list while I invited female strangers off the street. You know how sentences in telegrams end with the word "STOP"? That was me during Super Bowl week last year. Every statement ended with "B-to-G ratio. We need more G's."

And the seats! What if we ran out of seats? What if the place turned out to be insanely crowded? It is the Super Bowl, after all. This, this *too* I can control! The game started at 6:00 p.m., so I showed up at the bar at noon and scoped out the back. Stunningly, six hours before game time, there was no one there. Perfect! I had brought four different coats with me, and I dropped them at every possible booth. When anyone came to the back to sit, I stopped them. "Uh, somebody's sitting there." Three hours later, the same guy returned. "Er, yeah, that guy, um, he's in the bathroom right now."

People finally started filing in around 5:00 p.m. I immediately showed them to their assigned seat—I couldn't have her sitting with any Patriots fans, now could I?—and paced up and down, waiting for her to arrive. I suppose I could have kept myself busy by introducing the random assortment of women who wondered why the hell they had been beckoned here by a guy they hadn't talked to in months, but there was no time! She would be here any minute.

Kickoff. U2 bellowing at halftime. Third quarter. Still no sign of the girl. I don't remember watching a single play in the first half. At last, midway through the quarter, she arrived, looking exhausted and more than a little annoyed. I scampered to her like a dog awaiting a treat. "Sorry, I'm late. I think you gave me the wrong address."

I had. Sigh.

Well, you know how the game turned out. The girl? Well, she left me about four months later. Why? "Will, you barely give me any space to breathe. It seems like you have something for the two of us to do every night of the week."

This year, everyone can plan their own damned Super Bowl party.

ASS MEET CHAIR

I sit at a desk all day. Sure, sometimes I venture across the office to give some papers to my boss, or I head downtown to cover a press conference, or I slip downstairs to have a cigarette. But when you really break it down, my job consists of sitting on my fat ass, typing and talking on the phone. All day.

This is not what I grew up to believe a job was. In my family, a "desk job" was something people did elsewhere, in big cities, people who were bankers or businessmen or, if you were less fortunate, receptionists. (It wasn't until I later worked briefly as a receptionist that I realized that the position should require a doctorate in Homicidal Urge Resistance.) A job was supposed to be work, where you were on your feet, lifting something, carrying something, building something. My father, my mother, my uncles, just about everyone I knew, worked real, manual labor jobs, whether they were wiring circuit breakers, laying tar, cleaning toilets, or administering insulin shots. To them, sitting down was something you did when you finally made it home. It was something that you had earned.

For a summer during college, I worked at a paper factory, where I spent 10 hours a day feeding magazine pages into a large machine, which would compile them and glue them to other sheets. When it was done, *voila!* you had a magazine, or a company newsletter, or a hockey program. I was on my feet the whole 10 hours, save for one 10-minute break in the morning, a half hour for lunch, and another five-minute break in the afternoon. While on duty, if I stepped away or just daydreamed for longer than a minute, my stack of sheets would empty, and the machine, lacking its sustenance, would shut down. An alarm would sound, and everyone would know that I had stopped doing my job because a loud red light would flash menacingly above my station. Imagine if a big red light went off above your desk every time you stopped working for a minute. Your office would look like a strobe-lit disco.

Truth be told, these days I really don't know very many people who don't just sit at a desk all day. Do you? It feels like the biggest swindle in the world. Essentially, if I have this straight, the goal of this working world is to go to college in order to get a little piece of paper called a degree. With this little piece of paper—which you acquired pretty much by sitting down and listening to other people talk to you—you are somehow considered "educated," and when you show it to the right people, you are allowed to have a career where you sit on your ass all day. We call this success.

I feel rather guilty about this, as if I am part of an extensive nationwide conspiracy to mock those who actually have to work for a living. It's just confounding for me to classify interviewing people and writing stories as "work," even if evidence constantly mounts that I'm about as effective at manual labor as I am at menstruation.

When I was laid off by my first Internet company almost three years ago, a place that had the whole sitting-on-your-ass-doing-nothing thing down to a science, I suffered a similar crisis of conscience. What was I doing, lamenting the loss of a fundamentally fake business and the decadent dungeons of instant messengering and free music downloads, when I could be out there reminding myself what work is supposed to be like? Determined, I rushed out to a temp agency and told the recruiter, "I'm looking for a job. I don't care what I'm doing, but I want it to involve lifting something, carrying it somewhere, and setting it down. I want it to be out in the blazing heat or the searing cold, where I don't have to talk to anyone and all I have to do is get the job done, go home, and shut up about it." He smiled and said he had plenty of those, pretty boy, and, in fact, there's one you can start right now.

I showed up at a T-shirt factory. The job was to take large boxes of T-shirts, place them on a handtruck (and it is called a "handtruck;" no self-respecting man calls it a "dolly"), and cart them across town. I started at 2 p.m. For three mid-September hours, I put my hat on backwards and did the rounds with a burly man named Bruno (seriously) who kept calling me "fruitcake." Bruno's first impression of me was not, well, impressive. "You're kinda small, aren't you? You look like you don't have a muscle on your body." (Bruno apparently had been talking to my ex-girlfriends.) But for three hours, we worked together on an unseasonably sweltering afternoon, and at 5 p.m., we went our separate ways, and he said see you tomorrow, and I said yeah, and he said bye, and I went home and soaked my body in ice and slept until noon the next day. A week later, I was a receptionist.

But I still have my thirst for manual labor, but nowadays, I know my own limitations. So it manifests itself in another way.

If there is anything more painful than moving into a new apartment in New York City, it likely involves Tammy Faye Bakker, a tuning fork, and mayonnaise. Forget packing your life's possessions—inevitably thinned by space constraints—into a bunch of boxes, or renting a truck, or finding a place to park your moving van without compiling endless friendly notes from the New York City traffic authority. That's nothing. This city is jammed to its gills with people; it has no time, space, or patience to deal with frivolities like convenience. Its hallways and stairwells are designed for human beings exclusively, preferably thin ones. For one person to move his/her life from one dwelling to another, it requires, most of all, plenty of manpower, because the process of finagling a couch through a twisting, cramped corridor and up five flights of stairs is strikingly analogous to Lara Flynn Boyle giving birth to quintuplets.

So, as my penance for my inability to handle a "real" job, anytime anyone ever has to move, I gleefully volunteer my services. It's a horrible, wretched process, but it is real work, and I'm able to feel all manly, a sensation sorely lacking in other everyday activities. It makes no difference if I'm close to the person or not; I just want to feel like I'm doing something. (Personally, I'm not sure any of the people I help even like me.) It usually takes about four hours, involves the climbing of many stairs, and they usually buy me beer afterwards. But most of all, I feel like I accomplished something. It sure beats going to the gym and getting punched for staring too long at a sports bra.

Just yesterday, I helped a friend and co-worker move into his new place. I met his parents and his girlfriend's parents, and they were all very nice, and they just couldn't believe my generosity in volunteering to help them cart all his belongings across town. I tried to explain to them, after carrying the box containing five paperback copies of Cliffs Notes on Hamlet, how this was my atonement for a life of leisure, but they couldn't quite hear me through all the panting.

That said, perhaps I'm underselling the effort required to type out a story. As I can attest from the experience of writing today, it's not the least bit easy—at all—to type while soaking in an ice bath and injecting ibuprofen into your veins. Not in the slightest.

EVEN SWARTHY MINIONS MUST EAT

Once a year, New York City hosts Restaurant Week. The premise: Exorbitantly priced restaurants, for one week, set up a special menu for us swarthy groundlings. It's *prix fixe*—which is a fancy pants way of saying "fixed price;" why we give more cultural credit to phrases worded in another language will always escape me—which means you get three courses, four options each, for the low, low price of $30.03 per person.

Restaurant Week, like New York, is inherently insulting. Essentially, five-star restaurants are throwing a bone to the lower-middle class, allowing us to soak in their atmosphere, put on a nice tie and pretend like we're big shots, at least for one week a year. The wait staff is openly indifferent to your existence—like you're going to give a decent tip—and the general attitude of the whole joint is condescension. They know we're just there because they happen to be cheaper for the night, and don't think they're going to let you forget it.

This, of course, is exactly why I couldn't wait for Restaurant Week.

I was never really aware of my class issues until I came to New York. I'd always considered myself open-minded to notions of wealth. If people had money, and lots of it, good for them; they're people the same way my blue-collar middle-class parents are people, and it doesn't make them any better or worse because of it. It's about the way we treat other people, you see.

When I moved here, all that changed. I'm not sure when it happened; it might have been when my ex-girlfriend started dating an old-money stockbroker whose parents paid his rent from a trust fund and who lived in Manhattan but still owned two expensive cars. (Now that I think about it, yeah, that was probably it.) It also didn't help that I was working 12 hours a day and still struggling to pay the rent. It was impossible not to look at all the snots on the Upper West Side, with their Louis Vuitton handbags, belts by Prada, souls by Satan, with their sleek, shiny, artsy-modern seven-bucks-for-a-damned-Budweiser nightclubs, looking like they just stepped out of the fucking salon, and loathe them with all the envy I could muster. *Fuck* them and their smug self-satisfaction, their belief that they've done something to actually earn their lifestyles, their inability to earn an honest day's living, you know, if they had to.

This is not the right attitude to have when you live in New York City. It's an excellent way to become a sour, unpleasant person. Thankfully, um, I'm a charming drunk. Or something.

But, true to form, deep down, we really do all want to be these people, which is why I eagerly snapped up a reservation for a date and myself to Beacon, a schnazzy place serving "American" cuisine in midtown Manhattan. True, I wanted to impress the girl—for whom the most romantic gesture I'd made up to that point was offering her money for a cab ride home after a date—but what I really wanted was to feel part of the club, to play dress-up for the night. I put on my best tie, to go with black shirt and black pants and a long "stylish" trench coat that my uncle wore in the '50s. (I looked like a member of the Hives.) If only I'd had a top hat.

We arrived at the restaurant at 8:30, our appointed time. I checked our coats and ordered a bottle of the cheapest wine available, of course. We'd had a few drinks beforehand, so we settled into the atmosphere with warmth. Our waitress came by, had me sip the wine to make sure it was adequate (this ritual beguiles me; I inevitably crack a fake smile and chime "Mmm!" looking a lot like Harvey Keitel in *Pulp Fiction* after he tries Jimmy's coffee), and handed us our Grimy Proletariat Worksheet, the *prix fixe* menu. We both ordered steak.

An hour and a half later, when our waitress deigned to actually serve us our food, we'd blitzed through the wine and were beginning to doubt ourselves. We were halfway through a rather charred and tough steak when my date looked at me. "I feel kind of gluttonous right now, don't you?" I feigned ignorance. She continued. "I mean, we're sitting here, criticizing the food, and people all across the world would kill for something like this."

I took a deep breath.

"You see, this is what I'm talking about. We're in a position where we have to feel like we're just so incredibly fortunate to be in a place like this. But I work very hard, and I feel like I've earned the right to come here once in a while. But you and I, we're such noble, down-to-earth people that even on a night like tonight, when we're only here because it's the one week a year we can afford such a thing, we can't help but feel like we are being self-indulgent, that we're doing something wrong. We can't help but think about the less fortunate. The people here, the people who regularly come here, they don't entertain such thoughts. They just sit here and complain about their three-year-old's prep school, or how there are so many homeless people, or how the *Times'* arts section is becoming too liberal. This is the trap they have set for us. They make us feel guilty for wanting a brief taste of it all, for dipping our wick in their world ever so briefly. How dare they! We, you and I, we're the only two pure souls in here, and it's a battle for our souls that we have to fight every day. This is why we will never be a part of their world. We're just too real, you see? We're the only ones who get it!"

Well, OK, actually I said, "Hmmph" while cramming more steak down my gullet. But I think she knew what I meant.

I called for the check. With the wine and an off-menu dessert added to the *prix fixe*, and with tax added, I glanced at the damage. My "cheap" night out had become the most expensive dinner I'd had in years, maybe ever. I swallowed hard, paid the check and glanced at my date. "Um... can you pay for the cab out of here?" Four middle-aged women, whom we'd nicknamed "the hags" chuckled under their breath. It was Restaurant Week, and it brought out all kinds. At least we had bathed.

I am fooling myself if I believe that I will be any different if I ever come across any money. I will likely sit in my ivory tower on the Upper West Side, chortling over my copy of *Harper's*, savoring my vintage Napa wine, wondering why the rest of the world finds matters so damned difficult all the time, while some young punk plots my imminent destruction. I suppose I will have it coming.

"MR. LEITCH, IF YOU WERE A FLOWER, WHAT KIND OF FLOWER WOULD YOU BE?"

My father has worked for the Central Illinois Public Service Company (CIPS, before it was bought by St. Louis-based Ameren) since right after I was born. He works, essentially, as a troubleshooter for the electric company. You know those big, unwieldy metallic configurations with the power company's logo slapped on a chain-link and barbed-wire fence? They're usually siphoned off from everything else, because they're highly dangerous. When your power goes out, because of a storm or something, it's because one of those has broken down.

Well, my dad's the guy who fixes those and makes sure nothing goes wrong with them. He's been doing it for an awfully long time, and he's very good at it. My father has developed a reputation among his co-workers and bosses as a guy who never does a job half-assed, never complains, and never leaves work for others to do. Troubleshooting can be hazardous; while on the job, he lost his middle finger at the knuckle in an accident, and he has watched a man be electrocuted to death only a few feet away.

About 10 years ago, my father's union was threatening a strike. Management had been considering the possibility of locking the workers out as a preemptive strike, but they weren't quite sure if the union was bluffing. A large part of my father's job is overtime; he's on call 24 hours a day because you never know when your power's going to go out. In 15 years, my father had never once, for any reason, turned down overtime; when they called, no matter what time of day, no matter what he might have going on (he once left halfway through opening Christmas presents), he always dropped what he was doing and did the job. The union, as a matter of protest, distributed word throughout its ranks that, as a show of solidarity, when the dispatcher called, they would feign sickness to let management know they meant business. At 8 p.m. one night about two weeks before my high school graduation, our phone rang, and I answered. The dispatcher said, "Will, is your dad there?" I handed him the phone and watched as my dad looked down, saddened, going against his very nature, and said, "Sorry, Bob, I'm, um … I'm real sick. I can't make it."

If Bryan Leitch was turning down overtime, management knew the union wasn't kidding around. They locked out the workers the next day.

My father is the hardest working man I know. He has never sucked up to his boss, or played politics, or chummied up with management. He simply goes out and does his job, no complaints, no problems. He had a family to support and two kids to send to college. The notion of doing anything else has never occurred to him.

I bring all this up because this week, my father is doing something he has never done in his life: He is going on a job interview.

Can you imagine your father on a job interview? I don't think I've ever seen my father nervous, or apprehensive, or unsure of himself, even when I'm sure he has been. My father has the right idea about parenting; even if it's possible that he's wrong, he puts up a united front of certainty. Parents should not be namby-pamby. There were times that I just *knew* my dad was wrong, that he just didn't understand, but I never saw any doubt with him. It's more important to have a parent who is consistent than one who rises and falls with what his children think of him. Parents need to be tough and stable, not necessarily fair and nice. I don't think I've ever seen my father *flinch*.

But it's pretty tough not to flinch in a job interview. My father, the mythic alpha male, the man on our family's pedestal, sitting in a folding chair wearing a bad tie, handing over his résumé to three management schmucks? I mean, how in the world would my father answer the "What three adjectives would you use to describe yourself" question?

It's hard to imagine my father having to put on a happy corporate face to anyone, let alone try to convince a panel of people who probably aren't worthy to be in the same room with him (people who probably wouldn't know how to change a light bulb, let alone wire a house) that he's the right guy for the job. The job is still with Ameren, in a supervisor position; he would essentially be overseeing all the people he works with, correcting them when they're doing something wrong. Or, to put it another way, as one of his co-workers says, "He'd be doing the same thing he's been doing, he'll just be getting paid more."

But man… my father on a job interview? My mind spins just trying to imagine it. I once had a job interview where a guy asked me if I could be one kind of animal, what kind would it be? I have a higher tolerance for bullshit, so I can muddle my way through such ridiculousness. But my dad? I think his head would catch on fire. (Or maybe he'd just say, "I've always wanted to be a pretty kitten." Parents can surprise you that way.) I've never heard my father say a single self-promoting thing in my life. I can't imagine him coming up with a long string of them. It is not surprising that my mother reports he's been having trouble sleeping all week, he's so conflicted about the interview. Telling my father he has to sell himself to someone is like asking a cow to play the piano.

Yet I'm torn. Half of me wants the interviewers to just look at the body of his 25 years of work and realize there's no need to even talk to anyone else. The other half of me wants to feed them questions. That could be quite fun.

"Mr. Leitch, in 1985, as a joke, you told your son to climb up the television antenna tower to clean out a gutter. Halfway up, you pulled down his pants and threw them in the garage, forcing him to run around naked, horrified, while your whole family laughed at him. Now that your son is afraid to talk to girls and reportedly plays with dolls, do you regret that?"

"Bryan, you once claimed that St. Louis Cardinals infielder Gregg Jefferies would make the Hall of Fame. In light of his place as one of the most disappointing baseball prospects of all time, do you have anything to say for yourself?"

"Mr. Leitch, you often lie around your living room in your underwear, spraying Easy Cheese on club crackers and passing gas. We don't even have a question here."

"Mr. Leitch, a large part of this job will be training and supervising employees who aren't that skilled, intelligent, or capable of much of anything, actually. In lieu of your son turning out like he has, what makes you think you're qualified to teach anything?"

"Bryan, is this interview the longest you've gone without asking someone to pull your finger?"

Hmm. Well, good luck, Dad. You deserve it. They should ask you that thing about the TV antenna though. That was kinda mean.

THE PATHETIC SCOREKEEPER

There was this kid I went to high school with named Sammy Beck. Sammy was the best athlete to come out of Mattoon in 20 years. He was the star in football, baseball, and basketball, taller, faster, with an agility that seemed trained but was inherent. Sammy's big coming-out party as an athlete was his freshman year. At a school assembly, the principal, desperately trying to be hip, dressed inexplicably like a Blues Brother, tossed him a basketball from half court that Sammy threw down with a ferocious dunk. We had never seen anyone like Sammy at our school; that wasn't just because he was black, I swear.

Sammy and I didn't interact much. I usually tried to stay out of the way of guys like Sammy. He wasn't a jerk, really; he was just the most blessed, impressive student in school and tended to live his life that way. Whenever Sammy was in the room, he was In The Room. He was perpetually the pink elephant; just by his presence he elevated everyone else into something bigger than they were. *We're sitting here next to Sammy Beck*, we'd think. *This will be something to tell our kids someday.*

Sammy was the star center fielder for the Mattoon Green Wave, and I was the backup catcher/scorekeeper. I have told this story before, but it bears repeating, if just to sum up succinctly the legend of Sammy. It was my senior year, his junior, and Sammy had just been drafted by the Seattle Mariners in the 57th round of the amateur draft. Before he went into the on-deck circle, he walked over to the quiet kid with the scorebook.

"Hey, Will, how many hits has this pitcher given up today?"
"Um, six. You've got two."

He looked at me as if he were a paleontologist who had just come across the fossils of a specimen he'd long thought fictional.

"Will, if they ever have a draft for scorekeepers, you'll go in the first round."

This proclamation was welcomed with grunts and chuckles. When I've told this story before, I've made myself into some sort of dugout Dorothy Parker. I cock an eyebrow, turn my head warily in his direction, and proclaim, "Sammy, if they ever have a draft for people who blow their talent and end up working for the city, you'll go in the first round."

Problem is, that story is patently false. I said nothing at the time, and it is only through hindsight that the "witticism" makes any sense at all. No one would ever say that to

Sammy, not because they were afraid of him (though I was), but because no one thought Sammy would turn out to be anything other than a 10-time All-Star and the guy with the "Mattoon: Home of Hall of Famer Sammy Beck" sign welcoming visitors to town. I've made up the anecdote to pump up my own importance and make myself look like the high school outcast who always had his eye on the bigger picture; truthfully, I think that's the only time Sammy ever spoke to me.

Sammy graduated as I ended my freshman year at the University of Illinois, and, with much fanfare, he announced he would be attending the school as well, under scholarship as a rare-two-sport star, playing for the Illini baseball team and for coach Lou Tepper's beleaguered football program, which I was already covering for the student newspaper. I wrote an article for the *Daily Illini* about his impending arrival before the school year even started. He hadn't come to campus yet, so I spoke with coaches of both teams about where he fit in their plans. All were ecstatic about this special talent.

Sammy lasted a week. Classes hadn't even begun, and he had already begun to chafe under Tepper's workout regimen. At Illinois, he wasn't so important anymore; he was just another freshman grunt trying to catch the attention of his position coaches. Like any information about Sammy, all I gathered was through rumor and innuendo. I guess he missed his friends in Mattoon. He felt alone and without an anchor. He was never a student, not really, and he worried about the supposed advanced curriculum of a Big Ten school. He asked Coach Tepper for some time off, and next thing you knew, Sammy had dropped out and moved back home. He sat out a year, and then played for the Lake Land Community College baseball team. But a year without conditioning and the distractions and temptations that came with it were too much for him to overcome. He played two uninspired seasons, then left the school, and, alas, ended up working for the city.

He had been handed a singular ability, and he frittered it away. I looked at him with a mixture of disgust and melancholy.

Whenever I go home these days, all the Mattoon ex-pats pick one night to head to The Alamo, which is the only bar that has beers made by companies other than Anheuser-Busch on tap. That is to say, it's the classiest place you can find in the county; it even attempts to keep the Toby Keith jukebox quotient to a minimum, a small measure dearly appreciated. When I was home last Christmas, I filed in with some old high school pals, and sure enough, over in the corner, was Sammy; like me, he was with the same six people he was hanging out with 10 years ago.

He hadn't gotten fat, disappointingly, or at least not any fatter than I've gotten. I walked over to him, said hi, and after an agonizing pause, his face registered a faint trace of recognition. "Hey, Will Leitch. My man. How you doing? I didn't know you smoked." We made about 30 seconds of small talk, and he went back to his conversation with a "uh, good to see you. Merry Christmas." He looked happy, actually; healthy and content.

I could make some belabored argument about how Sammy has never really moved on from high school, and that inability to move out of his own way has cost him countless opportunities of which most people can only dream. I could say that he is stuck in Mattoon, in the past, and this quiet obsession with what is gone and can be nevermore is sad, almost tragic. But, then again, he's not the one writing this. I am.

CEMETERY

I f you hop on Old State Road, passing Ronchetti Budweiser and the old Broadway Christian Church, and take it out of Mattoon for about three miles, you'll see my Uncle Jimmy's place on the right, and if you take a left on the dirt path just after you cross Lerna Road, you'll be able to drop by and see Uncle Larry and his lovely wife Kay. For the purposes of our trip, however, you'll keep going past that, out to the quiet, open places where all the teenagers go to park, across that rickety one-lane bridge—be careful, because it's only wide enough to barely fit one car—and hang a right just past the Heartley house.

There's plenty of history in the Heartley house; an old buddy named Keith grew up there. I graduated with him; good solid guy, from a family of farmers, straight-arrow, married at 22, hard-working. My favorite Keith story was when we were in kindergarten, and he was a typically awkward kid with a pair of Harry Caray glasses that made you think he would fall on his face from the weight every time he walked through the playground. Keith had broken his arm that summer, and just as school started, he developed the chicken pox. Poor kid; he'd get those little itchy bastards right under the cast, so not only did his arm hurt like a sonuvabitch, but he couldn't even scratch those crazy fuckers. You'd see him in the corner of the room, bathed in sweat, shaking, biting his knuckles, trying not to cry. He made it out fine enough, though. And it was so long ago… dude probably doesn't even remember the pain, dulled like circumcision, mercifully happening too young to comprehend.

But you don't stop at the Heartley house, not too long, because we've got a final destination. Continue past there, and hang a cautious left and it'll be up there on your right. Supposedly some teenagers back in the fifties were all shit-faced and took the turn too fast, rolling over and bursting into flames in the ditch that runs up the side. They say their ghosts still haunt the place, though I've never believed that.

All right, now get out of the car—no need to lock the door; we're not in New York—and crawl over that little fence that appears to be there for no reason. You've probably noticed by now that we're in a cemetery, one of those old ones with headstones for people who died in 1893. Hope you're not spooked; this is why I asked you to come along with me while it was light out. I've been here plenty… there's nothing to be scared of.

OK… now take, oh, a good 20-25 steps to the left—we're not digging for lost treasure here, you don't have to be exact; ooh, watch out for those flowers though—and look down. You should be looking at a row of headstones. (If you're not, turn around, doofus.) On the far left is a man named Ethan "Whittie" Leitch, a great-great-uncle of mine who died shortly after birth around 1940-something. Apparently, he had some sort of effect on my grandfather because my grandfather always called me—his old fishing buddy—"Whittie" before he died in 1989. To Whittie's right is the headstone for William B. Leitch and his wife Anna, my great-grandparents. Willie B. passed on before I was born, but I used to sit next to Great Grandma in church as a kid, and she lived right across from the old Icenogle's Grocery, back before it burned down. I remember once, when I was about nine, I walked over to Icenogle's after school to get some baseball cards (Topps of course) and ran into her. I helped her carry her bags across the street and held the door for her. She kissed me, gave me a dollar, and said, "You be good now, Bryan." I could forgive her getting the name wrong; she was 80-something. She was a year away from a her final check-in at the nursing home, and my father's name was Bryan, as was her late husband's.

To the right here, it starts getting dicey. The next headstone, the lavishly crafted and sculpted one, reads William F. Leitch and Dorothy Leitch. This is my grandfather and my as-yet undeceased grandmother. (Deeply flattering, no? We can all hope someday to be referred to by the phrase "as-yet undeceased.") William F., who went by Bill, was an old railroad man—my one family memento is a pocket watch he kept attached to his belt—who later became one of the higher-ups at Howell Asphalt, a road tarring company that my father once worked for. Grandpa Leitch was a beloved figure in Mattoon, respected for his tireless work ethic, unfailing loyalty, and rock-solid common sense. He was also known as a bit of a grouch; years down the road, as he lay on his deathbed (still smoking his two packs a day), he wore out nurse after nurse, berating them, running them off. He finally found the only one who could stand him, and vice versa, when his oldest son's wife, who had gone to nursing school late in life, after the kids were already in school, when it was OK to work again, reluctantly volunteered for the job. They would jive back and forth with one another, but the banter disguised their obvious mutual affection. The woman who changed his bedpan, who regulated his IV, who turned down the TV when it was getting too loud, up until the day he died, was Bryan's wife, Sally, from nearby Moweaqua.

This might come as a surprise to you because you appear to know me so well already, but I was actually Grandpa Leitch's favorite grandson, and with eight kids, he had plenty. This was partly because I was named after him, of course, just like he had been named after his grandfather, but regardless of family obligation, we bonded almost from the beginning. The whole family—my parents, sister, grandparents and great grandmother—used to go to the First Baptist Church every Sunday, and inevitably Grandpa and I would be goofing off at the end of the pew. We played Hangman, we wrote notes to each other making fun of my dad, we would make strange, muffled, moderately disgusting noises when no one was looking, then giggle about it and hush up when Grandma yelled at us.

Grandpa loved to fish. He didn't have some big oversized boat with a deck, a bathroom below and cable TV in case the fish weren't biting. He had a little rowboat that he'd take to one of the various ponds around Mattoon, and he'd just go out there with rod and bait and a radio to listen to the Cardinals game. And I was the only grandson he would fish with. One time, just he and I went out to lunch, and he decided to get out the boat after I begged him for a quarter to play a video game at the Dairy Queen. ("Those damn things are worse than gambling," he'd say. "When you put money in a slot machine, at least you got a damned chance to win something back.") We drove to a nearby pond and plopped it in the water—stopping to pet a stray beagle on the banks—and rowed a bit out. A terrible fisherman, I cast my line a little too close to the pond's edge, and after a few minutes, I heard a horrible yelp. Being a particularly stupid child, I felt my line tug and pulled hard, and the yelp became louder, horrible, pained, piercing. Grandpa realized that the dumb dog had bitten my line and was flailing around, screaming and thrashing. We rowed to shore, and I'll be damned if that stray, untrained dog, upon seeing my grandfather, didn't open his mouth wide like a kid at the dentist and look longingly at him to please, please take this sharp object out of my mouth. Grandpa did, and that dog took off into the woods like the devil hisself was chasing him.

In my years of fishing, that dog was the only thing I ever caught. My dad still doesn't believe that story, but I swear, it's true.

So you see his stone, no? It's amazing how you can't fit everything on a stone that needs to be there. That dog story would be a perfect epitaph. Or the time, when I went to visit Grandma and Grandpa in Florida, where they lived for about a year until they decided they were too far away from Mattoon, that he chased off a big nasty swamp alligator that was scaring the shit out of me while I was pretending to be Cardinals pitcher Bob Forsch and bouncing tennis balls off the air conditioner. Honestly, that alligator took off like that dog with the hook in his mouth. Grandpa was strong, caring, simple, straightforward, worshipped by his entire extended family. You can't fit that on a stone. You can't even come close.

Instead, you just get his date of birth, date of death and his middle initial (not even the whole name!). And next to him is Dorothy, date of birth, date of death yet to be determined. And occasionally, he'll get some flowers, sometimes from me.

OK, let's keep moving. This is where it starts getting a little creepy, so bear with me. To William F. Leitch's and Dorothy Leitch's direct right… a plot that echoes the one that came two stops before it. There is the plot, with open spaces waiting to be filled, for William B. Leitch and his lovely wife, Sylvia Kathleen. These are my parents. I've never asked my parents exactly how long they've had this place all set up for them, had this imposing ground eagerly anticipating their arrival, and I'm in no hurry to. William B. was born in Mattoon, went to high school here, visited this very same cemetery to honor his grandfather and this mysterious Whittie character. Don't worry about messing up the ground; it'll all be dug up again... hopefully not sometime soon. My father has known since he was a boy where he would be buried. He knew that he had nowhere else to go. He still lives in Mattoon, where he has raised a family and cultivated a life that would be the envy of many, including myself. He doesn't like to leave Mattoon, whether it is to visit his daughter at the University of Illinois or to visit his son, making chaos in New York City. This is his land. He's not going anywhere.

He has three brothers and four sisters, and to be honest, I really don't know where they're planning on being buried. For some reason, the family tradition is naming its firstborns after their grandfathers, making Dad, technically, William Bryan Leitch II. And that tradition means being buried in the family cemetery, next to their fathers and their wives and their grandfathers and their namesakes, destined (sentenced?) to Mattoon for eternity, where the Leitch boys are supposed to be. Where they want to be.

You might have an idea where this is going. My name, dear readers, is Will Leitch, or William F. Leitch, or William F. Leitch III. I am the son of William B. Leitch and Sylvia Kathleen, of rural Mattoon, and the grandson of William F. and Dorothy Leitch, and the great-grandson of William B. and Anna Leitch.

It's too gruesome to face... but you must.

Because, if you'll kindly take a look over to your right, there it is. Right now it's just a free space, might easily be mistaken for an open area, where you can grow grass or plant flowers or simply play in the dirt. There is no headstone—not yet anyway—nothing placed there to make you think it's anything but dirt. A headstone shall be placed there, it's already been picked out and paid for and fussed over and everything. I think I've probably only stepped on that area three or four times myself—go ahead, step there, it's fine, not disturbing anyone, not yet—and that's just when I've been aimlessly frittering about, wondering why I decided to spend my Saturday afternoon at a cemetery. But there's a good chance I'll get to know the area pretty well.

I will be buried there. It is my space, all paved out and reserved, just for me, and my presumed eventual wife. It has been saved for me since my parents had the thought that I would exist.

Actually, that's not exactly true. In August 1973, almost exactly 26 months before I was born, my mother gave birth to a son. It was the first child of William B., 21, and Sylvia Kathleen, 20, married June 19, 1971. His name at birth, of course, was to be William Franklin Leitch, after his grandfather, after his great-great-grandfather. The name was all ready to be set in ink on the birth certificate. The young couple planned on building a new home in Mattoon, out in the country part of town (as if there were any other), with a room and a crib and a matching wallpaper and a little table for changing diapers.

But something went horribly wrong. The infant escaped my mother's womb… and he was gone. Dead, right on the spot. Dude never even opened his eyes. Never had a chance. My mother shot him out, and next thing you knew, a corpse lie there on the doctor's slab. He'd come out all wrong, this poor sad dead baby. There is some sort of fatal condition he had, something the doctors made very sure, most sure, to check for when Sylvia Kathleen's next baby came around, but, for the likes of me, I can't tell you what it was. I think my sister knows. I've always been afraid to ask, myself.

This poor sad dead baby, this kid whose world was taken away from him before he even had a chance to see it, lost not only his life, but his name. Once it became clear the family tradition, the family name, would not be able to continue, the Leitches went into action. Suddenly, William Franklin became Keith Vincent. He does get a spot in the cemetery— look, he's up a couple spots, small stone, small boy—but by dying, he forfeited his rights. He gets a substitute name.

That makes me scab labor. I've swiped the kid's name, pilfered his identity. I'm Sean Payton, replacement player, fill-in quarterback for the Chicago Bears for three games during the 1987 season. Sure, Payton wore a uniform with his name on the back, and he even threw a couple of touchdown passes. But we all knew he wasn't the real quarterback. He just had a brief chance because the real guy was gone. The guy who was supposed to be there.

Which just means I enjoy a bigger plot, built for two. I called ahead for reservations, and I got 'em. Whatever road I take, I know where it ends. What happens in between now and then, it's all just details, filler.

I left Mattoon—the city in which I grew up and which held everything I knew and held dear and not-so-dear—10 years ago, in August 1993. When I was a young man, all I knew was getting out, fighting to see more of the world out there, wondering if there indeed was some sort of life outside the rural community I called home. I fought against what had been expected of me. I wanted more. What more I wanted was never clear, just that I wanted it. Since then, I've lived in Los Angeles, St. Louis and New York City. And it is all a waste of time.

You see, no matter what, no matter how the story plays itself out, I end up back here, in the ground, back in Mattoon, next to my parents and their parents and their parents. Back where I started. There is no escaping it. I can pretend small town life is in my past, that I'm a sophisticated urbanite now, that I know how to use the subways and everything. But it's no use.

Because Mattoon still has me. It knows I'll end up back there anyway. It's willing to wait me out. It's just a matter of time.

So, now that I come to think of it, yeah, try to watch where you step.

A FULL LIFE

About 20 minutes after a cab picked me up from the airport and dropped me off at an apartment I'd never seen in a city I'd never even visited, I went to a bar. I was meeting a woman, another writer, who had written for some of the same publications I had. One of her friends was having a birthday party there. I had been in town for an hour, with a feathered hair and a center part, and I looked about 16 years old.

Everyone seemed so fancy. No, not fancy—*urban*. Everyone seemed to be snickering at a joke I'd never heard but wanted desperately to figure out. They all lived in the East Village—I had to be told that East Village wasn't the same thing as Greenwich Village— and they smoked and they talked really fast and they laughed really loud. It was a large table, packed with about 15 people, and I was the curiosity of the moment. After all, I was literally just off the bus.

I tried to make dopey jokes and self-aware references to my greenness, asking where all the cows were, wondering aloud if anyone knew where to find Woody Allen. They chuckled knowingly at my naiveté, and I played along, because I wanted to be like them; I wanted to be as sharp and vibrant and smart, smart, smart—man, they seemed so smart.

We drank for about four hours, and at around midnight, this guy named Karl took me aside. He appeared a bit fey—a *lot* fey; even this intrigued me. Gay people are openly gay in New York! Wow! And something about my corn-poke nature intrigued him.

"So, you're here to be a writer, huh?" He said this with the soft condescension of a parent whose child has just told him he's going to be an astronaut. I told him, yeah, that was the plan, with a side joke about being rich and famous that hopefully let him know that I was aware I was a cliché but was forging forward nevertheless. I asked him how long he'd lived in New York. "Seven years. I've lived in the same apartment for seven years." He said he had grown up in New Jersey.

I told him how excited I was to be a New Yorker, to be part of this special club of rejects and miscreants and dreamers. He laughed and took a deep drag off a long, slender cigarette.

"Oh, honey, you're not a New Yorker yet. Far from it. You're not a New Yorker until you've lived here five years." He stubbed out his cigarette and cocked his head slightly. He looked me dead in the eye. "Until five years, you're pretty much just playing with your dick around here, doll."

By my count, there have been three different occasions when I have been 100 percent, absolutely sure, no doubt, that I was leaving New York for good. My first year began with unlimited opportunity, a rather surreal succession of success, and ended with me in poverty, with no job, living in my cousin's guest room in Mattoon. If just to prove some kind of point, I forced myself to return to New York at the beginning of 2001, using my last $65 for a bus ticket, though I had no apartment and no means of support. In retrospect, it would seem a horrible decision. I spent three months looking for work, sleeping on friends' couches, stuck in a deep chasm of depression; I had gone from the biggest shot among shots to a cautionary tale people whispered about. My parents, when I swiped a friend's cell phone to make a rare long-distance call, would beg me to come home. Maybe the job I'd left would take me back.

I hung around, just to prove to myself that I wasn't the failure I so obviously was.

I finally found a regular job, a shit job, really, one that paid just enough to survive, but then a girl left me, and I looked at my life, and saw that I still had no real reason to stay. On a trip home for a wedding, I told my parents that this was it; without her, New York was pointless. I said I was looking for jobs in Chicago, where I had friends—an urban area where I'd be closer to home, safer, without feeling that I had somehow taken a step back. I was convinced of this; my parents even spoke about giving me a cheap used car as a return-home gift.

And yet I could never really leave. I found excuses: My lease runs out in a few months, and I'll go then. I'll finish up this freelance project, then I'll go. I'll live recklessly, as if there are no ramifications, because I'll be leaving soon enough.

But I never did leave. I fought through it, and found a better job, and settled my life down, and realized that New York isn't just a grownup Disneyworld, for me to play with and discard as I saw fit.

I've now been here four years—longer than I've lived anywhere since college. I'm not just playing with my dick anymore. I have a stable of friends, I have professional opportunities, I have stability. It took me three years to find it… and now I can't ever imagine leaving.

I'm not a New Yorker yet, even if I finally understand where all the subways go. But this is my home, and I'm as proud of its continued hospitality as I am of my own persistence. This place is chaotic, and confused, and scary, and everything that's full of life and hope and the feverish rush that life is supposed to have in abundance.

Perhaps there is a time, upcoming, where I will tire of it, when I will retire to strip-mall suburbia, when I eat at the Outback for my special Sunday night dinner, when I placate myself with digital cable and the Elks Club and the treadmill in the basement. There is nothing wrong with these things. But I don't want them, not yet. I go to bed every night exhausted and wake up without refreshment. I slog through long, hard days and endure endless subway rides home. I carry my laundry five blocks just to overpay an Asian man to wash it for me because I just don't have time.

But it is all worth it. This is a time to celebrate this city, which has let me stay here, for which I am eternally grateful. I might not be a New Yorker just yet, but I'm getting there. I'm immensely lucky for the opportunity and glad I never left when I had the chance, when it made absolute sense to leave. I have stayed, endured, and am blessed to have done so. Even my parents understand now. They've transferred their nagging from "When are you coming home?" to "When are you going to settle down with a nice girl and make us some grandchildren?" Which is nice, really, I guess.

But this is my home, and they'll have to blow the place up to get me to leave now.

Which is good, you know, because, um, they might.

POSTSCRIPT:
Decisions I Will Have To Make Once I Am Famous

Which late-night talk show will I become a regular guest on?

Ideally, Letterman's the Mecca, and after a couple appearances that bring down the house, he might even ask me to fill in for him when he's stricken with shingles, or rickets, or sickle cell anemia, whatever it is he has these days. I could toss him a bone and show up on maybe an anniversary show or something. Perhaps I will sing to him. Leno's out, no way.

But the real question is which upstart show that could use the immediate spike in ratings—ratings I would inevitably provide—will I appear on as a show of solidarity? That guy on E! is obnoxious, and Craig Kilborn is too tall. I could possibly serve as a guest host of the Jimmy Kimmel show for a week. But that's probably taking it too far; someone of my stature wouldn't stoop to a week-long shoot. I wouldn't show up on Bill Maher's program, unless it were to wilt Ann Coulter with my liberal charm. Howard Stern would call, obviously, and I'm sure gossip tongues would wag when I artfully dodge inquiries about that Page Six photo where I'm holding hands with Nicole Kidman. "She's a very special woman," I'll say, "but, really, we're just friends."

I would host Saturday Night Live, though I'd of course insist on writing all my own sketches, preferably ones which end with me making out with Tina Fey. I would have to turn down repeated requests to take over for Steve Martin as Oscar host, however; if they didn't like Letterman, they're clearly not worthy. I could conceivably present an award, but it would have to be Best Picture, or, at the *very* least, Best Actress; I'll leave the technical awards to the Ben Stillers and Cameron Diazes.

Who will be my first celebrity wedding?

J-Lo? Naw. *Way* too much trouble. If I'm for a 20-minute marriage, Drew Barrymore should do the trick, though, let's face it, in between *Charlie's Angels* movies she does tend to pork up a bit. When I was young, I had a rather intense infatuation with TV-movie diva Margaret Colin, but she's gotta be, like, 90 now. Pop music stars are out; it would be difficult to explain away Christina Aguiliera in the *New Yorker* profile.

Perhaps an athlete? Mia Hamm is taken, but maybe softball star Jenny Fields? The language barrier would probably be too much for Anna Kournikova and me, but she certainly would be invited to visit me in my room, provided she signed the relevant nondisclosure agreements. Other famous writers are out too; too high-maintanence, and I wouldn't want our union to be perceived as an endorsement of her last novel, which, honestly, was a little too precious and affected for my refined tastes.

I suppose I could marry someone who isn't in the public eye, but, let's face it, with all the starlets lining up, it will be difficult for her to understand the trappings of my life of wealth and adulation. Nobody worthwhile does that anyway. Denzel Washington, maybe, but I think he might be trying to prove some sort of point.

What about running for office?

Obviously, I would be an ideal candidate, particularly with a nearly 95 percent approval rating, appealing both to your blue-collar union man and your upper-class urban sophisticate. My appeal also crosses gender and racial lines; all demographics feel as if I am one of them, understanding their fears and raptures, siding with them against a cold world that never has its better interests in mind.

But would I want to soil my hands with something as shameless as campaigning? Surely, those jealous of me, those flushed with desire for power, those not as altruistic as myself, they would attempt to bring me down to their level with shameless slinging of mud. It would likely serve the public welfare better to work outside the system, use my influence to remind those in office what this country is about, using my tale of hard work, dedication and natural talent as an impetus to pull the nation up by its proverbial bootstraps. I would contribute to both parties, but I would only make public appearances for those who truly believe, those whose values mirror mine and those of my infinite constituents.

What about commencement addresses?

My alma mater, the University of Illinois, would receive first dibs, but it would have to first renounce famous alums Hugh Hefner, Dave Eggers and Roger Ebert who, while certainly advancing in their little niches in an admirably plucky way, don't really have the broad-based coalition-building skill I inherently possess. The Ivy League schools would call, surely, but any speeches there would have to come with the caveat that I could publicly chastise the private boys' clubs the schools have become.

I could speak at a high school graduation, but only if they agreed to my terms, primarily that my high school girlfriend would introduce me as "the one who got away." But I must be careful about accepting invitations; there will be far more requests than I will have time to embrace. Still, my story, one of determination and perseverance, is one of such inspiration that it would be irresponsible of me not to pass it onto future generations. My agents will weigh offers to compile my most touching speeches onto a "The Wisdom of Will Leitch" compact disc; concerns about overexposure will have to be addressed, as will issues of digital piracy.

What about past enemies and doubters?

All past enemies and doubters will be crushed, preferably in the public square.

Will Leitch is an editor at BlackTable.com. He has written for *Salon, Nerve, The New York Press, Ironminds, The Sporting News,* TheSimon.com, *The St. Louis Post-Dispatch* and *The New York Times on the Web.*

ACKNOWLEDGMENTS:

The notion of an acknowledgments page serves one major purpose: to offend people who have been left off. So, at the risk of sounding windy, I have a lot of names. This might be the last book I ever write. I apologize in advance.

First off, I must thank R A Miller, this book's publisher, and everyone at Arriviste Press. I hadn't intended to do anything like this; their faith and their persistence are the only reasons you're holding this book. Along the same lines, Kate Lee at ICM either has been unwavering in her belief in me, or she has done an astounding job faking it. (Either is fine.) Matt Dorfman is responsible for how sharp and professional the book looks, along with the cover design; it almost makes up for his pedophilia. Tom Perrotta, whom I've never met in the flesh, gives this whole endeavor a desperately needed shot of class; the man is brilliant, and receiving his endorsement justifies just about everything I do.

As with any leap of faith, it's your friends who guide you and carry you most of the way. Cindy Nowicki not only carted my sorry carcass to Boston from New York and back for this, she has also been the wise sage of the whole process. She has an unerring instinct for what will work and what won't, and I'd be lost without her. A.J. Daulerio not only had to read 200 columns to help me decide which ones to include; he actually had to pretend that he liked some. If it hadn't been for his influence, I might have quit this game a long time ago. (Yep. His fault.) Eric Gillin is a universe with a gravitational pull all his own; without his force and driving energy, I don't know if I would have ever pushed myself to do much more than log agate text. Aileen Gallagher is the best line editor I've ever come across; she's right so often, I wonder if we'd have been better off just having her write everything in the first place. Tim Grierson has not only provided me with a vessel for a column that could have died years ago, he has served as a mental raised eyebrow anytime I was about to do something stupid. Sometimes I wonder if I'm doing all this just to impress him. Matt Pitzer and Mike Cetera have been rocks for me since the beginning. If you're looking to find people who have figured it out and are living life as it's supposed to be lived, there they are. Greg Lindsay has been a reminder that you can be a professional in New York City and still not lose your soul. Lindsay Robertson is a wonderful reminder that life is supposed to be a vacation. Mike Bruno is not only the lone white man who can say the word "whack" and not sound lame, he's also fought back from a lot of the same shit I have and emerged considerably more victorious than me. Amy Blair and Erika Croxton have been the best roommates, drinking buddies and late-night commisserators a man could ask for. If it hadn't been for Chris Bergeron, I would have never started writing a column about my foibles in the first place. And Denny Dooley saved my life three years ago, and I'm still not sure he understands why.

And, of course, my family, specifically my parents and sister, whom I love dearly.

OK, now the list. The following people, in one way or another, have contributed to the whole Life as a Loser experience, whatever that means. Their contributions to this book, and the column, and to my life, are impossible to quantify but absolutely vital. They might not even know why. But to not include them would be a sin.

Rafat Ali, Woody Allen, Meredith Artley, Jami Attenberg, Marc Balgavy, Matt Barthel, Heather Benz, Tim Black, Hillery Borton, Emily Bozeman, Russell Brown, Jack Buck, Clare Bundy, Elinore Carmody, Emmy Castlen, Rick Chandler, Kurt Cobain, Jim Cooke, Aimee Crawford, Brian Desmet, Mandie DeVincentis, Mary Dooley, Mike Dooley, Ron Dooley, Brian Doolittle, Jennie Dorris, Roger Ebert, Erin Franzman, Kathie Fries, Dave Gaffen, David Geracioti, Ali Gerakaris, Mary Gustafson, Christine Hammel, Linda Hammel, Steve Helle, John Herr, Frances Huffman, Chris Jenkins, Kim Keniley, Jimmy Kimmell, David W. Klepper, Ken Kurson, Andy Kuhns, Marisa Laudadio, Lewis Lipsey, Katie Lukas, Eric Mack, Neeti Madan, James McKenzie, Kelly Mercein, Joan Mocek, Johan More, Jim Norton, Theresa O'Rourke, Dave Oaks, Grady Olivier, Jesse Oxfeld, Jamie Paquette, Jen Philion, Abigail Powers, Dave Plotkin, David Propson, Aimee Rinehart, Tom Rosinki, Bob Sassone, Jessica Seilheimer, Shlomo Sher, Choire Sicha, Jessica Simmon, Dakota Smith, Michael David Smith, Elizabeth Spiers, Brian Styers, Benson Taylor, Betty Taylor, Matt Tobey, Lynda Twardowski, Andy Wang, Otis Whightsel, Del Willison, Liz Zack, Claire Zulkey and, of course, Wu-Tang.

And, lastly, to Mattoon, Illinois, the town that has made me into who I am. It only has itself to blame.

Printed in the United States
1533100002B/163-170